THE DESERT RAVEN

PEGGY A. WHEELER

"I looked everywhere like you told me to, and at last I found my voice, but when I did all I could hear was my own screaming."

–Maggie Tall Bear Sloan to her psychiatrist soon
after discovering the corpse of her best friend,
Sally, with her heart cut from her chest.

DMP

THE DESERT RAVEN

PEGGY A. WHEELER

The Desert Raven

Copyright © 2019 Peggy A. Wheeler

ISBN 13 p 978-1-77400-008-3

ISBN 13 e 978-174400-008-3

www.dragonmoonpress.com

My most profound appreciation to my husband, Steve, the first to read and edit my manuscripts. He always gives my work total honesty. I love you for that, and everything else, honey. Gratitude to my wonderful publisher, the Queen of Dragon Moon Press, Gwen Gades. *The Desert Raven* is my fifth DMP title, and I expect it won't be the last. Thank you as well to Denise Dumars, my dear friend of nearly forty years and my mentor, who was also my one-time literary agent, and my all-the-time gal-pal and support system.

Thank you so much to all my readers, those who have spent their hard-earned dollars to buy, read, and sometimes even review, my books. My wish is that *The Desert Raven* entertains you, sometimes frightens you, sometimes makes you think or wonder, and above all, reading it brings you some measure of joy.

A note of gratitude and a huge hug to my favorite son-in-law, Tom Anselmo, for giving me a new character for Maggie Tall Bear Sloan to hang out with. Thanks also go to your lovely wife, my only child, Aimee Anselmo, and to your daughters, my grandchildren, Brittany and Gianna. You all inspire me.

CHAPTER 1

IN THE PRE-DAWN hours of a Sunday, during the season Maggie Tall Bear Sloan christened, 'The Summer of the Desert Ravens,' the crack of gunfire, two shots in quick succession, startled her from a sound sleep. "Shit! Right in front of the house."

Jake Lubbock, Maggie's live-in lover, reached for his cell. She jumped from the bed, grabbed her Glock off the nightstand, and ran into the street wearing only a pair of faded blue panties, and a coffee-stained tank top.

House lights snapped on one after another as neighbors peered through curtains and blinds, none daring to emerge from the safety of their homes.

Across the street, a young man, still in his teens, splayed spread-eagle, face-up on the sidewalk. The first shot left a clean hole in his chest, and the impact most likely flung him to his back. Maggie had seen enough fatal gunshots to know. A wound from the second shot to the head as he fell told Maggie the bullet was high caliber. Bits of brain, bone, and scalp had sprayed in a fan pattern across the cement behind him like a surreal halo.

The shooter had scored his second hit, point blank, between the eyes, creating a small neat pit in the front, and blowing off the back of the boy's head. Maggie said to no one, "From the angle of the shot, the killer must have stood directly over the body, straddling it. Forensics will know for sure." She laid her Glock on the ground, stood over the body with one foot planted on the cement walk on one side of the boy, and the other foot on the opposite side, and took aim with an imaginary gun, "Yeah, that would be it."

Although his legs and arms still twitched, Maggie knew the boy would have perished from the shot to chest alone within minutes before the second bullet shattered his brain into gelatinous, raw, nuggets, and finished the job.

She knelt by the body, and as she did explosions of light and sound blasted at her as someone stuck an arm out a moving car window and fired at her, once, twice, three times—bam, bam, bam. She scrambled behind a dense shrub and spread herself flat.

In the hazy light cresting the hills, Maggie could not identify the model or make of the car—a mid-sized sedan of some sort, black, or maybe dark blue. She rose to her knees, raised her Glock, and aimed, but didn't take the shot. Instead, she lowered her arm, and let the gun hang limply against her thigh. The car had already sped far down the street, swerving onto the sidewalk, knocking over mailboxes before making a hard left onto an alley, its tires screeching. Maggie struggled to her feet, and with her free hand swiped at the blood trickles from her shins where the cement had scraped them.

"Jesus, Maggie! Are you okay?" Jake ran across the street to her but stopped short when he reached the dead boy. He knelt and felt for a pulse. "Backup is on the way, but no need to rush the ambulance." Jake shook his head. "He's no more than a kid. Such a fucking shame." Jake stood and attempted to step forward, but one foot slipped in blood, and he had to struggle to keep his balance. "We've landed ourselves in a goddamn dangerous town."

"Tell me about it." Maggie turned her gun in her hand, inspecting it as though it were a curious artifact. As sirens wailed, an unkindness of ravens circled close overhead, knocking, cawing, and krawing. The louder the sirens, the louder the ravens.

"I better get a robe." Maggie sprinted across the street into the house; the ravens followed not far behind. By the time she and the birds returned, she found Jake leaned against a squad car talking to a deputy while the medical examiner busied himself with the corpse. Investigators erected a barrier and delineated it with yellow tape. They pulled on white latex gloves, flipped on their flashlights, and combed the area, searching for evidence, placing markers here and there.

Jake covered the body with his jacket, leaving the arms and jean-clad legs exposed. From half a block down the street a barefoot woman in a pair of SpongeBob SquarePants pajama bottoms and a ripped man's t-shirt, her home-dyed black hair matted, stumbled toward the squad car. When she saw the body, she halted and wailed. "My Tony!" She clutched the front of her t-shirt with one hand and gestured at his feet with the other. "He just bought them Chukkas with his own money he earned himself at the car wash. That's him, my baby! God, no. He's only fifteen." She attempted to rush to the boy's side, but Jake blocked her way, sparing her further the sight of her only son in his new shoes with the back of his head blown to chunks.

The woman slumped against Jake. She rested her head against his chest, sputtered and hiccuped. Her snot mixed with tears and soaked the front of his shirt. When her knees buckled, and she collapsed, he grabbed her from under her arms to prevent her from falling onto the pavement. Maggie put her arm around the woman, pulled her away from Jake, and supported the woman's weight on one arm. "Let's get you back home. I'll stay with you until the ambulance arrives." She slipped from Maggie's grasp and fell to one knee. As Maggie pulled the woman to her feet, she smelled it. Cheap whiskey, skunk weed, stale urine, and when Maggie checked her eyes, she could tell the boy's mother was stoned out of her wits. Barbiturates, or heroin, most likely.

The volume of the ravens' caws increased and decreased and increased again as the mass of them blackened the sky. The woman leaned her chin back and looked to the sky. "All those crows. I've never seen..." As she fainted, her eyes rolled back into her head and drool slid from the corner of her mouth, and rather than lending a hand, Maggie permitted the woman to sink to the pavement into an unconscious heap.

—

Maggie fooled herself into believing she'd finally achieved a time in life when she could pursue a normal existence, but the viciousness of this town twisted her guts into knots. The killings and incidents of gang-related violence were bad or worse than anything she'd experienced in Oakland where she'd served in the police force, or in her hometown, Wicklow, where she and Jake spent years tracking a child killer. As though the nightly gun blasts, rapes, robberies, helicopters, car jackings, and stabbings were not enough, Sheriff Mack called her and Jake into the sheriff's department where Maggie and Jake served on the reserves.

"Have a seat." Mack gestured to two metal chairs across from his desk. "You're going to be glad you're sitting when I show you this."

Mack turned his screen so Maggie and Jake could better view images of a family charred over a fire, turned on spits like a trio of suckling pigs, their legs cleanly severed from their hips. "The coroner says the vics were still alive when the killer or killers cut out their livers; their legs were sawed off post-mortem. We've been investigating for months, and we keep running into dead ends."

Jake gagged. "Sorry about that. I've seen some gruesome things in my life...but this..." He wretched again and the sheriff handed him a napkin. "How about you, Maggie? Are you okay?"

"I've seen worse." But she didn't know if she *had* seen worse.

"We are going to need your help on this one," Mack said.

And, that was the last thing on the planet Maggie wanted to hear. "Let's go home, Jake."

—

"You almost barfed in the sheriff's office. That's not like you." Maggie handed Jake a chilled bottle of Sierra Pale Ale and settled next to him in an Adirondack chair on their back deck. "You've seen children with their hearts cut out, half-rotted corpses in shallow graves, people with their heads blown off. What could have possibly made you sick?"

"I think it's the desert heat. I'm a mountain boy."

"I'm making sure you aren't getting soft on me."

"So, what if I am?"

"Maybe you've had your fill." Maggie felt his forehead. "You aren't sick with a summer cold, are you? Those are a bitch. Maybe you need a good rest. Maybe we both do. After all the shit we went through in Wicklow we've earned our neighborhood block parties, slothful Sunday mornings, and evenings of insipid T.V. sitcoms, right?"

They'd checked the crime stats before moving to the ratty, beaten town of Hemacinto, with its boarded storefronts, graffiti, and tumbleweeds. Crime. Higher than the national average. Higher than the California average. Gangs from East Los Angeles migrated inland, staked territory, cooked meth, and murdered one another. Back when they first discussed it, Jake did his best to persuade Maggie to find a safer, more pleasant town to settle in. She wouldn't hear of it.

"Hell, it can't be any worse than anywhere else in southern California, besides, what are we supposed to do? My entire family is there now, and we agreed we need a change. Don't forget, too, in Hemacinto, we can afford to buy a little house outright. Anywhere else near Los Angeles the same house would cost us half a million dollars or more. I'm moving to Hemacinto."

"You aren't going to listen to me at all, are you? Or even consider an alternative?" Jake shook his head. "I learned years ago there was no use in arguing with Maggie Tall Bear Sloan. It's always going to be your way or the high way, is that it?"

"Pretty much."

In Maggie's opinion, the best thing about Jake is he never said, "I told you so," when it turned out she'd been wrong.

One sweltering night over a pint of ale, she said to him, "I miss my mountains, but I thought our move to southern California last summer would be perfect, or damned well should have been. What's the old saying? If you want to make God laugh, tell him your plans, or make plans, or something like that? It seems to me if there were such thing as a God, he'd be laughing his fucking head off."

From the rebellious days of her caustic-mouthed adolescence, nightmares of shapeshifting into a green-eyed raven from Yurok legend plagued Maggie. "I thought once we moved to Hemacinto my raven dreams, or whatever they are, were over for good," she said to Jake. "Why do there have to be ravens following me here, too?"

"And I thought by now you'd understand that's who you are, Maggie. You know those aren't dreams, right? Besides, when have ravens not been a big part of your life?"

"But so many? Never have I've experienced such a concentration of these damned noisy corvids."

Night after night in what she insisted were "visions," Maggie shapeshifted into a raven and flew over the San Padrino mountain range behind Hemacinto, often alone. Sometimes not. In one episode, she encountered an unkindness of ravens, among them a female albino with the red eyes of either a prophet or a demon, Maggie couldn't tell. The raven spoke in flawless English. "Your grandniece will follow you. When she has her first bleed, she too will become a pukkukwerek."

"No. Another monster killer? Which grandniece?" She ruffled her feathers. "It doesn't matter. I don't want it for either of them. They both should have good lives, and I'm going to put a stop to this."

"It is destined. You are foolish to think otherwise." The bird laughed. "Jajajajaa. Humans are ridiculous with their false notions. You, in particular, are ridiculous, Pukkukwerek."

CHAPTER 2

THEN THERE WAS the ghost, the one Maggie thought she'd left behind when they'd moved from Wicklow, the apparition of her murdered friend, Sally Winters, who made startling appearances at the oddest and most inconvenient moments.

Nights at O'Malley's Pub-N-Grub, the Irish tavern and grill Maggie bought after their move, were busy enough, not quite so crazy that Maggie couldn't handle the bar solo, but she preferred never to work alone because of the ghost. The pub was precisely what she had hoped for. At over 100-years-old, the red brick building stood alone in the middle of a gravel lot, flanked by a few scrawny acacia trees struggling to survive.

When the realtor first showed her the business, Maggie right off fell in love with the heavy oak door that creaked as it opened, the original wood floors, warped and worn, the high back hickory booths, and the expansive bar with the original mirror and fixtures from the early 20th Century.

On the wall closest to the bar, the former owner had constructed a raised platform framed by a set of stained-glass windows, perfect as a stage for the weekend live Celtic music. Maggie went nuts when she laid eyes on the vintage National Cash Register, bronze and brass, probably from the 1920s, and beneath it, a secret cubby she could slide open, the best spot to store a handgun for protection. On the wall adjacent to the bar, an ornate shelf might have held a small figurine or plant would be the right size to keep her keys and cell phone.

Everything dark and comfortable inside, the entire building smelled of wood and whiskey, and on one wall an Irish flag lit by a dim spotlight gave brightness to the otherwise dark room. But without warning Sally appeared and disappeared in the pub, always preceded by the scent of jasmine.

One night, Sally manifested in the pub's bathroom as Maggie pulled down her jeans and panties to sit on the toilet. She'd not seen Sally's ghost since they moved from Wicklow, so caught off guard, she nearly peed herself. "What in damn hell are you doing here?" Maggie balanced mid-squat over the loo with her pants halfway to her knees. "You aren't real. Get out."

She squinted her eyes shut. When she opened them, Sally laughed. "Sorry. I guess I did arrive at a bad time. You're out of toilet paper, you know. You might want to pull up your drawers and put on a new roll before you pee." Sally popped out of existence as fast as she'd popped in, and the jasmine scent she'd come in with faded.

Maggie wasn't up for a haunting, and anyway she'd been sure she'd hallucinated Sally's ghost. I've gotta slow down on the Jameson or see a shrink or something. I'm going ape-shit bonkers.

———

Maggie's excellent Irish cook, Diego Juan José Miramar-Sanchez Ramirez she'd known from the northern mountain town of Wicklow, CA, handled the kitchen alone. He'd grown up in Hemacinto, but moved to northern California for a change of scenery where he first worked for Maggie. To her delight, Diego moved back to Hemacinto a year or so before she did and when Jake and she moved to town, accepted her offer to work the pub kitchen. "This is home for me," he told her. "I have always loved this pub, and my mother and sister are here in Hemacinto, and all my old homies. My older sister, Graciela, divorced her loser husband. She and her two little girls moved in with Mom. We're pretty close, my big sister and I." He put his fingers together to show Maggie the tight bond between brother and sister, "and we've missed each other. I love my little nieces and I want to help Graciela so she and the kids can get their own place."

———

Diego prepared the expected fare, corned beef and cabbage, and Irish stew. But more than a cook he was a master chef trained at Darina Allen's Ballymaloe Cooker School, a prestigious Irish culinary academy located in Shanagarry, County Cork. "I was the only Mexican ever to graduate from there," he told Maggie. "In fact, I never saw any Latinos in Ireland anywhere, let alone in Shanagarry. I was a genuine novelty, the only brown boy around, and because I was different, that helped me get laid a lot. *Híole,* those Irish chicks are hot." He snapped his hand down in a sideways motion creating a cracking sound with his fingers.

Diego eternally experimented with lamb and pork, and when bored, he scoured his menu portfolio for new dishes. "I'd die if I had to boil *pinché* cabbage my whole damned life," he told Maggie. "I'm gonna add Killarney smoked salmon to the menu, a classic."

"You need to open your own restaurant."

"I don't want the headaches. I'm good here."

Maggie hired ginger-haired girls from the Music Academy to play Celtic fiddle on weekends. Diego and Maggie kept the place humming.

"Don't those things hurt your earlobes?" Maggie asked one night after closing as they cleaned the kitchen. Diego wore Dayak hardwood ear lobe plugs bigger than silver dollars, and tattoos, mostly of lizards, covered his muscular arms and neck. She sometimes referred to him by Jim Morrison's moniker, The Lizard King.

"Naw." He reached with one hand to finger one of the plugs.

"What happens when you take them out? Will your earlobes have huge holes in them forever?"

"I don't know, *Patróna.* I never take them out." He hefted a pail and dumped sudsy water down a drain, sloshing some on the floor. "Dammit. Now I gotta rewash the floor." He reached for a mop. "Adding those traditional meat pasties seem to go over pretty good with the customers. How 'bout we consider corned crubeens? And, if it's okay with you, let's build a grill out back with a spit. We can roast whole pigs over applewood. *Muy deliciosa.*" He put his fingertips to his lips and kissed them.

"I'm not sure about the crubeens. Not many come into an Irish pub in this part of California for pig's feet. That's more of a southern thing." She stretched for a rag to dry a stock pot. "I suppose we can try them. There's a new butcher in town making good deals on pork. I bet he can supply us with feet. His wife came in the other day with a business card and flyer. I stashed them under the bar somewhere. I'll get them for you."

"I saw her. She's fine looking but reminds me a lot of a blonde Amazon hooker. If that chick ever got me in a leg lock, she'd crush me to death."

"She's the one, all right."

"What about the grill? I figure we'll start the..."

Maggie's thoughts shifted back to the day Sheriff Mack showed the gruesome photos. Someone had roasted a handsome but heavy-set local dentist, his plump as a ripe berry wife, and their chubby amber-eyed teenage son over separate fires in a remote area of the San Padrinos. From evidence at the scene, the murderer or murderers may have eaten parts of the bodies right there, then balanced a container of Aunt Lorrie's Seasoned Salt on the wife's corpse. "Aunt Lorrie's Seasoned Salt? Really? What a sick, sick bastard," Maggie later said to Jake.

"And we can start building the grill near the door to the kitchen," Diego said. "I can do most of the labor myself if you buy the materials. I want a big spit, a strong one."

Maggie snapped back to the present. "Let me think about it."

"Okay," Diego shrugged his shoulders. "If you want to do this, let me know because I can get some of my cousins to help, and they'll work for beer."

The door swung open and dusty light flooded the pub. A mammoth of a man with dark hair, a handlebar mustache, and yeasty beer gut entered and straddled a stool at the end of the bar. Diego retreated into the kitchen.

"What'll it be, Hank? The usual?"

"I need a cold one in the worst way. Shit, it's hot out there. I gotta wash this grit out of my mouth."

Hemacinto summers sucked the moisture out of lungs and dried flesh to sandpaper. The desert broiled everything—plants, lizards, and insects—into crispy rinds, and humans suffered the heat as the sun fused thin shirts onto sweaty arms and backs.

Maggie pulled the tap handle, drew a mug of Coors Light, and placed it on the bar in front of the truck driver. He guzzled a measure in one noisy swallow, spilling some down his chin. She passed him a napkin. "You must be damned thirsty."

"Kinda. Gimme another."

Hank held the second mug in both hands and stared into the beer as though peering into a crystal ball. His long hair hung in oily ropes down the sides of his face, and his bloodshot eyes, puffy as dirty cotton balls had almost swollen shut. Black stubble sprouted from his cheeks like tiny porcupine quills, unusual given his penchant for neatness, his affable demeanor, and his bright slice of a fast grin. As a general rule, Hank's clothes were clean and pressed, his hair tied back with a rubber band, his mustache waxed, and his shirts buttoned to the top. Today, he looked and smelled as though he had slept for days without changing his boxers and hadn't bothered to brush his teeth. He even wore mismatched and ragged socks, one brown as toast with a hole at the ankle, the other faded from black to dingy gray as though it had taken one too many spins in the washing machine.

"What's up, Hank? You aren't yourself. You okay?"

"You heard about the murdered dentist, his wife, and kid the hikers discovered in the mountains a while back?"

"I know about that, yes." Maggie wiped the bar with a white rag. "Awful how they died."

"I know the dead guy, and I hope he fries in hell forever. It's too bad about his wife and boy, but that fat son-of-a-bitch got what he deserved, to be roasted and eaten like the pig he is, or rather was. Asshole." Hank wiped his mouth with the back of his hand.

"You knew him?"

"He was our dentist—until I caught him bonin' Rosie."

"He slept with your wife?"

"Yep." He threw back a long swig of beer. "I'd been on the road deliverin' a load of chickens to Denver. I made good time so decided to come home a day early. I thought I might surprise Rosie with a bouquet of daisies and an iced bottle of Cold Duck." He pulled his lips back over his teeth into an expression so gruesome it couldn't have been either a smile or a grimace, but something much more sinister. "I surprised her all right."

He drained the rest of his mug and handed it to Maggie. Without asking, she drew a third beer and put it in front of him.

"I came in the front door at the same time the prick was runnin' out the back. I chased him, but the chubby shit-head was fast. He got into his BMW and punched the gas pedal as I grabbed the driver door handle. Nearly ripped off my hand." Hank rubbed his fingers as though massaging away the memory of the wound. "I found Rosie in the bedroom trying to pull on her pants. I've never seen her move so fast. 'Let me explain, let me explain,' she kept sayin', and she was goin' like this the whole time." To demonstrate how Rosie was "goin'," Hank flailed his arms as though swatting away hornets. "The whore." He screwed up his face as though he'd bitten into a rotten lime. "The whole house smelled of sex."

"God, I'm sorry," Maggie said. "Are you sure it was the dentist?"

"He's the only guy in town with a gold BMW. You know what's weird?"

"What?"

"He's a fat fuck. I never thought Rosie would want to have sex with a fatso. I can't blame him. His wife was cute but chunky like him, and Rosie? Hell, she looks better than Dolly Parton in her prime." The trucker gulped his beer. "I'd recognize that twatwaffle from a mile away. All his perfect blond hair. Probably uses hair gel, the pussy."

"What did you do?"

"I'd never hurt Rosie, not for nothin'. But when I saw what she'd been up to with that goddamn weasel, I lost it. I backhanded her and split her lip. 'Go ahead, bitch. Explain.' I smacked her again, and when she fell, it took all my willpower not to stomp her to death."

"Wow, Hank. Is Rosie okay? Where is she now?"

"She jammed a bunch of clothes in a bag and took off. I don't care if that filthy, cheatin' slut ever comes back. I gave her everything. Worked my ass off to buy her that fancy double-wide, her real amethyst and sterling silver ring, and that hot pink Volkswagen Bug. The custom paint job cost me a month's pay. The bitch."

"How long ago did this happen; when did you find out?"

"A few days before they discovered the bodies. A Monday. I'll never forget it, because it was the worst day of m'life."

"Monday, you say? And, when the dentist ran from your house that was the last time you saw him or had any contact with him?"

Hank pushed himself back in his stool. "What's with all the damn questions? I came in here to get me a cold brew, and maybe find a little comfort, not to get interrogated." The truck driver hung his head and sniffled. "I haven't slept since Rosie left. I don't know what I'm gonna do now." He let loose a loud plaintive sob like a yowling cat in heat, then hung his head.

Maggie reached over the bar and patted his hand. "It's okay. Have another beer on the house."

When he looked up, instead of tears and sorrow his face registered the vilest, purest hate Maggie had ever seen.

"I'm glad the son-of-a-bitch is dead." He drained his freebie. "I wish she were dead, too." He stood and rummaged through his jean's pocket for a tip and tossed a crumpled $5 bill on the bar. "Thanks for the beer, Maggie," He walked out, letting the door slam behind him.

After the truck driver departed, Maggie picked up her cell. "Jake, call Mack. We're going to have to question Hank Peterson. I don't think he's our guy, but he could be. A few minutes ago, he gave me a powerful motive for murdering the dentist and his family. So glad tomorrow is Sunday because I need a break in the worst way." She yawned then took a deep breath through her nose.

The next morning, the sunlight blasted over the San Padrinos. A dense row of ravens perched on the white vinyl fence in the back yard. "Okay, okay," Maggie said to them. "I'm buying more corn today. Can't I even enjoy a Sunday off without you pestering me?" One expanded his chest and looked sideways at her.

"If I didn't know better, I'd think you can understand me. Now, quit shitting all over my fence. Go away, all of you. Shoo." She swiped her arm at them. One of the birds puffed up and let loose a slimy white dropping that ran the vertical length of the fence.

"You little bastard." She turned to her bloodhound stretched out asleep on a lawn chair. "Chester, you useless lump." The dog raised his head, folded his ears back, and yawned. "Can't you chase those damned birds off the fence like a normal dog would?" Chester put his head back down and closed his eyes.

Jake emerged from the house and folded her into a loose embrace. "Want something to wet your whistle? I thought I'd make us margaritas to go with lunch."

She leaned into him and pressed her face against his cheek. "How's the book coming along?"

"I'm to the part where we found the second set of twins with their hearts cut out."

She disengaged from the hug and brushed a strand of hair from his eyes. "You've made good progress since yesterday. You're a helluva writer, you know? I can't wait to read this book. On another note, how'd the interview go with Hank last night?"

"He looked surprised as hell when we picked him up. We don't have anything on him, so we had to release him. We rattled him, though."

"Did he talk about the affair?"

"He wanted to know how we knew about it."

"It'll come out soon enough that I'm part of the investigating team," Maggie said. "Can't keep news like that a secret in Hemacinto, and Hank is going to pissed off big time when he finds out I broke our sacred bartender-customer confidentiality pact."

"Be careful, Maggie. There's no proof of his innocence, and

he could be dangerous." Jake raked his fingers through his scalp as always when tense or upset. "I don't want you working at the bar alone or walking through the parking lot at night without an escort, at least until we find the killer."

Maggie whipped her head around and fixed her green eyes on him. "I can take care of myself."

"I'm not trying to...oh, hell, Maggie. I have a right to worry about you. Besides the recent murders, the crime rate is on the increase in Hemacinto, especially against women."

"I wish I'd never let you talk me into joining the reserves with you."

"We agreed when we moved down here from Wicklow we'd use our experience to help our new community and join the reserves to assist when needed. So, now we're needed. But I want you to be careful because I love you. Is that so bad?"

Jake first met Maggie in eight-grade math class. Her glossy long black hair and vivid green eyes enchanted him, but the pretty girl who sat in front of him did not return his affection. It took over thirty-five years of friendship for Maggie to finally recognize her feelings for Jake, although she never could tell him how much she loved him. He'd grown up in Wicklow, as she had, and was an only child who spent most of his young life caring for his mentally ill single mother, went on to study criminal justice, and afterward, the town elected Jake as sheriff. In all that time, even though he married someone else, who a few years after, died of virulent inflammatory breast cancer, he was in love with Maggie Tall Bear Sloan.

"I guess you're right. I'm sorry, okay?" Maggie flipped open the grill lid and stabbed a thermometer into a hunk of meat. "I'll take that margarita," she said. "Make it a double. But, can you run down to the feed store first and pick up a bag of corn for these damned ravens? Otherwise, they'll bug us all day. Lunch won't be ready for at least twenty minutes, so you'll have time."

"Sure. I'll go." Jake inhaled. "Whatcha' grillin'? Smells great. Pork?"

"Lamb shoulder. I'll never eat pig again."

—

Dead as usual on a Monday night at O'Malley's, Maggie and Diego sat side-by-side at the bar drinking beers. Maggie put on a Clannad CD and cranked up the volume. The cook's favorite bands were The Red Jumpsuit Apparatus and V.A.S.T.

"At least you're not into gangster rap and hip-hop garbage," she said when the two of them talked music. Moya Brennan's honeyed voice spilled out of the speakers, and Diego grimaced. Maggie pulled the lever and poured herself another Harp. "Sorry, bud. You're going to have to tolerate my Celtic tastes because this is the music I listen to." She made it up to him by providing as much free Guinness and Harp as he could drink.

Although Maggie usually favored sweat pants, Vans, and rarely wore make-up, for work she dressed up a bit. Tonight, she wore high-end jeans, black patent leather pumps, and a pale green cashmere sweater that clung to her breasts. Her salt and pepper braid hung below her hips and brushed against the bar stool.

Diego wore a sauce-stained, ripped cook's apron over baggy chinos, with his dark, unruly hair imprisoned under a net. A black t-shirt, with a wide hole on one shoulder, showed off his muscle bulges and tattoos.

The doorbell tinkled, and Jake entered. "Hey, anyone but me walking into O'Malley's might think you hired a gang banger or ex-con to work kitchen duty, Maggie."

Maggie scoffed. "I thought I'd locked the door. What are you doing here?"

"The critique group finished early, and thought I'd stop by to see if you were still around, and join you for a drink."

"Sure. Ale?"

"I imagine you two could be a mismatched pair of shoes— Maggie, a patent leather six-inch heeled Prada, Diego, a scratched and worn motorcycle boot."

"Nobody has ever compared me to a boot, before." Diego snickered and took a sip of his beer.

"Pay no attention to him. He's now a hot shot writer and has to demo his creative skills for us. Shoes, my ass!" Maggie grabbed Jake's collar, pulled him down to her, and kissed him on the cheek.

Diego cleared his throat. "Not to keep bugging you about this, Maggie. But what about building the grill and spit? The barbecue could boost business."

"Oh, I guess so." She sighed and stretched her arms overhead. "How much will this set me back, and what'll you need?"

"I'll do it cheaper for you than I did for that butcher."

"What do you mean?"

"When he first came to town before he opened Bond's he commissioned me to make a barbecue for him with a spit. He said he'd thought about opening a catering business and wanted something big but portable. I charged him plenty, but I'll do it for you for under a grand. I'll need cement to start with, and I'll check around to find out where we can get a large enough spit to handle a young boar hog, a heavy-duty motor, and if we are going to add barbecued meats to the menu, I'll need a case of my super-secret magic spice."

"You use a secret spice?" Asked Jake.

"I put it on everything I grill. Don't laugh when I tell you what it is."

"Okay. I'm game. What is it?"

"The master chef's touch, Aunt Lorrie's Seasoned Salt."

CHAPTER 3

O'MALLEY'S HAD BEEN in Hemacinto for so long most of the regular customers' parents, grandparents, and in some cases, great grandparents had patronized the pub. The original owner, Paddy O'Malley, a Dublin transplant, constructed the red brick building in 1909 with the help of his brothers a few years before the Volstead Act passed and prohibition slammed shut and padlocked every saloon in the United States. The brothers converted the tavern into a family-style root beer house. Paddy prided himself on brewing the best root beer and sarsaparilla in America.

The O'Malleys added a windowless back room with a secret entrance, and the addition became a favorite speakeasy. According to Hemacinto lore, raids on O'Malley's were frequent and harsh, until Paddy buckled to pressure and issued weekly payola to the local Chief of Police, a fellow Dubliner by the name of Murphy.

One slow afternoon at the pub, Diego filled Maggie in on the details. "I hear that pinché hypocrite Chief hung at the speakeasy himself with a hooker known as 'Wee Betsy,' but there was nothin' wee about that chick, a half-breed from Louisiana with titties as big as a cow's udder." Diego cupped his hands over his chest.

"Watch the half-breed stuff, my friend."

"Sorry. I didn't mean it that way."

"What way, exactly, did you mean it?"

"I said I'm sorry, okay? Can I finish my story?"

"Go ahead."

"That broad outweighed the skinny-assed cop by a hundred and twenty pounds at least. Anyway, the *puto* came around every Friday with his greedy hand extended for his $50 payola, with that whore always hangin' all over him. After they stuffed their pockets, they'd go into the speakeasy, and drink bathtub gin for free until they puked."

"Fifty bucks would have been a lot of money back in the twenties and thirties," Maggie said.

"He drained most of the bar's profits, and the O'Malley's knew they had no way out. The sonofabitch deserved what happened to him."

"What happened?"

"A couple of drunks stumbling home to their wives found the cop's body in an apricot orchard. His head missing." Diego made a sawing motion across his neck with the side of one hand. "I hear they found it a few miles away with the flesh gnawed off by a coyote or dog. His wife and kids ended up okay. The widow married a wealthy banker, and they moved to a mansion somewhere in Pasadena. No one knows what happened to his whore."

"And the speakeasy? Did the police shut it down?"

"No cop would come anywhere near O'Malley's after what happened to the Chief. The speakeasy did damn good business until 1933 after the prohibition repeal. The brothers closed the root beer operation, re-purposed the back room for storage, and reopened the bar, but after a beer delivery truck ran Patrick over in 1935, things got strange."

"How so?"

"Bar patrons complained of noises from the back room, old-time jazz-age music, people laughing, and glasses clinking. Every time the barkeep investigated, he found only boxes, dust, cobwebs, and rats."

"Good thing that's over with, you know, the bizarre noises."

"Who says it's over? I hear strange-ass old fashioned music from the 20s and 30s, voices, and other stuff all the time coming from the storage room. I put in my earbuds and ignore it."

"No way, Diego. What you mean is you've listened to all those spooky stories for so long you believe them, and now you imagine you hear that shit. There's no such thing as ghosts." She tightened her jaw. "This is a bunch of bull crap, and I don't want to hear any more about it, okay?"

"*Tranquilla, jefa*. Whatever you say, all right?" He put both hands up as a shield against her temper.

——

Sheriff Mack put Jake and Maggie in charge of the investigation. Some of the other deputies made their dissatisfaction with his decision well-known. When he introduced the pair to the rest of the investigating team, the room full of male deputies dripping sweat and testosterone leaned back in their chairs and gripped their arms across their chests. The men made furtive eye contact with one another.

"Questions?" Mack asked.

Hands flew into the air.

The sheriff gestured to a short, balding man seated at the front of the room. "Yes, Deputy? Speak up."

"Jack or uh, Jake, and, uh, Maggie...those are your names, right?" The short man waved his hand at the pair. "How long have you lived in this county?"

"We moved here end of August," Maggie said.

"So, less than a year. What do either of you know about our town and how we operate around here?"

The sheriff intervened. "I didn't put Jake and Maggie—and, yes, that is their names—in charge of this case because of their knowledge of the area, but because of their long track record of solving tough murder cases and high-profile crimes. You're all good men, but these two are the best choice for the job, and I expect you to cooperate with them. If any of you don't feel up to it, I'd be more than happy to take you off the investigation. Understood?"

Most of the men nodded. The short one stood and left the room.

Mack looked from deputy-to-deputy. "Any more questions?"

——

"Jesus H. Almighty Christ," Maggie said to Jake when they returned home from the station. They sat on lounge chairs on the backyard, Samantha curled into a fur ball on Maggie's lap. The harsh sunlight reflected off the brick and cement patio, creating a mirage so real it looked as though a rainbow trout might leap from it. During times like this Maggie missed her mountains the most, and the cool air wafting through the pines in the late afternoons. Summer in the southland even punished Maggie's tomatoes to the point where she had to cover them with shade cloth to keep them from blistering in the 116-degree heat. "God, I need to get back to Wicklow and my cabin by the river. I hate it here. Since you're up, would you go in and fix me a cool drink? I need it. Make it a strong one."

"Vodka tonic?"

"Whiskey and water over ice. Double. No, triple. Man, those guys hate us. What the fuck are we going to do if they won't cooperate? The way they looked at us...I thought they were plotting to slit our throats. Did you see that short bastard in the front get up and leave? What a little jerknozzle."

"Those men have worked in the sheriff's department for a long time, some of them for decades. We newcomers show up from out of nowhere who know nothing about their town or its people and are put in charge of what is the most important homicide investigation in the history of Hemacinto. I get their resentment. They don't know how we'll treat them. They don't know if we've got their backs. They don't know squat about us. How would you feel in their place?"

"I don't know. I guess the same as they do. Where's my whiskey?"

"Comin' right up."

"Wait. I changed my mind."

"You don't want the whiskey?"

"Hell yeah. But add a lemon twist. I have to go to work, and after all the bullshit in the sheriff's office today, I need fortification to deal with the drunks."

"So, you're getting drunk to deal with drunks?"

She laughed and smacked him on the thigh, and in return, he kissed her.

After Jake departed for the house, Maggie stood and stretched under the dappled shade of an acacia. A raven flew in a circle and perched overhead.

"How you doin', buddy?"

The bird puffed his feathers and tilted his head to get a good look at her. She stuck her hand in her pocket and withdrew some corn. "Want this?" The bird flew down and perched on her outstretched arm. "Watch the talons, will ya? You're going to poke holes in me." The bird pecked a kernel from her palm.

Jake pushed open the French door and walked out with two high ball glasses. In an aggravated rustle of feathers, the bird flew from Maggie's arm back to the tree branch.

"Did I see a wild raven eating corn from your hand?"

"I guess so. My drink?" She dropped the rest of the corn onto the brick patio, dusted her hands against her jeans, grabbed the glass from Jake and slammed down the whiskey. She handed the empty to Jake. "See you later. If you can take a break from your writing, come on down for some smoked salmon and a cold one." She grabbed her purse and took off.

Before the investigation, Maggie worked at the pub every day from first thing in the morning until closing, except Sunday, her one day off. Since heading the investigation with Jake, there was no way she should be at the pub more than a few hours a day, but O'Malley's was short-handed, so she had to fill in. After she promoted Diego to manager, she gave him a budget to bring on a full-time bartender, a server, and some kitchen help. He hired his cousins.

"Damn it, Diego. I hoped you'd find someone who at least looked a little bit Celtic. This isn't a Mexican cantina, it's an Irish pub."

"Salvador is light enough to pass. He's working the bar a few nights a week. We'll dye his hair red and tell everyone his name is O'Tool or some Irish gringo shit like that."

Jake showed up around 5 o'clock and inhaled a plate of salmon. "God, this is good. Why doesn't Diego open his own place?"

Maggie pushed another pint of Fat Tire toward Jake. "Lucky for us, he's happy working with me here."

"You better give him a raise. We don't want to lose him."

"Already did. I made him pub manager, too."

"Is this a slow afternoon? I thought Sundays were busy." Jake scanned the bar. One customer sat at the end, Tom Anselmo, watching a Seahawks pre-season game, drank from a bottle of Stella Artois. Real tall, like 6 foot three or four, with short cropped hair and a brilliant smile, Tom dropped by for a beer and sometimes to watch a game or sports commentary on weekends when his wife, Aimee, had to be out of town on business. Maggie looked forward to seeing his Seahawk Blue truck pull into the pub parking lot.

"In about an hour, customers will pour in. Between four and five is the calm before the rush," She said to Jake.

Maggie stood and walked around the backside of the bar. "Hey, Tom, need another Stella?"

"Sure, I'll take one."

She smiled at him, brushed hair from her forehead with one hand, and popped the cap off a bottle of Stella. She handed the beer to Tom. Although she wasn't one given to frequent smiles, she kept a solid grin on her face.

Jake shifted on his stool, and the muscles in his neck tensed. "Maggie, isn't Diego or Salvador handling the bar? You shouldn't even be working today. Sunday is your day off, remember?"

"Diego is in the back, making chili. Salvador is not on duty tonight, and we're going to get busy, so I need to be here. What do you want?" She lost her grin, wiped the bar top with a rag, and circled around to sit next to Jake.

"You seem a little cozy with that guy."

"And you seem a little jealous."

"I'm not jealous, only curious. Who is he?"

"Local fire captain. Married to a pretty blonde and they've got two daughters in their late teens. I hear his mother-in-law is a real witch, though. She had a stroke and lives with them, but she's demanding with a volcanic temper, so whenever his wife is gone Tom comes here looking for a way to get out of the house and away from the pitiful virago."

"How do you know so much about him and his family?"

"He's a regular. We talk sometimes. What the fuck is wrong with you? You're acting like an adolescent who caught his seventh-grade girlfriend holding hands with his best friend. He's a customer, and nothing is going on between us. What's the harm?"

"Look, I...never mind. Any way you can get off early? We have to discuss the case, and you haven't gotten much sleep lately. You've gotta be exhausted. I thought I'd make you a light dinner, and we can strategize on the investigation, and maybe we can fall into the sack early tonight?"

"Sorry, that won't work. We've got more help coming in next week, but I'm not leaving Diego on his own. It'll be a busy night, and he's going to need my help, so I'll be home around 2ish."

"Shit, Maggie. You're going to get about four hours sleep tonight, even less than last night. We have to be at the station at eight tomorrow to meet with the investigation team." He lowered his voice. "You know we are going to have to question Diego. That Aunt Lorrie's Seasoned Salt thing is incriminating."

"Let's hold off on bringing Diego in for a day or two, okay? He's slammed in the kitchen until our new employees start."

"I don't know if that's smart, Maggie."

"Please. Give it a couple of days."

"All right. It's your call. But he's a suspect and if...are you sure you can't come home early tonight or get any time off this week? Besides, we haven't had much time together lately." He scowled at Tom, so wrapped up in the televised game and his Stella he apparently didn't notice or care.

"It's only for a few more nights, then Diego's whole damned family is going to be here working the bar and kitchen, and I'll have Sundays off again."

"I don't want you to overdo it, that's all, and we have a lot of work on the investigation."

Maggie's face tensed. "I appreciate your concern, but you don't think I'm aware of what we've got facing us? I know what I have to do, and how much sleep I require to do it. I don't need you patronizing me, and I'm stressed out enough as it is without you making it worse. Quit pushing." Maggie hadn't realized she'd raised her voice until she noticed Tom staring at them. "Sorry," she said to him. "Just a little lover's quarrel."

"We've got to get a lot of documentation in, Mag. Mack is becoming annoyed, and he'll have words with you if you don't pony up the docs."

"I'll take care of my end when I get home."

"Sheriff Mack is waiting..."

"Look, I told you I'd get to the damned documentation. If it's a slow night, I'll close early. Back off a little, will you?"

That night ended up being the busiest in over a month. Maggie kept a pot of French Roast going, but no matter how much of it she sucked down, she struggled to stay awake because she'd burned all her energy reserves. Between taking orders, mixing drinks and serving, she half-dozed on her feet, but kept moving anyway. As the evening progressed, Diego and Maggie had to scramble to keep up with the customers' demands. They ran out of smoked salmon and pasties before 7:30, which pissed off a couple of tipsy good old boys who threatened never to come back.

"Are you kidding? You're out of salmon so early?" One said. "If this is how you run the place, we ain't comin' back."

Since she'd only slept for a total of five hours over the past twenty-four, Maggie's testiness had stretched to the snapping point. "Fine. Don't come back. You can get out of my bar and go somewhere else if you want to play it that way." She knew these guys. They'd be back, but she didn't care. All she wanted to do was close out the night, get home to Jake, Chester, and Samantha, finish the damned documentation, and fall into bed. Please, no raven crap tonight. I'm too damned tired to deal with any spooky shit.

Tom stood and stretched. "Well, better get home. See ya, Maggie,"

31

and headed out. A little after midnight, the last two patrons departed. "' Night, Mag," one said. The other lifted a hand in a sleepy wave.

"Get home safely, guys. If you die in a drunken' wreck, or the cops haul you off on a DUI charge, your wives will kick my ass. Can I call you an Uber?"

"Naw. We live close and can walk. We're good. We'll pick up our cars tomorrow if that's okay."

Maggie followed them to the door and turned the OPEN sign to CLOSED. "Diego, let's shut down a little early."

"You bet, *Patróna*. Why don't I make another pot of coffee? You'll fall asleep at the wheel on your way home."

"I'm going for a Jameson. Want one?"

"No thanks. I want to put the kitchen in order and get home."

Maggie helped carry empties to the back room and wiped the counter. She upturned chairs on the tables in preparation to sweep and wash the floors but decided to pour herself three fingers of the whiskey and take a break before busting out the mop and pail. She pulled a stool down from a bistro set, swallowed her Jameson, and put her head down on the table, using her crossed arms as a pillow.

In her drowsy stupor, she heard Diego banging pots and pans as he dried and stowed them. She dozed until he woke her when he rested his hand on her shoulder and gave it a gentle shake. "Hey, *jefa*," he whispered. "You gonna be okay? Need a ride home?"

"I'm fine, thanks. Go ahead. I'm right behind you." As his car engine turned, and the wheels kicked up gravel, she put her head back down on the table and fell into the deep, comforting dark hole of sleep.

She didn't shapeshift, but she did dream. There were no ravens. It was as though Maggie watched a grainy home movie, "The Sally and Maggie Show." There they were on the beach as toddlers in their matching yellow bathing suits, covered in sand, playing in the shallow surf. Their mothers sat nearby on towels under red striped umbrellas. "Come, girls. Time for lunch," Maggie's mother called out to them.

In the next scene, on a Saturday morning in Sally's pink checked bedroom, they sat side-by-side on Sally's bed braiding one another's hair. They were in the fourth grade or fifth.

"I wish I had long shiny black hair like yours." Sally wove a Kelly-green ribbon into Maggie's thick dark plait.

"You aren't half Yurok like me. You're a white girl, even a blonde, that's why you don't have hair like mine."

There they were in Jr. High at a soccer match checking out the hot boys from the rival school. Then as high school sophomores in tight jeans, tank tops, and bare feet, sitting on a rock on the lakeshore sharing a joint and drinking from a bottle of Red Mountain Burgundy. A few years later, getting blasted on tequila shots the night before Sally's wedding. Later, a tearful Sally helping Maggie pack her '54 cherry red Chevy pickup on her last day in Wicklow before heading off on her own to attend UCLA.

Everything about their life together packed into one dream, including Maggie's retirement and return to Wicklow, where they often sat together in Sally's coffee house and bookstore, Mama Winter's, hot mugs of French Roast in-hand. "You do make great coffee, Sally."

It was all there, up to the night Maggie arrived home late and found Sally face-up in a dark lake of her own blood, her heart cut out and eaten by a monster, the same monster Maggie took pleasure in pumping full of bullets later.

"Maggie? I know you don't believe it, but I'm still here," Sally said in the dream, chatty as always.

"Why are you here? You're dead."

"Depends on what you think 'dead' is. I'm here because I love you. You were my best friend, and you need my help now."

"With what?"

"You, girlfriend, are going to be faced with a tragedy, a huge one. This investigation will bring more sorrow down on you than you can imagine, and when it does, I intend to be here for you."

"What do you mean? Sorrow for me? For whom? We'll catch the sonofabitch before he can cause any more pain."

Maggie awoke. A damp stain spread on her blouse sleeve where she'd slobbered on herself. "Mother of Christ. What a dream." She lifted her head from the table. At first, the overwhelming scent of jasmine filled the room, then there sat Sally across from her looking very much alive. "Maggie, you need to go home now, finish the police stuff you're behind on, and get some real sleep. Look at what you did to your silk blouse."

"Holy goddamn shit! Why don't you leave me alone? You aren't here. There's no way you can be real. No. Fucking. Way."

CHAPTER 4

WHEN AT THE pub Maggie first met Nola McCabe-Bond, owner of McCabe's Gym and wife to the new butcher in town, she could not envision this fit and firm beauty as ever having been overweight, let alone more than 200 pounds beyond the standard cultural definition of "heavy."

Their second meeting occurred after Jake and Maggie had compared bellies side-by-side in their bedroom full-length mirror early one morning and decided they both needed to work off one too many servings of shepherd pie and way too many pints of Harp Ale.

"Damn that Diego. It's his fault my favorite jeans don't fit." Maggie patted her belly.

"Yeah? Well, since I've been chowin' down on his fine cooking, I've had to let my belt out another notch." Jake poked his finger into his spongy spare tire.

"That's it. We're joining that new gym today."

——

They stepped into a bright gym with all new equipment. A pretty, slight-built girl with curly chestnut hair, an intense smile, and a tight butt greeted them when they entered. "Welcome to McCabe's. Can I help you?"

"Only if by joining you can guarantee I'll end up with an ass like yours," Maggie said.

The girl's laughter made her coppery curls shake. "We can work on that." She clasped hands with Maggie and Jake. "I'm Skye Miller. I do a little bit of everything around here."

"I'm Maggie. This is Jake." Maggie indicated "Jake" with her thumb.

"I'll get the paperwork for you, and let the owner know you're here. She likes to personally meet new gym members."

The girl disappeared behind a counter, pulled out two packets attached to clipboards, and two pens. "Go ahead and complete those. I'll be right back." She turned and tapped on the door to a glassed-walled office with the blinds pulled.

"Yes?" A female voice answered.

"Nola, two new members, Jake and Maggie, are in the lobby."

"Good. I'll be out in a minute."

As Jake and Maggie handed their completed paperwork to perky Skye, the office door opened and out walked a golden woman looking as though she'd stepped from a pre-Raphaelite painting into the modern world. She'd pulled her strawberry blond hair into a high ponytail, wore a pair of snug pink gym shorts, leaving little to the imagination, and a matching spandex top, barely covering her implants. Maggie thought the woman carried eight percent body fat at the most. *Where have I seen her before?*

The moment Jake, busy checking out the gym equipment, turned his head and the goddess came into his view, he gasped.

Maggie elbowed him in the ribs and whispered, "Don't even think about it, you old...Crap! That's the woman who came into O'Malley's with the meat flier, the butcher's wife," she whispered.

"Hello. I'm Nola, and you must be...wait...I know you." She pointed her French-manicured forefinger at Maggie. "Aren't you the new owner of the Irish pub, hon? Your cook...Dano, is it?" Nola cocked her head causing her blond ponytail to hang over her shoulder.

"Diego." An unmistakable sweet fragrance hit Maggie and overwhelmed her with a childhood memory. *Nola wears White Shoulders, the same perfume Grandma Sloan used to wear. I haven't smelled that in years.*

"Right, Diego. He ordered a pulled pork special from us from the flyer and price list I left with you. I know our prices are a little steep, but we do have the best pork. Even Diego says so. You've got a great tavern there, and by the way, I'm hiring León."

"León?"

"Your cook's cousin, or nephew, or something."

"Figures," Maggie said.

"León is working his way through USC doing odd jobs and delivering meats. He's a super smart kid and a hard worker, and kind of cute for a youngster. In fact, so cute I noticed even the gay men in the gym follow him around like smitten puppies." She raised an eyebrow then winked. "You haven't met him?"

"Not yet."

"I'll introduce you when I next come in; he'll be delivering pork for our shop."

Maggie decided even though this woman was a major bimbo, and called her "hon," and despite the fact Jake couldn't keep his eyes off those tits, she thought Nola might be okay after all.

"Come into my office. I want to show you something." Nola turned and walked toward the office. Jake glued his eyes to her butt, and Maggie elbowed him again. "Knock it off, you horny crapweasel," she whispered.

"What was that you said about Tom Anselmo? What's the harm?"

"Shut up." Maggie elbowed him.

"What?" Nola asked. "I'm sorry, but I didn't quite catch what you said."

"I commented to Jake on how clean you keep your gym."

"Why am I not surprised?" Maggie whispered as they entered Nola's office. The first thing Maggie noticed was the cold. The air conditioning turned full blast reminded Maggie of the time she'd visited the Grewingk Glacier on a trip to Alaska, and in response to the chill, she unconsciously wrapped her arms around herself. Pink was the next thing she observed. The walls were painted rose pink, the pile carpet dyed a deeper pink, and all the white furnishings were upholstered in costly pink floral fabric. Lots and lots of pink.

A male blue point Siamese curled on a velour upholstered settee opened his eyes, stretched, and yawned. *She can't be all bad. She's got a Siamese.* "Hey there," Maggie said to the cat.

"Allow me to introduce you to Sir Jasper. He's the king of the gym." Nola stroked the cat's back then took a seat in her high-back carved chair.

"Male? Is he neutered?"

"Nope. I know I should get him fixed, but…"

"I've got a female seal point. We can mate them." Maggie reached to scratch the cat under his chin. He closed his eyes and purred.

"That would be great. I'd love to have a Siamese kitten or two." Nola waved her hand toward the chairs opposite her desk. "Sit anywhere you feel comfortable. Do you want water with lemon, or Skye can bring a pot of peppermint tea if you'd prefer?"

"No thanks. We're good." Maggie sat next to the cat who climbed into her lap and rubbed against her arm. Jake dropped into an overstuffed wingback.

Maggie leaned back into the chair, still stroking the cat. "You had something to show us?"

Nola pulled a white leather binder from a drawer on her desk and positioned it so Jake and Maggie could see. She opened to a page of photographs, one an 8 x 10 of a woman wearing a shapeless printed mu-mu. In the photo, she sat in an armless chair she could barely fit on. Her buttocks hung over both sides. She was big, maybe 400 or more pounds, and rolls of fat hung like loose sacks of raw bacon from her arms and face. In an opposing photo, another woman, buff, cut, stunning, and at most, 130 lbs., in a barely-there white bikini accepted a second-place ribbon for Ms. Fitness Competition, Las Vegas.

It took a second for Maggie to register that both women were Nola.

"Jesus," said Jake.

Maggie looked from one photo to the other. "That's you?"

"Yes. I weighed 408 in this photo," Nola pointed to the photo of the woman in the mu-mu. "In this other photo, I weigh 126 and still do. I'd weigh less if it were not for the muscle." She flexed her bare arms, swelling her triceps and biceps.

"My God. Amazing. Good for you," Maggie said. "How'd you do it?"

"Over four years of dieting, excellent quality protein, extreme exercising, hon, and a great personal trainer, my husband."

"No kidding?" Jake said.

"That's how we got together. Before becoming a butcher, he worked as a personal trainer. I knew I had the best man in the world when we finally got into a real relationship, yet at first, I had no interest in him, partly because my non-existent self-esteem as in 'heaven forbid if he were to ever see me naked at my weight,' so I pushed him away hard. In fact, the more he pursued me, the more I pushed him away, and he never gave up. You would have thought from the flowers and love notes I had to be the most beautiful and desirable woman on the planet. James Bond fell in love with me when I was at my heaviest, and though things have cooled down with us between the sheets, if you get my drift, I'm crazy-in-love with him to this day, and he still..."

"Wait, your husband's name is James Bond? As in 'shaken not stirred' James Bond?" Maggie asked.

"As in his mother had a crush on Ian Fleming, and since she'd married a man with the last name of Bond, I guess she figured 'why not?'"

"That's pretty damned hilarious," Jake said.

"What's hilarious is once he completed his training and we moved here, he wanted to name his new shop '007 Meats' with the tag line 'Try our top-secret spy sauce so good, you'll need a license to kill for a taste.' I put my foot down. We're simply Bond's Butcher Shop."

"I bet the poor guy had to deal with a lot of bad jokes and some bullying growing up," Jake said.

"Oh, no he didn't. No one touched James or teased him, not ever, I assure you." Nola flipped the page and there stood James Bond, all 6 ft. 5 inches of him with muscles like Conan the Barbarian, and lush brown shoulder-length hair.

"He still looks like that, too, only his hair is shorter and a bit more silver these days. He's put on a few pounds, but it suits him. James is my very own hunk. You'll meet him soon, I'm sure." Nola closed the photo album and put it on the desk.

"Most likely your husband thinks the same of you. You look as good now as you did in those last photos, maybe better," Maggie said.

"Well, I've had a little work done." Nola patted her cheeks with both hands and laughed. "Sure I can't get you tea or something, hon?"

I wish she'd quit calling me hon. "Our dog's in the back of the truck waiting for us, and has to pee by now." Maggie stood, and Jake followed.

Nola rose from her chair reminding Maggie of a mermaid rising from the Aegean Sea. "Will you two be here tomorrow to try the machines?"

"You bet. We have to go to Target and buy some work-out togs, but we'll be here," Maggie said.

"Wait a minute." Nola leaned over her desk and opened an online calendar. "Good. I'll be in. When you arrive, ask Skye to let me know, and I'll give you a more thorough personal tour, and show you how to use the equipment." She grinned and pulled her fingernails through her ponytail.

Even her goddamn teeth are perfect. Maggie rubbed her tongue across her own teeth.

"So good to have you both here with us at McCabe's." Nola extended her hand to shake.

As Jake and Maggie headed across the parking lot, Maggie asked, "So what do you think?"

"Damn. Nola is something else. Whew. She's nice, I mean not as nice as you, naturally, but..."

"That's not what I meant, you cockwad. Of course, you think she's great, especially her ass, I'm sure. I'm talking about the gym."

"Hell, if I didn't know better, I'd think you are the one who is a little jealous. At least I'm not drooling all over Nola like you do on that Tom guy."

"Fuck you." Maggie gave him a playful shove.

———

That night, the raven dream took a twist. Instead of shapeshifting, Maggie found herself in a darkened movie theater, deserted except for Sally sitting next to her, snacking on popcorn. The two old friends watched a movie with talking ravens in the starring roles. Maggie reached into Sally's popcorn bag and took a handful of the buttery stuff, and then another, shoving each fist full into her mouth, chewing and swallowing so hard she nearly choked. "God, this is good. Too bad this stuff is so fattening." Then she grabbed another hand full and stuffed it into her mouth. Butter dribbled down her chin.

On the screen ran a cartoon with a 40's vibe, like something out of the old Heckle and Jekyll magpie cartoon series. It should have been fun, silly, but no. The images on the screen loomed menacing and shadowy. Loony Toon type ravens with goofy eyes pulled off chunks of road kill. No, it wasn't road kill but the liver from the charred body of a corpulent man. No, the corpse wasn't burned, but cooked, though, with the corpse face up, both legs missing. The ravens sliced open the cooked cadaver's bulbous stomach with their beaks and pulled out entrails. On the body's left hand, a ragged stump where a raven had bitten off the thumb left a clean, red, wound. They ate the man's face, pulling at the skin, so it snapped like rubber bands until nothing remained except bits of scalp and a toothless skull. One raven worked to pry open the jaw, grabbed the tongue and yanked it out, causing the cadaver's head to jerk forward. Maggie overwhelmed with nausea, stood to leave.

Sally placed a restraining hand on her forearm. "Wait a minute. Sit. They have something to tell you."

"I'm listening." Maggie eased back into her chair. One of the ravens, a big fellow, hopped onto the corpse and looked at Maggie. Blood and pieces of raw flesh hung his beak. His yellow eyes spun in opposite directions. "Caw, kraa. You, Maggie Tall Bear Sloan, remember you are what you eat. Bon Appétit, Pukkukwerek."

Unable to hold back, Maggie doubled over and retched.

Sally grabbed Maggie's hair and held it off her friend's face. "It's okay, sweetie. I'm always here for you, my dear, always."

Maggie vomited liquefied yellow fat, gallons of it, butter.

Mixed into the grease were bits of partially digested popcorn and unidentifiable meat particles. When sure her stomach had nothing left to regurgitate, she sat straight and wiped the back of her hand across her mouth. As she was about to ask for water, her gut contracted violently, and she dry-heaved dull green bile, gagging so hard she thought she would suffocate. When something solid moved from her abdomen through her esophagus, she bent over further and expulsed an entire human thumb.

CHAPTER 5

MAGGIE AWOKE THE next morning to the strains of Eric Clapton's "Lay Down Sally." The song title reminded her of the horror of last night's dream with Sally, and the grotesque cartoon ravens.

Although early, Jake had been awake for hours working on his novel in the small guest room he'd commandeered as his 'writing space'. When he wrote, he always played classic late 60's/early 70's rock. Canned Heat, Grateful Dead, and Eric Clapton were his favorites, not the kind of music Maggie thought anyone would expect a good 'ole boy ex small-town sheriff to enjoy.

"Classic rock 'n roll stimulates my creative impulse," he told Maggie. Once he closed the door of the guest room, and turned up his tunes, except for when he emerged for a pee break, to get something to eat, or to read a juicy passage to Maggie, she might not see him for hours. She knocked on his door. "Jake. Hey, Jake."

He dialed down the volume. "Come on in."

"Nope. Come on out. We gotta get to the sheriff's office. We're interviewing Diego this morning."

"Ugh. I almost forgot. Let me finish this one last paragraph where I'm..."

"We're late. Gotta go now."

—

The air conditioning in the sheriff's office blasted cold air that could in no way begin to compete with Diego's frigid glare. He sat in the metal chair across from Maggie in the interview room. "*Jefa,* what's this about? If it's because of that little recreational reefer I sold back in..."

"I don't give a damn about the pot, and I'm sorry I had to ask you here. Bear with me, but I need you to answer a few questions."

"About what? Mexicans don't much like cop stations, and I've got a lot of work back at the pub. We got customers coming in today, you might remember." He crossed his arms and set his jaw.

At Maggie's request, Jake and Sheriff Mack steered clear. They observed the interview on a monitor from an adjacent room. Maggie believed Diego had nothing to do with the murder of the dentist and family, but her shoulders were so tense they pulled halfway to her ears. I've been wrong before. "Do you recall where you were on the 15th between the hours of midnight and 3 a.m.?"

"Hell no. That was a while ago. If the 15th fell on Sunday, I'd be out drinking with my homies and would have gone to my apartment after to sleep it off. Why?"

"Can anyone verify you were drinking with them or knew you were asleep during those hours? And I don't want to get too personal, but were you alone while you slept?"

"I don't even know what I was doin' last week, let alone last month, or who I was with. C'mon. What's this about?"

"We are investigating the murders of the dentist and his family and we..."

"Are you saying I had something to do with that? I don't understand."

Maggie searched Diego's eyes. She spoke in a slow, deliberate tone. "You always use Aunt Lorrie's Season Salt on all your grilled and barbecued meats, don't you?"

"Yeah. So what?" Diego's expression shifted from annoyed to perplexed. "What does seasoned salt have to do with people gettin' killed?"

Her shoulders relaxed a little, and she exhaled. "It's okay, Diego. I've got what I need. Go back to work, and I'll catch up with you later."

"I'm free to go? You sure you don't want to ask me for my marinade recipe, or question me about the brand of cooking oil I prefer? What *pinché* crazy shit is this?"

"I appreciate your coming down, Diego. Sorry for taking your time."

Diego rose and stormed out the door, shaking his head,

muttering in Spanish. Maggie followed him out of the interview room, and once he left the building, she approached Jake and Sheriff Mack. "Not our guy," she said.

"How did you figure that one out?" Jake took a sip from a chipped coffee mug.

"Did you notice his reaction when I asked about the seasoned salt?"

"No, not really." Jake looked at the sheriff. Both men shrugged their shoulders.

"That's the point. He didn't react, at least not the way we could expect. What about Hank? Is he coming in for questioning?"

"Can't locate him," Mack said. "No one has seen him in days. We're looking for him, but he might not even be in town."

"Interesting," Maggie said. "Is he on the road?"

"His rig is parked beside his house," the detective said.

"Think he bolted?" Jake asked Maggie.

"Maybe so, and maybe he's scared. Could be our killer because he certainly had motive and opportunity. We have to find him and bring him in."

⸺

Maggie returned to the pub late. Diego and the crew had their hands full with serious drinkers and famished customers. Tom sat in his regular seat with his Stella. When Maggie smiled at him, he smiled back. "Hi, Mag."

Maggie stepped into the kitchen and shouted over the din of clanging pots and pans, and the sizzle of meats and vegetables frying on the stove. "Hi, Diego. Sorry to be late. I'll take over the bar."

The cook glowered at her, turned his back and with a wooden spoon stirred the contents of an over-sized bowl with such ferocity Maggie thought he'd break his wrist. She worked her way through the kitchen and rested her hand on Diego's shoulder. "I'm sorry we had to call you in."

Diego threw the spoon into the bowl so hard the contents

splashed over the counter and onto the wall. He ripped off his apron and tossed it on the floor. "I gotta talk to you, *Patróna*. Right now. I gotta talk to you." He barked orders in Spanish to the dishwasher and stomped toward the back door, Maggie behind him.

Once they were both outside, he turned to her and put his face a few inches from hers. "If you think I had any goddamn thing to do with the dentist and his wife and kid gettin' murdered, fire me right now. I work my *cajones* off for you, and you think I'm a *pinché* killer?" His face livid red, his eyes wild as a cougar's, Maggie could tell Diego struggled to keep his temper in check.

"Hold on there, guy. Back down. I told you already I had to question you. I had a good reason."

"Well, you better tell me 'the good reason' or I'm walking outta here now. I sat in that damned cold sheriff's office, and you got in my face like I'm some sort of lyin' crazy-assed outlaw gang-banger. You examined me like you think I'm a murderer. Then you gimme' some bullshit questions about spices I use on meat? You think I killed and cooked those people, is that it, eh?"

"I can't discuss the details of the case, Diego. I don't think you had anything to do with the murders, no, and, again, I am sorry I had to question you." Maggie looked down at her feet, then back at Diego. "I can't handle this place without you. You're the best damned cook in Hemacinto, maybe the state, and one helluva manager, reliable, smart, and professional. I'd be crazy to offend you. I need you, and I'm asking that you trust me, please."

He nodded. "Okay." His voice softened. "I trust you, but it pissed me off so bad you pulled me in to that police station and...what you did...it wasn't right, it just wasn't. You disrespected me...and I felt like..." He broke off and gazed into the night sky as though searching for something.

"I know." Maggie gave Diego's arm a squeeze.

—

The last of the late-night crowd dispersed, and Maggie wiped down the bar. "Diego," she called. "Come on out and have a drink with me. You've earned it."

He emerged from the kitchen, drying his hands on a towel. "I could use a Don Julio shot."

"Have two. Hell, have three." She took the Don Julio Silver from the top shelf, pulled out two shot glasses and poured. "Take off your apron and sit. I'll clean the rest of the kitchen later."

Diego removed his apron and tossed it on the bar. He held his glass to Maggie in a toast. "*Salud*," and threw back his shot. Maggie followed suit. She reached for the bottle to pour a second round but stopped short when her cell phone buzzed. Jake's name appeared on the caller ID.

"What's up, Jake? Diego and I are having a nightcap. Why don't you come by and join us?"

"I received a call from Mack. They think they found Hank."

"Great. Is he at the station? I'll head on over, and we'll talk to him. I'm glad you..."

"Maggie listen."

"...found him because I'm pretty sure he's our guy and he'd skipped..."

"Maggie, will you please shut up for a second, dammit?"

"What?"

"We think he's dead."

"Oh no. What happened?"

"Your boyfriend, Tom, called it in. He found a body when his crew putting out a grass fire in the open space that borders the property line behind Hank's house. Legs and liver missing like the others. We are waiting for the forensic report. Looks like Hank's killer...or we think it's Hank...carved pieces out of the body because, in addition to the missing legs, there are hunks of flesh missing from his sides and butt. The killer left his calling card, the Aunt Lorrie's Salt container, balanced on his chest."

"Jesus! Any note? By the way, Tom isn't my boyfriend, you jealous asswipe."

Jake laughed. "Yeah, I'm an asswipe alright. No note, but a weird thing: Ravens or crows or something had gotten to his head and eaten the skin from it, leaving nothing but pieces of scalp and skull, and what's even weirder both his teeth and tongue are missing. Whoever did this tore him open and gutted him, and what's stranger…"

"What the fuck can be any stranger than what you told me, Jake?"

"The killer folded the vic's hands across his chest and left what Sheriff Mack considers another clue."

"What?"

"The killer severed the thumb from the left hand."

CHAPTER 6

MAGGIE AND JAKE sat hip-to-hip on their sofa. Although later than late, adrenalin kept Maggie awake. She opted not to share her dream of Sally and the cartoon ravens. *It was a damn dream, nothing more, and the severed thumb thing was coincidental, I'm sure of it.*

"When do we get the results of the forensic test?" Maggie asked Jake.

"We'll know in a day or two. The coroner sent tissue samples to the lab for DNA. Fingerprints cooked off, and it looks like the perp or perps tortured before killing him. Forensics report says the killer yanked the teeth before death. Without teeth and prints, it's difficult to make a positive ID. We'll have to run DNA."

"Are we sure the vic is male?"

"Yup. About Hank's age, too, but we don't know for certain. One thing, though, this guy might be Hank, but if so, he'd put on weight awfully damned fast. We can't jump to conclusions about the ID until we get the lab results." Jake scratched Chester's head, and as he patted the old bloodhound, he continued. "Who would torture someone, cook them, carve out the liver along with chunks out of the muscle meat, and leave seasoned salt at the scene?"

"A murdering asshole who gets a major kick out of taunting the cops, that's who. The Aunt Lorrie's Salt is more than a calling card. It's a morbid joke. When I run a profile, I'm guessing I'll find that this guy, whoever he is, is a psychopath with an ugly sense of humor who has been killing for a long while."

"We're investigating other cannibalistic murders, hoping to find a similar MO. Nothing yet."

Maggie sat back, folded her arms behind her head, and put her feet on a wooden footstool. She stretched and yawned. "I'm exhausted, but no way I can sleep right now. How 'bout a brandy and coffee?"

Jake stood. Chester pawed at his leg in a bid for more petting. "No more, boy. I need a break. Maggie, I think the body has to be Hank's."

"I think so, too. If you put on the coffee. I'll pour the brandy."

—

Maggie didn't recall falling asleep on the couch. When she woke the following morning, she found Jake had tucked her under the quilt her sister-in-law, Cathy, years before had made for her as a birthday gift. The images on the quilt were of salmon, bear, quail, with a Wintu pattern around the border. Cathy, a full-blooded Wintu, took it upon herself to remind Maggie that although she had immersed herself in her Irish heritage from her father's side, Maggie was Yurok on her mother's side. Cathy often scolded her. "You listen to all that Irish music, and run that white Irish bar, and it makes you forget you're Indian."

"I'm not forgetting, Cathy. I identify more with my father's culture. Nothing more to it."

"That's because you ain't listenin' too good to your Native half. But your grandnieces — them little girls with Modoc from their mommy, and Yurok and Wintu from their daddy are more Indian than you, and since they ain't got no ma or grandmas 'cept me, they need their great aunt to show them about their culture, too. You can teach 'em stuff if you knew somethin'. You don't even talk much Yurok and no Modoc. No Wintu."

"I know. I know."

"You gotta help me and Jimmy teach them little girls about their Indian side. They should grow up proud, and it ain't good for them otherwise with all them white people runnin' things."

"I'll do my best, Cathy."

—

The cell rang, and Maggie pushed the button.

"Hello."

"It's me, Cathy."

"I've been thinking about you. I slept under your quilt last night."

"I hope it gave you dreams, so you remember you're a Yurok woman."

"It reminded me, all right."

"Danny and me gotta go up north on tribal business. I'm on the Wintu council now, and the tribe is talkin' about disenfranchisin' a band. Bad stuff. Jimmy gotta good job dry wallin' at a fancy house in Los Angeles. Can you take Flower and Bird for a couple of days? School ain't startin' for 'nuther two weeks, and we got no one else."

"Of course, I'll take them." *Oh, crap...the investigation.* "I have to work. I've been called in on a case, but we'll figure things out."

Flower and Bird were Maggie's twin grandnieces. Her brother, Danny, had married the teenaged Cathy, four months pregnant with the only child they'd ever have, Jimmy Tall Bear Sloan. The nephew and his aunt, Maggie, had their differences, but when his wife, a half Modoc/half French beauty had abandoned him and their twin daughters who were but toddlers at the time, Maggie did her best to mend things with Jimmy. She loved her grandnieces with their shiny black bobs and their dark eyes. But Jimmy resisted reconciliation and jabbed Maggie at every opportunity.

—

"Any ravens, recently?" Jake asked Maggie. "Did they tell you anything to help with the case?"

"Almost every night I fly with them, but no info. Did I tell you about the albino? Not a speck of any color other than white, female, blue eyes."

"An albino raven?" Jake looked at Maggie as though he'd seen a three-headed purple Martian.

"More common than you think, and sacred to a good many Natives. Almost every tribe has some spiritual belief about albino animals."

"White ravens?"

"All albino animals. Leni Lenape, a storyteller from the Susquehannock Iroquois, says albino animals are not to be trifled with or killed. It's a big taboo, and if broken the consequences are harsh because of the nasty curses attached. Bear Two Arrows from the Delaware tribe, an expert in Owl Medicine, says the taboo extends to even non-Native hunters because the white animals are easy prey, and the hunter would have an unfair advantage. It's considered bad form even among modern-day hunters to kill albino prey. Unsportsmanlike. In any event, white animals are supposedly connected with sacred spirit medicine, especially buffalo and owls, but ravens, too. The question I have to ask myself is this: are those spirits always good or sometimes evil?"

"How'd you find this out about the white animals, and why the renewed interest in Native American mythology?"

"I promised Cathy I'd learn more about Native ways. She wants me to help Jimmy and Danny with instructing Bird and Flower about their culture. I'd rather teach them about The Troubles in Ireland and talk to them about their Belfast tribal history. But...I promised, and so there you have it."

"Do you think the albino is around to give you insights into the case?"

"I hope so, but there's something different about that raven. It's almost like she's not a bird at all."

CHAPTER 7

MAGGIE MISSED SALLY. The two had grown up together, and other than Jake, Sally had been Maggie's only real friend. "I loathe it here," she'd told Jake, "and I need Sally, not her ghost, but the live, beautiful friend I shared wine with on the banks of Wild River and talked to about everything."

"You could make a friend here if you wanted to."

"I doubt it. Why would I want to hang around with some vapid bitch whose primary concern is if her lipstick matches her shoes, or the scuzzy barfly interested in banging her?"

"I'm not talking about those cheap tarts who hang out at your pub."

"Screw you." She laughed and gave him a quick hug.

But in spite of herself, Maggie did like Nola. The next day when Jake and Maggie showed up at the gym, Maggie tapped on the office door.

"Come in."

Maggie plopped in a chair across the desk from Nola. "Gotta minute?"

"What can I do for you, hon?"

"We're new in town."

"Yes?"

"The thing is, I'm working on this tough case, and I own a pub, and like I said, Jake and I are by ourselves, we're under a lot of stress, me especially, and I..."

"Would you like to go out for a glass of wine sometime?"

"Yes. Exactly." Maggie's face lit with a wide smile. "It would be great to have the opportunity to bounce things off another woman and relax a little."

"How about this Friday?"

Maggie shook her head. "Can't. Friday is one of O'Malley's busiest nights, and I have to work."

"When's a better time?"

"It's difficult for me to get away any night. How about you show up at the pub some Wednesday or Thursday early, and I'll order us a bottle of wine. We'll get a corner booth. Diego can run things while we talk."

"Let me check my calendar." Nola keyed something into her computer with the tips of her hot pink fingernails. It sounded like a woodpecker on the roof of a barn. Click, click, click. She halted, leaned forward in her seat and squinted at the screen. "Perfect. I'll be there on Wednesday."

—

When Nola showed up at O'Malley's, three of the regulars sat at the bar, one of them, Tom. She wore a tight orange paisley dress so short as she walked, she flashed her black lace panties. As the door swung open flooding the dusky pub with afternoon sunglow, the men turned. She stood in all her glory in the open doorway back-lit from the outside brightness. Tom gave a quick look, then put his attention back on his beer. One of the others sucked in his breath, and the other issued a low whistle.

"Jesus, you guys. Show some class." Maggie greeted the other woman, gesturing for her to step through, allowing the door to close behind. Nola reached out for a hug, but Maggie stiffened, patted the other woman's back, and pulled away.

"Not much of a hugger, hon?"

"Well...I only...hey, Diego, could you bring us a good bottle of pinot noir? Okay with you, Nola?"

"Perfect. I always drink red, and pinot noir and old vine zin are my favs."

She likes the same wine Sally always drank. "Great. Let's take this booth in the back."

The two women scooted into the booth opposite one another, and Diego brought a bottle of Hirsh Vineyards, and when Maggie nodded her approval, he opened the wine and poured an inch for Maggie to taste.

Maggie took the glass by the stem and brought it to her nose. "Ummm," She tasted, letting the wine slip around her tongue and into her cheek. "Delicious. Thanks, Diego, and don't bother to pour. You can leave the bottle on the table."

Within a few minutes, the women talked like they'd known one another for decades. By the third glass of pinot, Maggie relaxed. "So, McCabe. Irish name?"

"Scots Irish. My great grandparents on my father's side emigrated from Ulster, County Louth during the potato famine, but the family, except for a couple of errant cousins who intermarried, kept to the Irish Catholic community and wed within their own. My mother, a Dubliner, a Kelly from an old family, came to California for college and stayed. Until the day she died, she kept that beautiful Irish lilt to her voice. Like music."

Irish. That seals it. I've made a friend. Maggie poured another glass for the two of them, finishing the bottle, then motioned for Diego. "One more bottle, please. I've befriended an Irish woman at last. Someone like me."

"Hey, *Patróna*. You're half Yurok, too."

Maggie's eyes narrowed to olive green slits. "My Dad was an Ulster man. He died for his beliefs, and my name is Irish. Would you get the wine, please?"

"Okay, okay, whatever you say."

Three hours later, and another two bottles gone, the women still talked. The tavern had filled with patrons, emptied, filled again. Diego and the servers kept on a dead run, but Maggie, generally attentive to the pub business, remained oblivious. She hadn't even noticed Tom had left. She told Nola about Sally, about her life in Wicklow, about her father, about her time as a criminologist in Oakland. Nola told stories of her life, her Irish mother, and of her childhood as a fat girl bullied by her classmates.

"I have a question about your perfume. White Shoulders?"

"It's my signature scent. My grandmother used to wear it, as did my mother."

"You're kidding? My paternal grandmother loved that perfume, too. Our family bought her a new bottle every year for her birthday until she died. When I smell White Shoulders, I cannot help but think of my grandmother."

Nola finished and put the empty on the table and reached for the water pitcher. "I hear this place is haunted."

"I dunno," Maggie said. She told Nola about the speakeasy and the story about Chief Murphy and Wee Betsy. "Some customers say they have seen them around, but almost always the spooky sightings happen to occur after someone has downed a half dozen whiskeys, and too much Jameson can make anyone see anything."

A few minutes past midnight, Nola's phone rang. She pressed the button on her cell. "I'm doing great...no, no...don't worry. Maggie and I are still talking. Yes. At her pub. We're fine... Don't worry, I told you. Yeah. A little tipsy. We're drinking wine. Yes. I promise. I'll get a ride home. Don't wait up. I'll be there later. Love you, too. Did you say León is with you? He's working late, isn't he?" She paused for a few seconds. "I love you too." Then she hung up and put her cell on the table.

"Your husband?"

"I told him I'd be gone a couple of hours, and it's more than double that." She took a sip of wine. "Damn, this is yummy. You know something? I haven't talked like this with another woman for years, Maggie. It's nice, and I'm so delighted to have met you."

"Thanks. I'm glad we met, too. Want something to eat?" She turned to motion for Diego, and that's when she caught a whiff of Jasmine. There on a corner barstool sat Sally with a glass of wine in her hand. Unsmiling, looking hard into Maggie's eyes, the ghost upended her wine letting the red liquid spill onto the floor. It seemed all the world to Maggie like blood.

What the fuck. My ghost friend is jealous of my new real friend? Bullshit. When Maggie looked again, Sally and the blood had vanished.

"Are you okay?" Nola said.

"So, would you like some fish and chips, or shepherd's pie? Diego makes the best.

"No thanks. I'll take another glass of wine, though." Nola held out her empty glass.

"You're my kind of gal." Maggie poured another drink for the two of them.

Diego brought the next bottle of wine, then returned with two glasses, a small bucket filled with ice, and a pitcher of water. "You two might want to hydrate a little."

The goddess tilted her head and smiled. "How sweet of you."

Maggie glanced at the cook, then looked at the still smiling woman across the table.

Diego poured the water and set the pitcher on the table. "Need anything else? If not, I'm going to clean the kitchen, and go home."

"Go ahead. Lock the door on your way out. Have a good night."

Another hour passed, and another. Although the conversation remained lively, Maggie could not stop thinking about Sally's apparition, the blood spilling from the wine glass, and Nola's unmistakable flirting with Diego. Her phone rang. "Hello."

"This is Jake."

"You don't think I know who you are? I sleep with you, remember?"

"Hey, I don't want to bug you, but we got some news on the body we thought was Hank's."

"What do you mean 'thought' was Hank's?

"Coroner's report came in. The dead guy was an escaped con from Hemacinto Jail on route to Folsom in a prison bus."

"What was he in for?"

"Murder. He cooked and ate his victims, too, like our guy. Might be the same. Can you meet Mack and me at the station right away?"

"Hold on a minute." She pressed the mute button. "Sally...I mean, Nola. I'm sorry, but I gotta go. Something has come up on the case."

This time when Nola reached out for a hug, Maggie hugged back. When they broke apart, a few feet behind Nola the ghost of Sally stood, her face rigid. Where there should be eyes were black holes that went on forever.

"So, you're not talking now? Quit trying to creep me out," Maggie said under her breath.

"What did you say?" Nola asked.

"No, no. It's nothing." Maggie smiled. "I enjoyed the evening. Shall we do this again?"

"You bet, hon."

I better call us both an Uber. Neither of us should drive anywhere tonight."

CHAPTER 8

JAKE'S OLD TIMEX watch read 2:15 a.m. when the Uber pulled up to the sheriff's office. He paced outside, waiting, his jacket buttoned to the top. "Finally, it's cooled the hell off," he said as Maggie exited the car. "Mack is inside and needs to confer with both of us. Are you okay to work?"

"I'm a little soggy, and my head hurts like someone took a ball-peen hammer to it if that's what you mean, but I'm coherent enough. You're gonna have to give me a ride to the pub tomorrow to get my car, though."

The heater had kicked on inside the office, giving off the particular odor that old heaters throw out when they've been off for a while. The smell nauseated Maggie. "Can I have some water and an aspirin?"

Sheriff Mack fished around inside his drawer and pulled out a bottle of Bayer. A clerk materialized with a paper cup of water from a cooler.

"Do you think the dead guy is our salt killer?" Maggie threw back the water and aspirin, crumpled the paper cup, and tossed it into a trash bin.

"The timeline doesn't make sense. We discovered our last bodies as this guy sat in a jail cell." Mack looked like he hadn't slept in a month. The purple circles under his eyes and his rumpled clothes made him look a decade older than his fifty odd years. The light glistened off his balding scalp, and despite the cold air of the station, sweat beaded into tiny crystals on his forehead.

Maggie and Jake pulled chairs to the metal desk and sat next to one another across from the sheriff.

"Tell us what you got," Maggie said. "You probably briefed Jake before I got here."

"Nope. I wanted to talk to you both at the same time. What we have here is 36-year-old Milton Newton. He was on route from Hemacinto to Folsom in a prison bus with three other convicts when he stuck a sharp pencil hidden somewhere on his person into the eye of the guard before he could pull his sidearm. Newton jammed the same pencil into the throat of the bus driver. The bus ran off the road, skidded, hit a boulder and landed on its side, killing everyone but Newton. He managed to kick out a window and got out that way. We don't know how he got his cuffs off—maybe snagged the guard's keys, and how he ended up close to Hank's backyard, cooked and partially dismembered, is beyond us. We're investigating, but no answers yet." The sheriff drummed his pen against the side of his desk, and the sound made Maggie think of bullets fired from a Glock. Bam, bam, bam. The noise pummeled her brain. "Do you mind not doing that? I've got a hellish headache." She rubbed her temples with the thumb and middle finger of one hand.

"Sorry." He dropped the pen into a holder on his desk.

"Either we've got a copycat," Jake said, "or, this is a revenge murder."

"Why do you always assume a copycat? You did that in Wicklow, too. Besides, this doesn't fit the pattern of a copycat," Maggie said. "Someone might have offed him in the way he killed their sweetheart or relative. So, you might be right in that this could be a revenge killing. But, he isn't our salt guy, Jake."

"Could be someone is trying to throw us off," Jake shrugged his shoulders.

"What did Hank say when you called him in, Sheriff?" Maggie asked.

"We've got an APB out, but no sign of him."

"He ran?" Jake asked.

"He knows he's a suspect," the sheriff said.

"Hank is distraught over his wife's leaving him. It drove him crazy with jealousy, crazier than a damned rabid raccoon in a hornet's nest." Maggie said. "We need to talk to the relatives and friends of Newton's victims, too. One of them might be his killer, that is if Jake's right and this is revenge. But why is Hank missing? What the hell?"

———

Morning came too soon for Maggie. When her cell phone rang, it took her forever to answer, and by the time she did, the call had gone to voicemail. Maggie listened.

"It's me, Cathy. Jimmy is bringin' the girls by in an hour, then he's gotta get to L.A. for that job. We're leavin' for up north right now. We need to be at the council tonight, and we can't be runnin' late."

I gotta work. God damn.

"Who called?" Jake rubbed his eyes and yawned, his hair a mess, his boxers rumpled and twisted at the waist, from tossing and turning in bed. They'd both spent a restless night.

"It was Cathy. Get dressed. Jimmy will be here in less than an hour with the girls."

"The girls? I thought they were coming next week."

"I did, too. I messed up the dates. I gotta get to the pub this morning because Diego's out of town, and there's no one to open. I can't take them there, but you can watch Bird and Flower today, yes?"

"Mag, did you forget I'm meeting Mack this morning?"

Maggie's shoulders dropped. "What the hell am I gonna do? I screwed up bad."

"Can one of Diego's thousands of cousins, or his sister, watch the girls?"

"I don't know any of them well enough to leave my nine-year-old nieces with."

"You don't trust Diego?"

"Of course, I trust Diego. I. Don't. Know. His. Relatives. I'm not leaving the girls with someone I have no knowledge of...wait. I've got an idea." Maggie pushed the buttons on her phone. "Nola, I've got a huge favor to ask."

——

Maggie waited on the front porch, blowing on the French Roast she'd poured into oversized chipped mug. Jimmy pulled up in his truck and opened the door for Bird and Flower.

"Aunt Maggie!" Bird ran to her aunt with her twin sister a few steps behind.

Maggie set her mug on the railing and opened her arms to embrace both girls. As they hugged, Maggie kissed the tops of their heads. "It's so good to see you two."

Jimmy stepped out to greet Maggie. "I'll be back in a week to get them. I'll call you when I get to L.A. You girls be good for Aunt Maggie. Love you both."

"Jimmy, I don't want to come off like an ass, but what's up with the weight gain?"

He patted his stomach. "Stress eating and beer. It's tough working down here, and I eat too much of mom's fry bread."

"When you get back, join the gym with us."

"I can't afford a membership, as if you didn't know."

"We'll pay for it. Call it an early birthday present. You have to stay healthy for your daughters. Even if you don't care about your own health, you have to think of these girls."

Jimmy spun around to face Maggie, his expression fixed and dark. "You know what, Aunt Mag? I get that you're trying to help, but my weight is none of your business, and how I take care of my daughters is also, none of your business." He jumped in the truck, slammed the door, and sped away.

Maggie and Jimmy, close as a nephew and aunt could be while Jimmy was a boy, had struggled with their relationship most of his adult life. They argued. A lot. Usually over minor issues.

"Why do you and Daddy fight all the time?" Flower asked.

"I don't know, sweetie. I guess we're different."

"Is it because he's Indian and you aren't?" asked Bird.

"I'm Indian, too"

"Not as much as Daddy is, and he says you're Irish."

"I'm half Irish, so is your grandad, and that makes your daddy and you part Irish, too, Snookers." With her knuckle, she thumped her grandniece on the head.. "Now, let's go in and get some waffles with whipped cream, then I'm taking you to meet my new friend, Nola. She owns a gym and is a lot of fun. You're going to hang out with her for a few hours while I work today, all right with you?"

———

A few days later, Nola brought León, Diego's nephew, to meet Maggie. The young man had eyes the color of old copper pennies, always spoke with perfect diction, pronouncing each syllable with care. Thin, with a birdcage of a chest, León, in his late twenties appeared for all the world to be a boy of sixteen or so. Although slender, almost delicate, León hefted fifty-pound boxes of meat like they were bags of feathers. The young man fawned over Nola, keeping his gaze glued to her as though if he'd turned his eyes from her for even a half a second, she'd vanish forever. Nola brushed her fingers through her hair and gave her head a little toss.

Christ, he's got a massive crush on her, and she likes that he does. Maggie put out her hand to León, and they shook. Diego emerged from the kitchen with a dish towel in his hand. *"Hola, Sobrino. ¿Que Tal?"* He said to León. "You're delivering the pulled pork from Bond's now?"

"Hello, Uncle. Yes. I will be making deliveries to and from Bond's Butcher Shop, as long as Ms. Nola's and Mr. James' are satisfied with my work and the quality of the pork."

León deposited the cases of meat where Diego instructed him. Nola gave Maggie a quick hug, and the two departed, she, passing through the door like a queen with León following, a loyal servant trailing his grand mistress.

"Not everyone likes León," Diego said. "Our own family think of him as too proud and make fun of him. 'You think you're some big shot gringo professor, too good to be a Mexican now. Is that so?' They say, but he's a great guy, he works his ass off, and he's sure to make something of himself. He'll be the first ever in our family to graduate from a real university." Diego inflated his chest with pride.

"Nola says he works hard and doesn't complain. He's polite, too, and I happen to like him. So what if he comes across a little formal and foppish to some people? Doesn't matter to me as long as he gets the damned deliveries to us on time."

"You can count on it, *jefa*. He's had a job delivering organically-fed pork to high-end farm-to-table restaurants for some time. León works with an organic pig farmer in El Centro, and a few days a week when not in class he drives there, picks up pork and makes deliveries to eateries throughout the Southland. Been at it for several years, so he knows what he's doing, and the boy is smart and professional enough to understand if he were unreliable with his deliveries, he'd lose a big chunk of his income. You don't need to worry about León getting our meat to us when promised."

—

One of those rare afternoons when Maggie worked the pub alone, the truck driver, Hank, walked in like he might on any Thursday. So surprised, she let a beer mug she'd been drying slip from her hand and clatter across the wood floor. "Holy crap!"

"Hi, Maggie." He pulled up a stool. "Good that thing didn't shatter. It would have made a mess."

His face was clean of stubble. He smelled of cheap men's cologne, reminding her of Hai Karate from the 70s her boyfriend used to douse himself in, and his socks matched.

"Uh, Hank, where have you been? People are looking all over for you."

"For fucksakes why? I wish everyone would leave me alone, dammit. I needed to get away after that thing with Rosie. I quit my job, parked my rig, bought a VW Van, and took off by myself to camp in a remote area of Colorado near Vail. I only rolled into town an hour ago, and haven't even checked my cell, or picked up mail. I showered and came straight here for a beer. Why would anyone look for me? If it's Rosie, I don't give a shit and she can..."

"A local fire captain and his crew were working to put out a grass fire and found a man's body right behind your property."

"Body? As in a dead guy?"

"Right. Someone murdered him in much the same way the dentist and his family were killed. Liver gone."

"God, that's damned awful, and right on the edge of town? Well, then, I'd say that's pretty brazen." The man paused and cocked his head. "You aren't sayin' you think I did it? I wasn't even here."

CHAPTER 9

MAGGIE WRAPPED HER arms around herself to stave off the arctic cold from the air conditioning in the sheriff's office. "It's gotta be forty-five degrees in here. Can't you turn that thing off?"

"Sorry," said Sheriff Mack. "It's not working right, so it gets a bit too cold, but since it's 112 degrees outside, it'll get too hot in here in a hurry, and I can't risk overheating the computers. Do you want me to interview Hank?"

"No, I'll do it. You gotta coat or something I can borrow?" After Mack handed a jacket to Maggie, she put it on, wrapped it around her, and pulled open the door to the interview room.

Hank paced like a nervous beetle. Despite the cold, dark sweat spread in an expanding patch across the back of his shirt, growing to the size and configuration of an elephant's ear, the fabric so thin, curls of brown back hair showed through like thin dark worms crawling over his skin.

"Please take a seat, Hank." Maggie gestured to a metal chair. "Can I get you some water?"

"Why the hell am I here? It can't be about the dead guy you found out in that wilderness patch in the back of my property. I told you I was gone when it happened." He scooted his chair backwards, and as he did it scraped against the ceramic tile making a sound like someone scratching paint off a car with a screwdriver. The noise set Maggie's teeth on edge.

Hank's eyes narrowed to malicious slits, and he leaned forward in his seat. "Rosie. That little whore. She filed a complaint because I smacked her. Didn't she?"

"Where were you on Tuesday the 20th?"

"Camping. I told you that already. In Arizona."

"Arizona? That's interesting because you told me in the pub you were in Colorado. So where then? Arizona or Colorado?"

Hank bit his bottom lip, rubbed his nose, glanced at the ceiling, then stared point blank at Maggie's face.

Shit, he's about to lie to me.

"I don't know. What difference does it make? I was in the damned desert. Okay? I didn't kill the guy."

"Desert?"

"That's what I said. Desert."

"In O'Malley's, you told me you were in the mountains."

He bolted straight in his chair, and his eyes flashed open so wide Maggie thought his eyeballs would pop out. "I didn't say that." He shook his head. "Nope."

"You mentioned Vail. You can't get more mountain than that, Hank. Can anyone at all verify you were camping that night? A camp host?"

Hank's gaze shifted to the ceiling and then back to Maggie again. "I was dry camping, meaning out in the wild by myself. No hookup. No formal campground."

"Why are you lying to me?"

Hank leaped from his chair and balled his hands into fists so tight his knuckles turned white. "I'm not lying!"

Maggie stood, and when she did, Hank stooped over and put his face close to hers. His jaw clenched.

She popped out of her chair, stiffened and fingered her holster. "Back away from me now and sit!"

Hank dropped into his chair and hung his head. "Okay, so I wasn't camping."

"Right. So where were you all that time we were looking for you?" She sat back into her chair.

He lifted his head. "I was hanging around. Keeping under the radar, following Rosie. I wanted her to think I was gone so I could watch what she was up to without her knowin' it."

"You do understand stalking is against the law, right?"

"I wasn't stalking...I was..."

"You followed her and observed her without her knowledge or consent. That's stalking. Where did you sleep?"

"Here and there. Sometimes in the Walmart parking lot in Riverside, sometimes in an alley, or next to a park. I outfitted the van so I could camp in it. Put in an airbed, and even got a little fridge for beer and bologna sandwich makings, and I got one of those portable plastic bottle thingies you stick your dick in to piss so I wouldn't have to get up at night. I learned about those back when I'd transport goods through areas where there was no safe place to get out of the rig, so sometimes had to take a wiz in the cab."

"You're no longer a trucker?"

"Not at present. Does it matter?"

"Can anyone at all confirm where you were on that night?"

"Nope."

"By the way, we're running a background check on you right now. Will we find an arrest record?"

"Naw."

"Sure about that?"

Hank grinned without humor and bared his teeth like a cornered badger. "I'm sure about this. You can't legally hold me without cause." He pointed a finger at Maggie's face. "You have to let me go unless you're going to charge me with something, and you don't have a goddamn thing on me. I won't say no more until I get a lawyer, and, by the way," he leaned back into his chair, still grinning like an ape, "if I were to kill anyone it would be some goddamn civil servant part-time cop who thinks she's entitled to harass a law-abiding citizen."

"Is that a threat? If so, I could arrest you right now." Maggie looked at the camera. "Got that, guys?"

⸻

Jake left the station without his customary "see ya at home." Maggie finished her paperwork and left. A solitary raven knocked and called to her from a conifer outside the station, and she looked up in time to see a flash of a white wing flying overhead, brightened by the moonlight. The albino raven.

When she opened the house door, Chester greeted her with a tail wag. She petted him. "Why's the house dark, Chester? Jake and Samantha asleep, are they? Thanks for waiting up, buddy."

She found Jake in his boxers sitting at the dining room table. Although he hadn't bothered to turn on a lamp, the moonbeams streamed through the window illuminating a slice of Jake's pale thigh. When she flipped on the overhead, he looked up at her and pulled his fingers through his scalp once, then again—the one nervous habit that always gave him away.

"You're pissed off at me, aren't you?" She pulled out a half-empty bottle of Jameson from the booze cabinet, grabbed two water glasses, and poured three fingers into each. Then without a word, she sat in the chair next to Jake's and put a drink in front of him. He shot down the whiskey in one swallow and slammed the empty on the table. That's when Maggie knew she was in big trouble.

He didn't even look at her. "Why in goddamn hell did you let Hank go?"

"It was my idea mostly, but Detective Mack and I both thought it would be good to trail him. To find out where he goes, what he does, and..."

"I don't give a fuck, Maggie. He threatened you, and for all you know, the prick has got a gun, or he could even be our Aunt Lorrie's Seasoned Salt Killer. He could...goddamn it all to hell. Don't you realize he's dangerous or could be? Goddamn..." He pulled his fingers through his scalp again and lifted his head to glare at her. "I know you will have a hard time believing this, but not everything is about you and what you want. Why don't you think about someone else besides yourself once in a great while? I'm sitting here in the dark worried sick that bastard might be coming after you, or maybe even already killed you and they'll find your bloody body somewhere dumped in the..."

"Hold on right there, Jake. Have you ever, even once in your life, thought I was incapable of taking care of myself?"

"Oh, for damnfucksake." He cocked his head and scrunched his forehead into a taut mass of ropey lines. "Why do I even try to reason with you?" He stood to leave but stopped short when Maggie's cell rang. Sheriff Mack. She put the phone on speaker so Jake could listen in. "You got something on Hank, Sheriff?" She asked.

"Yup. He was born and raised in Cochise County, Arizona in a small town, Crystal Cavern, but he lived there under a different name, Paul E. Luck. He did hard time for domestic abuse, and attempted murder. He almost beat his then wife to death. Broke her neck. She's now paralyzed from the shoulders down, and in a wheelchair for life."

Jake stared down Maggie hard. "I told you. Didn't I?"

"Is that Jake I hear in the background?" Mack asked.

"Sorry, Sheriff. I forgot to mention I've got you on speaker."

"Hi, Jake. You two might find this interesting. That butcher, James Bond?"

"Yeah?" Said Jake.

"Apparently, Hank, rather Paul, grew up with him. They attended the same middle grade, graduated high school together, and both played football for the team."

"No shit," Maggie said

"Yes. And guess what? We uncovered an arrest record for Bond. He was nineteen at the time. Assault and battery, and another charge for animal cruelty. The victim, a neighbor, an eighteen-year-old girl, rejected his advances. He tied her up, slapped her around a little, then he got her pet Doberman."

"He killed her dog?"

"In front of her. Bond slit its throat. And, get this. He skinned the dog, cut it into pieces, skewered the meat on a spit, roasted it over an open fire, and ate hunks of it with a fork and knife, a napkin tucked nice and neat under his chin."

"Disgusting."

"Pretty much. And take a guess at what seasoning he used?"

"Don't tell me," Maggie said. "Aunt Lorrie's Seasoned Salt?"

"That's it."

CHAPTER 10

SEVERAL TIMES EACH month on a Sunday, Maggie and Jake shared a meal at Danny and Cathy's. They ate in the spiritual center of Cathy's home, her kitchen. They sat together at a wooden picnic table Danny had years before built and painted her favorite color, a garish, ecstatic yellow with a high luster finish. It had been one of only three pieces the couple brought with them from the mountain town of Wicklow after they'd lost their land and their business to bankruptcy, and moved to Hemacinto to be nearer their son, Jimmy, and their granddaughters.

"I ain't movin' from Wicklow without this," Cathy said to Danny. Cathy told Maggie the table held family memory.

"It's in the wood," she said. "Even cut down as a tree, and made into somethin' else, wood has a spirit in it, and this wood here keeps our family history." She stroked the table top as though she might pet a beloved cat.

Years before, Danny had built the oversized table with long benches on both sides and matching stools on either end. Large enough to seat ten, in a pinch Cathy would pull up extra stools to squeeze in twelve. Cathy never turned anyone away from her kitchen who needed a hot meal or a cup of coffee. Today, there were seven, Maggie, Jake, Danny, Cathy, Jimmy, and the twins, Flower and Bird, seated around the table to enjoy Cathy's specialty, venison stew and fry bread.

Her jeans and hands covered in flour, and her black hair tied back, Cathy fried the dough in a cast iron skillet. "They say Navajo were first to make fry bread, but I think it was Wintu, 'cause our history with the bread goes way back."

"No matter who did it first, you make the best," Jimmy said.

"You want honey on yours?" Cathy asked Jimmy.

"No fry bread for me, Mom. Aunt Maggie says I'm getting too

fat." He leaned back on the bench and patted his corpulent gut. "What do you think, Aunt Maggie? Time for me to join McCabe's Gym with you and Jake?"

Maggie couldn't tell right off if Jimmy was sincere or sarcastic. Almost every cordial discussion with Jimmy devolved into a raging argument. She reflexively tensed in preparation for yet another nasty bicker session with her nephew but instead, to her delight and surprise, he grinned at her. Still smiling, he grabbed a Pacifico from the metal ice bucket on the table, popped open the top with a church key, and handed the beer to his aunt. "I want to talk to you about something."

Maggie reached for the bottle and took a swig from it. "Thanks." But when he stood from the bench, her delight soured, and her solar plexus tightened. *Now it begins. Can't we even enjoy one damned family dinner in peace?* "Do we need to step outside?"

"I want everyone to listen in. And what I want to ask of you the girls need to hear because they have to agree, too. That is if you don't mind." His expression turned from light to dark.

The color drained from Maggie's face. *Damn, I don't want to fight with him today. Not now. Please. Not in front of the twins.* Jake must have read Maggie's mind because, in a reassuring gesture, he squeezed her thigh.

But instead of coming off as confrontational, Jimmy's voice and demeanor expressed a quality of sincerity. "Aunt Maggie, I apologize."

"For what?"

"For the jerk I've been all these years. It's been tough since the girls' mom left us, and I know I've taken some things out on you, but I didn't intend to."

Maggie thought she might pass out from shock. She looked at Jake, and he squeezed her thigh again, then she mustered a smile for her nephew. "Jimmy, you are under a lot of pressure raising these girls on your own, and you..."

"Stop talking and listen, okay? This is not easy for me. Mom and

I discussed this, so I promised her I'd do this today, not only for her, for me, too. We need to set things right and be closer as a family. That's what I'm trying to say."

"Jimmy, thank..."

"I'm not done." He held up a hand to quiet her. "I want to spend more time with you like I did when I was a kid, and I want you and Jake to be more a part of Flower and Bird's lives."

"Cool!" Flower said. "Will you go to the Saboba pow-wow with us next month, Aunt Maggie?"

"Shhhh," Cathy said. "Eat yer fry bread and let yer daddy talk."

"I want to ask you and Jake something. You don't have to answer right now. Think it over, if you want, but here's what I need to ask: if anything happens to me would you two raise Flower and Bird?"

Maggie almost choked on a mouthful of beer. She looked to Cathy and to Danny. Her brother and sister-in-law loved the girls more than anything. "What about your father and mother?"

"We might be goin' back up north. Lots of tribal business," Cathy said. "Since I'm on the council now, there's responsibility that'll keep me plenty busy, and gone away too much. I know you got that salt killer to find, but once that's done you n' Jake are plannin' to retire here for good, right? And..." she paused to look at her husband. "Danny and me got other news, too." She shifted her gaze to her husband. "You wanna tell 'em?"

"Looks like we're getting the land back on the river," Danny said. "All sixteen acres, the house, and everything. We made an offer. Our credit's better, and I got a job already lined up at the lumber mill, and as a foreman, no less. If it all goes through like we think it will, we're going home in a month or two, and by this time a year from September, we'll be hosting a bear dance again. I'm going to build a new sweat lodge and everything."

"That's wonderful," Maggie said, "You and the girls, Jimmy? You're not going with them?"

"I'm doing good here and looks like I'm going into partnership with a local to open a high-end cabinet making business, plus,

I'm dating someone. Don't ask who. I'm not ready to share yet. There will be plenty of visits to see Mom and Dad, but what's most important is the girls like their school and have new friends. I don't want to uproot them. We're taking over the rental here with an option to buy, and I guess other than mom's table, which she won't leave without—right, Mom?—we don't have to worry about furnishings. Everything is falling into place, and all this will happen I imagine by the end of the year."

"Jimmy, you're young. You're healthy. Why would you think..."

He raised both hands. "Nothing is going to happen to me unless I get stupid and cut off a finger with a circular saw or something," he laughed. "I'm asking if I can make this formal, that is, if the twins are okay with it. Are you, girls?"

In unison, both girls nodded.

"Then, if you and Jake agree I'm making you legal guardians in case something ever happens to me. I need to know my girls can have a life with you and Jake if I...you know. I can't think of anyone better outside of Mom and Dad than you two to raise my daughters."

Maggie looked at Jake, and, in turn, he smiled his approval.

"We'll take the girls if you ever need us to," Maggie said.

Jimmy made his way around the table and motioned for Maggie to stand. She did, and for the first time in many years, he took his aunt into his arms and embraced her. "I love you, Aunt Maggie, and I am sorry for being such an ass all these years. You're the best."

She could barely contain her emotions. "I love you, too, Jimmy."

———

That night, the raven shapeshifting took a turn. Maggie felt herself transforming as she rested on the bed next to Jake. When her face stretched into a thick beak, Samantha hissed and hid under the bed, and Chester awoke and trotted into the living room. Jake, stretched out on top the quilt, snored, oblivious to the world. Maggie marveled that he never witnessed her transformation, even when in bed next to her. While she still could walk, more or less like a human, and still had hands with opposable thumbs, Maggie opened the bedroom window, and once her wings formed, she flew into the night air.

The albino raven awaited her on a fence post in an open field. "Took you long enough," she said.

"Where are the others?" Maggie alighted on the fence and worked to get her balance.

"It's you and me tonight, Pukkukwerek. We aren't flying anywhere so we can perch here for a minute or two. I have a matter of importance to discuss concerning the talk you had with your nephew about the girls."

"How could you possibly know what my nephew and I discussed?"

"I was there. I heard every word, and by the way, I didn't know you liked Pacifico. I thought you only drank Harp Ale."

"Harp is my go-to, but I drink others. How did you know?"

"I said I was there."

"You weren't. There were no ravens in sight, and I would have noticed an albino bird, even if you'd been only at the window."

"Jajajaaa."

"Why are you laughing?" Maggie ruffled her feathers in annoyance.

"You didn't even know I was inside the house with the yellow table, and you have never heard of a ghost raven? You think you know everything, but you don't know anything. Jajaja!"

"What is a 'ghost raven,' and what matter of importance do you have to discuss with me?"

"You'll understand about the ghost raven when you need to. But what I must talk to you about is your grandniece. Listen. Something big is coming your way, and you must watch Flower because she will need you."

"What about Bird?"

"I said Flower. Did you not listen?"

CHAPTER 11

MAGGIE WOKE NEXT to Jake propped on one elbow, staring at her. When she opened her eyes, he brushed a stray hair from her forehead. "You went raven last night, didn't you?"

"How'd you know?"

"You left the window wide open, and I found this." He picked a glossy black feather from the nightstand and held it to her. "One of yours, I presume? Did you get any info about our killer?"

"No. It's all so weird. I met the white raven alone, and she said I had to watch Flower. I have no fucking idea what she meant and, as always, ravens can't seem to say anything outright. There always has to be a game with them." She tilted her head like Chester always did when someone or something made a high-pitched noise. "I have a question. How come you have never seen me shift?"

"I don't know. Maybe the ravens don't want me to witness your transformation."

"I don't get this shapeshifting raven thing."

"You only started accepting this part of who you are a short while ago, and you need to give it time. You think you know everything, but you don't know anything. Not about this."

"That's what the albino raven said, almost exactly."

—

Fuck, what did I do this time? Maggie walked into the pub and encountered a fuming chef. So furious, Diego's face turned from brown to crimson, and his neck muscles bulged and pulsated in time with his heartbeat.

"*Hijo de puta!*" Diego continued to issue invectives in Spanish, stomping from one end of the bar to the other.

"Settle down and tell me what's going on."

"*Mi sobrino.* My nephew, *pinche* León. That's what's going on."

"What's up with León?"

"The little bastard dropped out of USC. He made the announcement at Sunday dinner with the family like he was proud of it. He's planning to work full-time with the meat company, Bond's."

"What?"

"He's gonna deliver meats to the butcher from the place down south, and from Bond's to the community restaurants and pubs, and train to be a butcher. It's a complete waste of his good brains, and he's shitting on his entire future. Do you know how hard he had to work for the grades to get into that school? The *idiota.*"

"Why would he do such a thing? He only had another year. It doesn't make sense."

"He's got it bad for that Nola chick."

"What in hell's name? She's married and is almost old enough to be his mother. What the..."

"I took him out to my place for some beers and talked to him, because I couldn't believe that shit, either. He's 'in love' with her, he says, and if he's delivering pork for her husband full-time, he'll get to be near her, he says. When I heard that, I wanted to beat the crap out of him."

"Do you suspect they are having an affair? I'll talk to her."

"Would you do that, *Patróna*? Please. He's gonna ruin his life over her, and my mother can't stop crying."

"I actually have a couple of things to discuss with Nola. I'll make sure to talk to her about León, too. I'll get to the bottom of this. I promise."

Maggie pulled her cell from her bag and punched in the number to McCabe's.

———

The gym was closed when Maggie arrived. Nola opened the door and offered a hug, but Maggie pulled away.

"Are you angry with me?" When Maggie didn't respond, Nola shrugged her shoulders and ushered Maggie into the office. The janitor vacuumed the empty gym; the noise grew loud enough that Nola had to shut the door. "Would you like some tea?"

"No thanks. I don't have time. I'm here to discuss a couple of matters of importance."

"All right. I'm game. Shoot." Nola sat behind her desk and pulled the elastic from her hair, allowing the golden stuff to fall in a bright mass. "I can tell something is up."

"You do know Jake and I are heading the investigating team for the Aunt Lorrie's Salt Killer?

"Yes. I know."

"I've got to talk to you about your husband, James."

Nola's stiffened, and she sat taller in her chair. "What about James? You don't think he's involved, do you?"

"We're going to have to call him into the station to ask him some questions, and you can't say anything to him about this. I'm already violating protocol, but you and I have become friends, and I like you, so I'm giving you a heads up."

Nola shifted in her chair as though sitting on a pebble. "Whatever could you have to talk to James about?"

"Two facts have surfaced recently involving your husband. First, his conviction in Arizona. And, then..."

"Shit on that!" Nola threw her hands into the air. "We have worked so hard to put all that behind us, and it's one reason we moved here because no one knows us and we wanted a fresh start. But this keeps coming up, and coming up, like vomit."

"I have to..."

"He was only nineteen when all that happened, almost thirty years ago when young and stupid, and crazy in love with a girl who really hurt him. He did his time and has been a model citizen since." Nola threw her hands in the air again. "Why in hell can't people let this go and leave him alone!"

"I'm trying to tell you if you'll listen, that is not all. There is something about the way he killed the dog that might link him to the case, and not only that, it appears he is childhood friends with one of our prime suspects."

"What do you mean about the way he killed the dog, and yeah, if you are thinking about Hank, he and James were friends way back in high school. What of it?" Nola wrinkled her brow and tilted her head.

"I cannot say. And, again, you can't say a thing, either, or you'll get me fired, and if you do tell him, and James bolts, you will be up against a charge of aiding and abetting or obstruction. You cannot warn him. Do you understand? Plus, didn't you tell me you and James don't know anyone here? It's a little weird that James is trying to get away from his past yet moves to the same town where the last guy in the world he should ever hang out with happens to live."

"I don't think they've seen one another since we've moved here. If so, it's news to me." Nola inspected her forefinger, then stuck it in her mouth to chew on a hangnail. "Damn it. I hate hangnails."

"Can we stick on point here, and talk about your manicures and hangnails later?"

Nola removed the finger from her mouth. "Maggie, how can I not tell my own husband he could be in trouble? If it were Jake, would you not warn him?"

"Promise me you'll not say anything, Nola, or you'll put us all in deep shit. Don't make me sorry I told you."

"I promise." Nola rose and started for the door. Maggie remained seated.

"Is this all, Maggie, because I've got work to do, and I don't have time to sit here with you tonight."

"I can tell you're upset."

"Ya think? Or, let me put it this way. You're damned right I'm upset."

"Regardless, I need you to sit back down. I have something of a more personal matter to discuss with you."

Nola sighed and inspected her thumb nail. "This morning, I

spent $80 for a deluxe manicure and look at this polish already flaking off."

"Nola, please get off your damned nails and listen."

"What is it? What can you possibly say to upset me even more?" She made her way back to her chair and sat with an audible plop.

"It's about León."

"León? Are you talking about his choice, as an adult I might add, to quit school and work full-time for us?"

"That's what I'm talking about. Do you have any idea what an opportunity he's throwing away? He only had a year left, then he'd planned on graduate school. He's a brilliant boy, and this is..."

"I tried my best to talk him out of it. I did everything I could, but he insisted, and as a grown up, he can make any decision for himself. It's none of my business, actually, and I have to respect his decision, and so do you. He's glued himself to James, and I know we'll get him trained as a butcher in no time. Butchering is an honorable profession, and once trained and certified, he can open his own business."

"Do you have any idea why he'd make such a rash decision, Nola?"

Nola looked at the blank wall as though peering out a window. She said nothing for a few seconds, then turned back to Maggie, and softened her voice. "Yes. I have an idea."

"Would you mind sharing?"

"León is in love with me."

"Have you given him any reason to believe he has a chance with you? Are you two having an affair?"

Nola made a strangling noise and her eyes brimmed with tears. "Once." She held up a finger. "Only one time."

"You had sex with León?"

"It was crazy dumb. James and I have had some problems lately, hon. James can be temperamental at times, and moody. We have both been under stress for a long while, with the new businesses, and all the work, we haven't enjoyed physical intimacy in a long while. León is always so attentive and adoring, and I'm ashamed to admit I ate it up. It happened only one time here in my office after hours. I told him it couldn't happen again, not ever, and I don't know what to do now. To compound things, Skye has a raging crush on him, and she knows he has feelings for me, so it's caused some problems. Skye won't talk to me, I'm afraid she's going to quit, and I need her. Everything is such a mess, and it's all my fault. I don't know what to do, and if James finds out..." Nola put her face in her hands. "I don't know what to do, Maggie. How stupid of me to let things get so far."

"Nola, what do you mean 'if James finds out'? And, bloody hell—León? He's only a kid, for crapsake."

"Like I said, James has a bit of a temper, and he might...please don't judge me for my moment of weakness. You're the only friend I have."

"I hate what you did with León, but I don't hate you."

"I promise to fix this. I'll do everything I can to talk León into going back to USC."

———

After leaving the gym, Maggie dropped by the pub.

Diego emerged from the kitchen; his apron soiled with a mass of gravy. "Had a little accident and spilled all over myself. Glad to see you here. It's busier than shit."

"I'm sorry I can't stay to help. I'm working on the case, and it's going to be a late night for Jake and me. He's waiting at the sheriff's office, and I must get going. But I wanted you to know I spoke with Nola."

"What did she say?"

"She's not in love with León, but she knows he's in love with her. They aren't having an affair, and she promised she'll do all she can to talk him into going back to college."

"*Gracias a Dios.*" Diego looked upwards to his God and crossed himself. "At last I have some good news for my Mom and my sister. They've been upset over all this, and they deserve to hear something good. Graciela is torn up. León is her favorite nephew for some reason I don't understand, because they aren't all that close, but he's always the family's beacon of light. When he made the announcement—she's already gone through so much with the divorce and everything. This will cheer her up."

——

When Maggie and Jake returned from the sheriff's office, the ancient clock in the living room chimed eleven, and a few minutes after midnight, a call came through from Mack. Both Maggie and Jake were asleep and so exhausted it took Jake almost four rings to get to the cell on the nightstand. Groggy from sleep, Jake sounded drunk. "Yuh, wad ish it? Waidaminute, I'm puddin' you on speaker so Maggie can get in on this." He nudged Maggie, and she sat in bed, tucking a pillow behind her back.

"So, what's going on?" The now fully awake Jake asked.

"A forest ranger discovered another victim in the San Padrino range. Cooked over a fire on a spit. Legs and thumb missing. Aunt Lorrie's salt left on the torso. The whole bit."

"Any evidence other than the salt?" Maggie asked.

"We've got a team out there now, along with the Medical Examiner. We found tire tracks. Looks like an RV of some sort."

"Like Hank's van?" Jake exchanged looks with Maggie.

"Could be. We're checking it out."

"Do we have an ID on the victim, Sheriff?" Maggie asked.

"Yed, we do. Graciela Ramirez, age 38. Maggie, I hate to tell you this, but she's your cook's sister."

CHAPTER 12

"NO. IT HAS to be me," Maggie said. "I have no idea how I'm going to break the news to Diego about Graciela, but I have to do it alone."

"Are you sure?" Jake asked. "Sheriff Mack and I are more than willing to..."

"I appreciate the offer, but no. I need you to take care of things today, can you? I'll be sending Diego home, and I'll have to fill in for a few days. How am I going to tell his mother?"

"I'll help you as much as I can, but, Maggie, you can't cook worth shit. How will you manage the kitchen?"

"I've got plenty of help. Salvador is there, and I'm going to ask Nola if I can borrow León. He's got some fry cook experience. We'll do okay."

—

The ten-minute drive to notify Diego of his sister's death felt like hours to Maggie. The brutal morning sun punished her through the windshield, and her head ached so much she thought her brains would explode in her head. At a stop light, she opened the glove box to retrieve a bottle of ibuprofen. She opened the cap with her teeth, threw back her head, and dropped a couple of tablets into her mouth. She managed to get the lid on and put the bottle back into the glove box when a horn from the driver behind blasted her.

The light had turned green the split second it took her to stow the ibuprofen. With her foot still on the brake, she twisted in her seat and gave the offending driver a middle-finger salute, which he returned with gusto.

Maggie pulled the parking break, and unlatched her seat belt in preparation to exit her truck with the intention of getting into the other driver's face up close and personal, but as she touched the handle to the door, a raven perched on her windshield, another on her back window, and others on her side windows, then another and another. They landed so fast Maggie lost count of them until a mass of black feathers, beaks, and claws completely obscured her view from all windows. She withdrew her hand from the door handle and idled until the ravens blocked all exterior light, leaving her in complete darkness. The driver behind her swerved around her, leaned on his horn, and sped away. Within seconds, the birds lifted off her windows and took to the sky.

"What the fuck was that about? I suppose they thought they were saving me from a road-rage infected butt taint. Why doesn't anyone think I can take care of myself?" She buckled her seatbelt and continued on her way.

Maggie arrived at the pub early, but rather than waiting for Diego inside, she stayed in her truck. He pulled into the gravel parking lot next to her, and she stepped out from the cab.

Diego met her with a big smile. "What's up, *Jefa*? I wasn't expecting you until noon or later. Why so early?"

"I am afraid I have some terrible news for you."

When Maggie told Diego about his sister, he stepped back, collapsed into the side of his car, and slid down into the gravel. She knelt in front of him, reached out and bundled him into her arms. He cried like a small child. "What am I going to tell my mother? What about my little nieces?"

"I'll go with you. We'll tell her together if it would be easier."

"She wouldn't want to get this news from a stranger. I have to go alone." He got into his car, put his head into his hands and sobbed.

Maggie's heart cleaved in two. She put a note on the pub door, "Closed today due to a death in the family. Sorry for any inconvenience." *It's going to be a bitch running this place without Diego. Shit. I don't even want to come in tomorrow.*

—

"León, this is Maggie Sloan. You deliver pulled pork to my pub?"

"Yes, Ms. Sloan. It is so very nice to hear from you."

"My condolences on the death of your aunt."

"Thank you. Although I was never particularly close to Graciela, her passing has been difficult on our family. Will you and your gentleman friend be attending the services?"

"We'll be there, but that's not why I'm calling. Diego says you're handy in the kitchen."

"I worked as a short order cook for three consecutive summers while attending high school. I am not the skilled chef my uncle is; but others have told that I am adequately competent."

"Diego is going to be away from the pub for a few weeks. I've spoken to Nola, and she says it's okay if you take time off from Bond's to help out here, if you want to."

"Most certainly. I would be delighted to provide my assistance."

—

"There have to be hundreds of people here," Maggie whispered to Jake.

Mourners packed in to pay respect to Diego's family and crowded into every pew at Saint Mary's Catholic Church. The Priest said the mass in Spanish for Graciela Ramirez, so Maggie and Jake couldn't understand most of what he said. A confirmed atheist, Maggie, didn't care about the mass anyway. She spent most of the time scanning the crowd. *Our murderer could be here.* Graciela had been a large woman, and to accommodate her girth, Diego ordered an over-sized white casket and covered it in pink roses.

"Jake, I noticed something in common with all our victims."

"This is a memorial service, Maggie. You aren't talking shop right now, are you?"

"It could be important to the investigation."

A mourner seated in front of Jake and Maggie turned, scowled, and put her forefinger to her lips.

"Sorry," Maggie whispered. She dug in her purse for a pad and pen, scribbled a note and passed it to Jake. "All the victims are obese."

Jake read the note, folded it, and stuck it in his coat pocket. He whispered in Maggie's ear. "Good observation. We'll call Mack after the service."

In the front pew, Diego sat next to his mother, his arm slung around her. She rested her head on his shoulder, and her body shook with sobs. Maggie was taken by the mourning woman's slight frame. *So fragile and delicate.* Maggie thought if the diminutive woman cried any harder, she would break into little pieces and dissolve. *That must be where León gets his thin build.* The two little girls, Graciela's daughters, were not present.

"They're too young, and don't need to see their mother buried," Diego told Maggie before the service. "León offered to remain behind and watch over them. Even though she loved him, he'd never been close to Graciela and would have only come for the rest of the family anyway. It's better he stays with the girls."

After the service, the procession wound its way to the Hemacinto Cemetery on the outskirts of town. The grass had long died because, due to the prolonged California drought, the city had turned off water to the cemetery.

The maintenance crew kept the grounds tidy. But the barren landscape, the blistering heat, and the desert wind made Maggie want to curl up in one of the graves and lie in a fetal position until winter when she could burst out like a butterfly from its cocoon, and fly nonstop back to her cabin on Wild River in Wicklow. She licked her chapped lips and tried not to inhale too deeply for fear the heat would scorch her lungs.

Nola showed up at the grave-site in a sundress that clung to her breasts and bared her knees to pay her respects to Diego and his family. *At least she's wearing sensible shoes and navy blue instead of hot pink flowers and eight-inch stilettos.*

Maggie poked Jake's ribs when he stared at Nola's butt a little over his "time limit," as the God's-gift-to-men shook hands or offered hugs to everyone she encountered.

"I see the men are enjoying this," Maggie whispered to Jake. "Funeral or not, I bet none of those horny jerknozzles will miss an opportunity to feel those Triple Ds pressed against their chests."

Nola reached to embrace Maggie who returned the hug, and as she did Maggie looked over her friend's shoulder. Beyond the grave site, in the distance, parked on the dirt cemetery path, a tan VW van with blue striping. Maggie craned her neck to get a better look. The van took off in a hurry, throwing gravel from its wheels. *He must have seen me looking at him.* Maggie disengaged from Nola, grabbed her cell from a side pocket of her purse, and punched speed dial to the sheriff's office.

CHAPTER 13

MAGGIE FIRST MET Nola's husband, James Bond, in the interview room at the sheriff's office. She had a preconceived notion he'd be affable and intelligent like Nola, and she'd prepared to forgive him for the transgression, as terrible as it was, he'd committed when only nineteen-years-old.

"I can't imagine she would marry someone like that. Who in fuck kills and eats a person's dog right in front of them? He must have really changed," she said to Jake.

"He's either a real asshole or a one-hundred percent sicko. He's not likely to have changed a bit."

"But he's Nola's husband, and they've been together for years. I can't understand how she'd fall in love with someone like that, marry them, then stay for all these years if he wasn't completely repentant. I bet he's a good guy who did a terrible thing as a kid. I'm reserving judgment until after I chat with him."

When she entered the room, James Bond scooted his chair back and stood.

Jesus Hamilton Christ. He's huge.

"Mr. Bond, I'm Officer Maggie Sloan."

He looked her up and down as though examining one of the hunks of beef he was about to butcher into steaks. "You're damned good looking for a cop. Nola should have told me."

"Excuse me?"

"You heard me, babe." He took a step closer to her. She stepped back. "Please sit, and you may call me Officer Sloan."

He did look like the photo Nola had shown her and Jake that time in her office. Thick salt and pepper hair, Roman nose, and straight bleached teeth. He flexed his muscles under his too-tight and too-thin t-shirt.

I hope to shit that muscle t-shirt isn't for my benefit. "Do you understand why you're here, Mr. Bond?"

"No idea." He leaned back in his chair and sucked his teeth like he had a piece of toffee stuck in his molars.

"You were convicted of assault and animal cruelty..."

"You mean when I was a love-struck teenager with a broken heart, and that was...oh, let me see, three decades ago? I did my time, and I've lived my life as a law-abiding, productive, tax-payer since. So, unless you have something else to chat about, babe, or you want to meet me at the Motel 6 on Florida Street for a little fun ride on my pony," he grabbed his crotch and stood. "I'm out of here."

"No. You're not 'out of here.' I've a few questions for you, and once you've responded to my satisfaction, you may leave, but not before."

He sat hard in his chair, spread his legs wide, and sucked his teeth again. "Go for it."

"I need to ask you about the dog...the seasoned salt, the Aunt Lorrie's. When did you..."

"What about it? I use Aunt Lorrie's to season everything. Tasty on grilled dog meat." He halted, smiled, and licked his lips. "I bet you look good in a thong bikini because for a woman your age, you..."

A vein in Maggie's neck pumped so hard she thought it might burst. "You need to listen to me, and you need to answer the questions. Do you understand, Mr. Bond?"

"I'm only being friendly." He shrugged his shoulders and raised both hands, palms up. "Most women are flattered when I tell 'em they're hot and invite them for a little play time with Larry and the Twins." He grabbed his crotch again and shook his package. "You might give this a try. It'll loosen you up and...wait a damn minute!" His eyes widened in an "ah-ha" revelation. "You're a lesbo, aren't you?" He nodded. "That's gotta be it."

After the interview, Maggie rushed James to the exit, almost pushing him through it. The men, who'd watched the interview on a monitor, guffawed. She gave them the a venomous look and continued shoving James toward the door. She would have slammed it after him had it not been an automatic slider.

"Holy fuck. What an inbred rock troll," she said to Jake and Sheriff Mack. "And, thanks guys for helping me out in there. Don't tell me you didn't hear and see everything, and you left me in there with him? Fuck all of you."

The deputies broke out into belly laughs so profound some of them choked.

"You seemed to be doing just fine on your own," one deputy said.

"Well, then, fuck you especially."

"An 'inbred rock troll.' He is certainly that," said Mack. Maggie watched him force a business face, struggling to keep his amusement under control. "Do you think he's our guy?"

"Could be. His responses were sketchy, but right now I'm leaning more toward Hank." Maggie said.

"Me, too," said Jake. "As it stands, we don't have other viable suspects." He turned to Maggie. "I'm pooped. Let's go home."

—

Maggie rarely let anyone drive her 54' Chevy truck. It had been her daddy's, and she'd been close to him. He taught her, protected her, and kissed her scraped knees and elbows when she fell, always there to help her to her feet. "Now, now. You're a strong girl, and you'll be right as rain in a bit."

Daddy is who she turned to for comfort and wisdom when life went wrong.

"Sometimes in life we get the velvet, and sometimes we get the brack," he often told her.

"But, mostly, if we look for it, we get the velvet."

After he died in a Belfast car bombing in front of The Europa, the most frequently bombed hotel during The Troubles, when she came of age she spent her own money and time to restore the old truck. From the beginning, it had been a head-turner with its bright cherry red custom paint, and because so many auto enthusiasts had offered to buy it, she finally developed a stock response she gave to anyone who inquired. "No way in hell."

When feeling particularly generous, she'd let Jake take the wheel, but only if she sat shotgun, and watched his every move. "Don't slam the breaks. Ease up to the light. You're crowding the car in front. If he makes a sudden stop, you're going to shove my truck up his ass. I hate when you tailgate. You're going a little fast, there, guy." As a result of her nervous and relentless backseat driving, Jake took his own car or rode as a passenger. Tonight though, after James Bond, she asked him to take the wheel. "I have to breathe through this," she said. "Can you drive?"

On the way home, she yammered on. "I've had two gal pals in my entire life. Two." She raised her hand and made a "V" with her fingers to emphasize. "Sally, who I grew up with, now dead, although she's still bugging me—may she finally move on so she quits haunting me—damn it, and after all these years, I make one other friend, Nola. And, what the fuck? Both of them, smart women, savvy, or so I thought, somehow manage to marry gormless dog shit tacos."

Jake stifled a laugh.

"For my entire life, people tell me I'm a crappy judge of character in my personal life, and okay, so I am, but these two women—holy crap nuggets on a stick. Talk about missing the boat on picking partners. At least I am smart enough to have hooked up with you."

"If I didn't know better, I'd think you were paying me a compliment."

"Here's the thing. I'm a Quantico trained profiler, right? I should be able to judge character, and I'm pretty good at it professionally, wouldn't you agree? I know I blunder sometimes. So what?"

Keeping his eyes on the road, Jake nodded.

"But other than you, I'm absolute crap at it in my personal life, and I know it. These two women—somehow, I thought they were better than me, or at least intelligent enough to know when to get out of a rotten relationship. I can at least recognize when I've gotten involved with festering pus ooze on a hermaphroditic midget's taint."

"Bwahahahaaa." Jake threw back his head and roared. "How in hell do you come up with these? You need to be the writer, not me. Hahahaaa."

"No thanks. I've got enough on my plate. You write, and I'll do my shit." Maggie's cell phone buzzed to signal she had a text message. She pressed the connect button. A photo of a man, naked except for his tighty-whites, grasped his penis through his underwear. "If you aren't a lesbo, you're gonna want some of this, babe."

"How in Mother of God's name did this idiot fart-nugget get my number?"

She turned the phone so Jake could see, and when he looked, that's when it happened. The Audi sedan in front put on its breaks and Jake rammed Maggie's precious Chevy right up its ass.

—

While the mechanic repaired the damage to her truck, Maggie had to rely on Uber or Jake to get her around. That put her in a foul mood. She confronted James Bond via text. "Look. Assswipe. You're still a possible suspect in the murder case I'm on. If you try to send even one more text or contact me in any way, unless it's to confess you're a slimy cannibalistic killer, I'll haul you and your pathetic 'Larry and the twins' back into the station and charge you. It's against the law to send texts like this, especially to an officer of the law. Understand? Nola and I are friends, and that's the only reason I'm letting this one slide with a warning. By the way, I've got a question for you? How in Jesus' name did someone as great as Nola end up with you — you needle-dick bug fucker?" She didn't wait for his response. She blocked him and shoved her cell back into her pocket.

—

"Nola. Good to hear from you." Maggie rattled the ice in her empty whiskey glass and handed it to Jake for a refill. She sat on the couch with Samantha on her lap and Chester at her feet. Occasionally, she'd reach down, squishing the cat a little to give Chester a scratch between the ears. Since Maggie had called "C.O.L." meaning "Cat On Lap," it was up to Jake to make the drinks.

"I called to see how it went with James. He's not saying much."

"I'm sorry, Nola. I cannot discuss the case with you." She leaned again to scratch

Chester, and when she did Samantha put her ears back and sprung off her lap. Jake mouthed. "Next time, you get our drinks."

"I'd so hoped you'd meet him another way, like at our house for dinner."

Maggie screwed up her face and froze it into a mask of disgust. "The circumstances for our meeting were unfortunate."

"He isn't a suspect, is he? He's a bit temperamental sometimes, and like everyone else, he has a difficult time handling rejection, but he's a good sort."

"I'm sorry, Nola. I can't say."

"I bet you liked him, though. Isn't he handsome? If I didn't know better, I'd think even León harbors a little crush on my husband."

Maggie took the whiskey from Jake and downed a gulp. "He's a looker all right." She finished off her whiskey.

Nola laughed. "Keep your paws off. He's mine."

"No worries there, my friend. I've got my own hunk."

"I've been thinking. Now that you've met James, perhaps once this investigation is over, the four of us—you, Jake, James and I—could get together for a few beers or dinner?"

Maggie paused to formulate a response.

"Maggie, are you there?"

"Yes. I'm here. The thing is, Jake and I stay pretty much to ourselves. We have stressful jobs, and when we have time off together, we prefer quiet time alone. We rarely socialize. It's fine for you and I to get together, though, and by the way, aren't we overdue for wine time? But, I hope you understand if Jake and I..."

"No problem, hon. How's León working out in the kitchen?"

"He's doing great, actually. You and León aren't, you know, hooking up any longer, are you?"

"No. It's over. I suspects he still harbors strong feelings for me, but he understands the one time would be the only. I'd hope the two of you would get to know one another better because he's a good kid, and you'd like him."

"I do like him. With the investigation, I haven't had much time to chat, but I'll invite him for a quick beer after work tomorrow." Samantha jumped back on Maggie's lap and groomed herself. Maggie held out her empty glass to Jake.

"A third?" He mouthed.

She gave him the middle finger in response. He laughed and took the glass to the hooch cabinet, then returned with the whiskey, handed it to her, and disappeared into the guest room to work on his book.

"He'd like that, hon. Oh...and, I know you can't talk about details, but have you a suspect in the case?"

"All I can tell you is we're getting closer."

"What happened to these poor people is horrible. After Graciela's death, I feel so sorry for Diego and his family, and I hope you catch the sonofabitch soon because, frankly, I'm scared."

A vehicle pulled to the curb, and its lights showed through the window. Maggie parted the drapes to look. A tan VW van with a blue stripe idled in front of her house. "Nola, I gotta go. Sorry." She hung up. "Jake!"

"What's up?"

"It's Hank. He's outside." Jake and Maggie grabbed their side arms and ran for the door, and as they did, Hank took off, leaving no time to get Jake's car from the garage, and pursue. "Call the sheriff," Jake said.

"Done. He wants us at the station. How in crap's name did Hank find out where we live?"

———

The next night business at the pub crawled. A few regulars popped in for a brew, then popped out. Tom showed up in the early afternoon for his Stella, and when there was no game on the tube, like tonight, he regaled Maggie with stories from the fires, and grisly auto accidents in which the victims were so mangled it made identification difficult.

"How was work?" Maggie asked.

"Quiet. One brush fire we put out in about ten minutes, and two calls from homeowners about rattlesnakes."

"Do you capture and relocate the snakes?"

"We relocate their heads from their bodies. Speaking of bodies, none of my business but I noticed that guy in the kitchen has got something going on with the butcher's wife all the men are drooling over. What's up with that?"

Maggie's throat tightened. "What do you mean?"

"I saw them coming out of that Mexican joint together the other night right as Aimee and I were going in for dinner."

Once Tom headed out, given the sparse food trade and slow traffic at the bar, Maggie decided to close the kitchen early.

"León, let's wash up. Stay for a while and have a beer with me, okay?"

"That would be quite nice, Ms. Sloan."

"Call me Maggie, please."

"All right, if you prefer it, Ms...Maggie."

"I prefer it."

The first thing Maggie noticed is León sat on his stool as though he might be an 18th Century baron. His back straight, his nondrinking hand in his lap, his head held high.

This guy is a little tight. "Tell me, León. Are you planning to finish college?"

"Not at present." He took a dainty sip, dabbing at his mouth with a napkin after. "I enjoy school, and may return one day, but for now I am quite satisfied working at Bond's."

"This is none of my business, so don't feel you have to answer if you feel uncomfortable, but is the reason you left USC to work full time delivering meats because...of Nola?"

León lost his composure. He slumped on his stool, and his eyes darted from the ceiling to the bar and back to Maggie. *The poor guy is in a frantic search to find a way out of answering my question.*

With his voice still formal, but a little softer, he looked at Maggie with such pain on his face she wanted to hug him and reassure him everything would be all right.

"I know you and Nola are friends, so it may not be a secret to you that I have profound...feelings for her...but she is a married woman, and I respect her, as well as her husband, my mentor."

"You had dinner with her the other night. Someone saw you coming out of the restaurant."

"We did not dine together. I had gone for take-out, and she and I met on the way out, so I escorted her to her car. I did not even know she had been in the restaurant. There is no further love relationship between us, and I harbor no false hope for future romance."

"I'm glad to hear it, León, and I do hope you finish your studies. You are a bright young man with a tremendous future. I know you aren't asking my advice, but please do consider returning to USC, will you?"

His eyes brightened. "Thank you. I appreciate you saying so. I have disappointed my family, and I have dishonored them. It had not been my intention to do so, and I am ashamed that I foolishly gave into my heart's desire. I promise to take your advice under serious consideration."

"Speaking of family, I have never asked. What happened to

your mother and father? Diego never speaks of any sibling besides Graciela."

"Perhaps he does not speak of it because what happened occurred so many years ago."

"I'm listening."

"I was five-years-old. My mother and father had taken me for a picnic to a local park. I recalled it later as a wonderful day, but as we walked home, a bullet came from nowhere and struck my mother in the chest. She died instantly in front of my father and me."

"That's pretty traumatic for a little boy. Did they find the person who did it?"

"No. Some years passed, and the police closed the case. I vowed one day to find the killer and avenge her death, but Diego is opposed to revenge of any kind. He says if I fail to forgive the shooter, it will be as though I had consumed deadly poison in hopes the murderer will die instead of me. I suppose he is right, but I cannot forgive the evil person who took my mother from me. This killer got away with murdering her without paying any consequences whatsoever."

"Your father?"

"Shortly after my mother's burial, he disappeared." Leon's eyes clouded. "No one has seen him since, and I no longer care where he is. I do not even remember him. My grandmother and Diego raised me."

He smiled, and when he did, Maggie almost understood how Nola had slept with him, and how it could be that everyone, young, old, male, female might fall for his handsome face.

"Let's have another ale." Maggie walked behind the counter to the taps.

—

Sally's ghost never appeared anywhere other than the pub, so Maggie nearly fell out of her easy chair when Sally popped into her living room late the next night as Jake met in town with his critique group.

"Why are you not working tonight?" Sally asked.

"Unlike you, I have a real body, and sometimes my real body needs a break. I thought I would listen to a little music and catch up on my Gaelic lessons while I wait for Jake. Is that okay?"

"You still don't understand I'm here for you."

"And for what reason? I love you, Sally. You were my best friend ever, and I miss the shit out of you. But, girlfriend, you need to move on."

"I can't."

"And why the hell not?"

"Because you will need me."

CHAPTER 14

MAGGIE PROMISED TO go with her nephew, Jimmy, to take his daughters, Bird and Flower to the Soboba Reservation Pow-Wow. Cathy and Danny were still in Wicklow, getting ready for their move back.

"Are you coming with us, Jake?" Maggie asked.

"I'd like to, but I'm behind on my novel, and my critique group meets tomorrow night. I need to have something to take."

"Okay. I'll call Jimmy and let him know."

"Aunt Maggie, I'm glad it's just the four of us," Jimmy said on the phone. "We haven't done anything with only us together in years, and the day will give us time to reconnect."

"I look forward to it, too. You're going to have to drive, though, because my damned truck's still in the shop."

"I'm surprised you didn't kill Jake over that."

"Trust me. It crossed my mind, but I don't want blood all over my custom upholstery."

"You do realize you love him, right?"

"I suppose I do...a little."

"Hahaha. You love him a lot, but you can't bring yourself to say it, can you?"

Maggie would have said anything to get him off the subject, even "how about those Dodgers?" would have been okay, but instead she said, "Tell me about this woman you're dating?"

"I can't right now, but you'll be the first to know who it is when I can say. I can tell you she's beautiful and smart, everything I'd ever hoped for in a woman."

Her nephew was obviously in love, but Maggie didn't know if she should be happy for him or worried about him.

—

When Jimmy pulled into the driveway, Maggie waited on the front porch. Dressed in Wintu regalia, the girls leaped from the truck and ran to their great aunt.

She took them both into her arms. "Aren't you two pretty?"

"Grandma made our outfits." Bird said.

"Why Wintu? For all the other pow-wows you wore Yurok regalia." For some reason, although disconnected from her Yurok heritage, it bothered Maggie to see the girls as Wintu rather than Yurok.

"Next year, we're going Modoc," said Flower.

"Not Yurok?"

"We're Yurok, Modoc, and Wintu. Mostly Wintu, and French, and Irish, and I think it bothers you that you're only Yurok, and Irish."

Just what I need, a precocious nine-year-old trying to analyze me. "It makes sense you honor all three traditions." She tugged on one of Flower's braids.

"No! You're gonna mess up my headpiece." The little girl raised her hand to straighten what Maggie had pulled askew.

"Headpiece? Looks like an upside-down basket to me."

"Stop it, Auntie." She laughed and gave Maggie a hug.

"Are you girls dancing in the competition?"

"Nope," said Flower. "Grandma didn't have time to teach us the Wintu dances for this year. Besides, Bird only wants to look at boys."

"Boys?" Maggie said. "You two are not even ten-years-old. Aren't you a little young to be thinking about boys?"

"Flower is going steady with a boy, and he has red hair, and it's always messy. I don't think he's cute at all," Bird said.

"Yes, he *is* cute," Flower said, "and he's smart, too. The smartest boy in the class. I'd rather have a smart boyfriend with messy red hair than a cuter boy who's dumb, like the stupid ones *you* like."

"Going steady? What?" Maggie looked at Jimmy.

"No worries," Jimmy said. "It means they hold hands at recess when the teachers aren't around, besides, these relationships only last a week or two at most."

"Seems young to me to be even thinking of such things." When Maggie saw the mind-your-own-damned-business warning in Jimmy's eyes, she backed off. "How 'bout we get started? I'm craving Navajo tacos."

The pow-wow was in full swing by the time Jimmy, Maggie, and the girls arrived. Tribes from all over the United States, Canada, and Mexico displayed their colors. The fragrance of hot oil and frybread filtered through the atmosphere, as did the rhythmic strains of Native song and drumming.

Maggie, Jimmy, and the girls found a seat in the bleachers. Representatives from northern and southern California tribes danced in the arena. Standing on the sidelines or seated on benches tribes from other states waited their turn, Apache, Sioux, Crow, Hopi, and Choctaw, and even some Aztec from the Yucatan talked among themselves. Other attendees, white and non-white, browsed the vendor tents or stood in long lines at the food trucks, fanning themselves with folded dance programs. Jimmy put his arm around his aunt. "This is a big damned pow-wow." "Yes, it is. One of the biggest we've ever attended."

"Being here with you reminds me so much of when I was a boy you'd take me to these things. I'm glad we're doing this."

"Me, too, Jimmy. You don't want to tell me about this person you're dating?"

"Not yet. I haven't dated anyone since the girls' mother left, and I don't want to jinx this before I know if it's going to work out."

When the Yurok dancers performed The Brush Dance, Maggie swelled ever-so-slightly with pride. "Check these performers out," she said to Flower. "This dance is meant to honor and protect children."

"It is? Cool!"

After the performers exited, a young dancer from the arena, a Yurok woman, climbed into the bleachers and sat in front of Maggie. When the dancer turned, Maggie thought it might be to address Flower or Bird, but instead, she talked to her.

"Grandmother tells me you are the Pukkukwerek. Thank you for killing the monsters and protecting our tribe." The young woman stood, worked her way through the crowd, and got in line at a hot-dog-on-a-stick truck.

Maggie, too stunned to talk, watched the young woman.

Jimmy pulled away from his aunt. "Two times in my adult life I go to a pow-wow with you, and something weird like this happens. Remember the old storyteller last year who called you a monster killer? What's up with that?"

"What's a pukk-whatever-thing?" Bird asked.

"I'll tell you the story another time, Okay?" Maggie said.

A Cherokee elder who'd been on the drums, cried out, "Aiyee!" He pointed to a fence post. "Look! A sacred white bird to honor us today!" A collective gasp drifted through the crowd.

"What a pretty white bird!" Flower said.

Perched on the fence the white raven preened. Maggie shook her head as if dislodging a spider from her ear. "Can't be."

"Can't be what?" Flower asked.

"Can't be what I think I'm seeing."

The bird flew from the fence and circled low over Maggie. She heard its voice in her head, an echo. "Beware." The bird clicked and cawed, soared into the sky and away until it disappeared into the afternoon light.

Maggie's cell rang. Since she left the phone off more than on these days, she found the ring both foreign and disconcerting. She checked caller I.D., Jake. She answered.

"Hey, Mag. I'm at the station."

"Any new developments? I thought you were going to stay home and work on your book."

"I needed a break, but I'm meeting with Mack to go over what we have so far. Are you enjoying the pow-wow with Jimmy and the girls?"

"We are having a great time. Why are you calling?"

"To check in, and, well...if you have time, and later this afternoon after the pow-wow can you stop by the station? We're hitting a wall with this investigation, and the sheriff and I thought it might be a good idea if you joined us and the three of us noodled some stuff out together."

"I'll swing by." She clicked off the cell.

"Gotta go to work?" Jimmy asked.

"In a little while. Right now, let's enjoy one another's company."

The girls watched the performers. Jimmy and Maggie talked.

"What happened between us, Aunt Maggie?"

"I'm not sure I understand."

"We were close. As a kid growing up, I thought of you as one of my best friends. We did stuff together. You took me to my first pro baseball game, you took me hiking and camping. I'd stay over your house, and we made pizza. Then..."

"...life happened. I went away to college, and off to work out of state, and during that time, you grew up and became your own person. I may have influenced you when you were a boy, but once you hit adolescence, my effect on you ran thin. Over the years, you and I kinda grew apart. There are fundamental and philosophical differences between us, too."

"Like what?"

"As an example, you, along with your father and mother, were always so much more in tune with our indigenous heritage, while I am fascinated with my Irish roots. I'm sure that's why you're surprised to hear me say I am a Pukkukwerek, right? There's that difference between us, but there are more. I'm politically progressive. You are politically conservative. So, there's that. You've a spiritual bent. I'm an atheist. You have children. I have never had children, so that..."

"...you had a child. I'm sorry I never got to meet her before she... died...but still, you had a daughter."

An ice-dagger tore into Maggie's heartstrings, ripping them into frozen shreds. *Bridget, my sweet little dark-haired lass.* As a UCLA student, Maggie had fallen in love with a married professor, but after five years of their affair when she ended up pregnant, the professor abandoned her and left her to have the baby on her own. The child suffered a congenital defect, died within days of birth, and Maggie, broken-hearted, knew she'd never have another child.

Maggie often dreampt of the dead—her long-gone mother and daddy, her ghost friend Sally, but most of all her dreams were filled with visions of the little girl, and the young woman, Bridget might have become. She had wanted the baby and wondered how different her life might have been had she been a mother instead of a law enforcement officer who hunted murderers, a monster killer. She mourned the loss of motherhood, sad to never know how her life might have gone had she raised the daughter she wanted.

—

"Can't you guys ever get the goddamn temperature right in here?" Maggie fanned herself with both hands. "If I didn't know better, I'd think the minute I stepped into the station a hot flash attacked me."

"Air conditioning busted," Mack said. "We had to bring in ice and a fan to keep the computers from melting."

Maggie poured water from a cooler into a paper cup and gulped it. "No new leads on our Aunt Lorrie's Salt killer case?"

"Nope," said Jake. "We've turned over every rock and can't find anything."

Maggie tossed her cup into a trash receptacle. "Let's go over our suspect list again."

Jake stood at a whiteboard with a marker in his hand. "Okay. So...we've Hank. He keeps disappearing on us, and it looks damned suspicious. We know he has a criminal record, even though it's some years old." Jake wrote Hank's name and under, he wrote: "Who else do we have?"

"We ruled out Diego. We've interviewed James Bond, and although he's an asshole, and has a record, I don't think he's our murderer." As Maggie paced, she wiped the back of her neck with a napkin.

"What makes you think he's not our serial killer?" asked the sheriff.

"Because the guy is dumber than a shoelace," Maggie said. "Whoever is murdering these people is smart enough not to leave traceable clues and has probably been killing for years. We would have caught Bond a long time ago."

"Could be an outsider," Sheriff Mack said.

"We need to figure out who is targeting overweight people and likes liver. And why in God's name can't we find Hank? He's shown up twice since he disappeared, and he can't be that hard to find in a town like this," Jake said.

"He could be smarter than you think," Mack said.

———

"Where is everyone?" The day after the pow-wow, Maggie found León working alone when she opened the door to O'Malley's.

"Since business is slow, and I am capable of handling both the kitchen and bar today unassisted, I did not think you would mind if I released the staff from their duties and spend the afternoon to prepare pork dishes for this evening, and to organize the kitchen pantry and refrigerators. Would you like to see what I have done? If you disapprove, I will put everything back exactly as you had it."

The minute Maggie followed León into the kitchen, she smelled it. The rich aroma of roasting pork...blended with the unmistakable fragrance of White Shoulders.

"Uh, León? We need to talk."

CHAPTER 15

WHEN SHE ENTERED her house, Maggie found Jake waiting for her. He sat on the sofa with pages of his manuscript spread out on the coffee table in front of him. The oversized hound and the undersized Siamese cat jostled for space next to him. All eighty-eight pounds of Chester attempted to climb onto Jake's legs, but the cat, already on his lap, wouldn't budge.

Jake smiled at Maggie, "Glad you're finally home. We need another lap."

She plopped down next to him, and Chester crawled over Jake and put his head on Maggie's thigh. She scratched the dog behind his ears and cooed at Samantha before she spoke. "I didn't expect to see you. I'm surprised you're still awake."

"I finished another Chapter of the novel and want to read it to you." He paused and wrinkled his brow. "Not tonight, though, eh? You look spent. Busy night at O'Malley's?"

"The opposite. It's so slow León told everyone to go home and I found him working the pub on his own."

"You aren't worn out, then? You look awful...I mean, you're pretty, always, but..."

"I'm a little tense. While we were at the station, Nola was at the pub in the kitchen alone with León."

"What? Do you think they are still having an affair?"

"He said she'd only stopped by to deliver pork, but we had a meat delivery on Thursday. There is no reason for her to be there with León, especially when I'm not around. Something about the whole thing doesn't feel right to me, and even though they both swear there's nothing more going on between them, I can't help but think..." A cacophony of caws and clicks caught Maggie's attention. On the ledge of the living room window, dark figures of ravens perched like wraiths tap tap tap tapping on the pane as though asking permission to enter. Maggie opened the window and pounded on the screen until they flew into the night. "I'm going to call Nola in the morning and ask her what's going on. Right now, I need a bubble bath then I gotta get some sleep."

———

Maggie poured two fingers of brandy into her morning coffee to work up the courage to call Nola. She hated grilling her only living friend beside Jake and Diego, but she had to know. She crossed her fingers in hopes the call would immediately roll to voicemail, but Nola picked up on the first ring.

She laughed when Maggie asked her about being alone with León at the pub. "Hon, I am telling you, although León is as cute as they come, and I'm flattered by his attention, there is nothing at all between us any longer. Besides, he's spending most of his time with James learning the butcher trade. One time only I got stupid with him, but that was it. Cross my heart."

"Why were you there, then?"

"I'd forgotten the pork when I made the Thursday delivery, and I thought I would bring it by."

"León didn't mention to me our order was short, and why not James? Doesn't he usually make the deliveries when you're working at the gym?"

"What is this about? I told you I'm not screwing León. For Christ sake, Maggie, I had other errands to run, so I stopped by the shop to pick up the pork, and I delivered it to the pub. I put it in the kitchen where León asked me to, and then I left. Are you all right with that?"

Maggie paused to take another big swallow of her spiked coffee. As the hot drink hit her stomach, it burned in a good way. She closed her eyes and took a deep breath.

"Earth to Maggie. Are you there?"

"Sorry. Listen, Nola, I don't mean to sound weird or accusing, and I'm not judging you. I'm on edge with this Aunt Lorrie's Salt killer, and I can't handle any additional drama right now. Anything between you and León could result in repercussions for me here at the pub, especially with Diego, and I need in the worst way to keep my chef happy."

"What drama? There is nothing at all going on between León and me. I've got James, and I love him, not León. What I did that one time was stupid, but I'll not jeopardize my marriage to such a great guy for a fling with a youngster with an adolescent crush. Do you believe me?"

"I believe you, and I'm sorry if I got too personal. Let me make it up to you. Drop by the pub next Wednesday after two, and we'll share another bottle of wine. My treat."

—

The next night at closing the "great guy," James, showed up at the pub. Tom, the only customer left, decided to use the men's room before leaving. Maggie started to clean up, but as she turned the OPEN sign to CLOSED someone knocked. She opened the door a crack and there on the front porch stooped James Bond trying to squint through a shuddered window.

"Can I help you, James?"

He straightened and backed away from the window. "Hi, Maggie. Let me in. I've got something for you."

She opened the door, and he filled the room with his size. "We got our meat delivery the other day, James. León said after Nola delivered the pulled pork the order is now complete, and I don't need anything."

"You do need something." He moved like a locomotive at Maggie, backing her into the bar. She reached around and felt for her Glock she kept in the pub, the one generally within easy reach, but out of view of customers. Of course, she knew where she'd hidden it, in the secret compartment under the vintage cash register. Diego and Jimmy knew, as did Jake, but no one else. No matter, she couldn't quite reach it anyway. She looked around the room for another weapon but saw nothing handy.

She glared at James and mustered a loud authoritarian voice she hoped Tom would hear. "Get the fuck out of here, or I'll..."

"You'll what? We both know you're attracted to me, Maggie. Why not admit it and let's get this thing between us going, shall we?" The second he put his hand out for her, she twisted out of his reach and tried again to get to the Glock. He grabbed for her again, held tight to her arm and yanked her to him.

"Get your goddamn hands off me." She brought her knee up hard, smashing it directly and squarely into "Larry and the Twins."

The big guy doubled over and crumpled to the floor, all the while grasping his penis and testicles with both hands. Still holding himself, he curled into a fetal position and let out a wail. "Owwwww...Shit! Why did you do that? I only meant to give you a friendly kiss. I thought you wanted me to. What the fuck?" He stood and reached for her again, and that's when Tom grabbed him by the neck and threw him back to the ground. Bond whimpered like a little girl who had fallen from her trike and scraped her knee.

"Get out. Now." Tom grabbed Bond by the shirt collar, pulled him to his feet, and pushed him to the door. "You come around here again, and you can deal with me instead of Maggie. Got it?" Tom told the lesser man.

Bond said nothing but hobbled toward the pub exit holding his penis and testicles with one hand.

"Thanks," Maggie said to Tom, then she spat venom at the retreating Bond. "I don't know what Nola sees in you, you pathetic virulent slice of crap cake, or why you think I want anything at all to do with you. Get out. Don't come back. If you show up anywhere near me again, I will arrest your sorry ass, and if it weren't for Nola, you'd be in cuffs right now, so you best get home and thank her. Go before I change my mind, or before my friend, Tom here, tears off your skanky head and sticks it on a pike outside."

James limped out, and Maggie slammed the door behind him.

"You gonna be all right?" Tom asked her. "I have to pick up Aimee in the morning from the airport early. I gotta go, but if that asshole comes back, call me, and I'll be right back."

"I'll be fine, Tom. Thanks again. See you later."

She sat for a moment to regain her composure. She heard Tom's truck on the gravel, but she also heard another vehicle, not Tom's. She bolted from her seat and opened the door in time to see a tan VW with a blue stripe, peeling out of the moonlit parking lot.

Maggie picked up her cell, turned it on, and dialed the sheriff's office.

———

As a raven, Maggie understood the meaning of freedom and light. Flying as a bird had been the closest she came to anything spiritual. Although the transformation came unbidden and often as a surprise, Maggie sometimes welcomed an opportunity to climb through the skies like Icarus, higher and higher, always in danger of getting too near the sun and scorching her wings, but not caring. As she soared through the air unfettered, her head and heart overflowed with the excitement that comes with experiencing life in all its expansive exuberance. The sky belonged to her, and she to it.

That is why when the ravens summoned her to sit on a fence and talk rather than to fly she'd grow antsy with disappointment. She heard the call, grew her wings, and preened her glossy feathers in preparation to soar over the mountains and towns, but then filled with anticipation, she'd skim out the window only to find the ravens sitting on posts, and she'd know. *We aren't going anywhere, are we?*

Tonight was different, though. An unkindness of ravens waited for Maggie on the fence, among them, the albino. But when the albino spoke, it didn't talk to her in Raven, or English, or Yurok. It spoke in a voice like a violin in a tunnel, the words incomprehensible at first but then syllables and words took form. "Say—leee," the bird said.

"What? I don't understand."

"Say—lee."

"You ravens and your riddles. Can't you tell me what you want to say?"

"Say—lee. Saylee. Sayley."

"Dammit. You aren't making sense. How can I know what you want to tell me?"

"I...Saylee."

"You Saylee? Are you trying to tell me you have a name?"

"I am Saylee. Not name. Who."

"You make no sense. All this time you're communicating with me just fine, and now you sound like you've eaten too many fermented peaches or something. I'm going back to my house and get some sleep—as a human. I've had enough."

"Saylee! Sal! Sal! Sally!" The raven's voice took on a quality of desperation and urgency.

"What did you say?"

"I...Sal. I Sally.."

"Are you trying to tell me you're Sally?"

CHAPTER 16

ALTHOUGH THEY ANNOYED her with their endless riddles, their ceaseless demands for corn, and their bossy ways, the ravens were Maggie's family, every bit as much as Danny, Cathy, Jimmy, the girls, and Jake. Ravens had been a part of Maggie's life since her adolescence, and many had followed her for years. Some had even trailed her from Wicklow to Hemacinto.

When Maggie discovered the identity of the white raven, she'd come to know Sally as, it somehow seemed right to her. Sally had re-entered her world in a corporeal way. No longer only a ghost, Sally had turned into a beaked and feathered bird who would fly alongside Maggie, so once again, Maggie and Sally could be friends in the world of flesh and bone.

"I don't understand, Sally. How did you get to be a raven? How is it you had trouble talking to me as a ghost those last appearances in the pub? How is it you were so articulate the first few times we met as birds, but when you tried to tell me who you..."

"You ask a lot of questions."

"Because I *have* a lot of questions."

"I'll do my best to explain. When a detached human spirit ..."

"You mean a ghost?"

"I mean, let me talk, okay? When a 'ghost' enters a new body or moves on, there is a transitional phase in which things grow distorted and fuzzy for us. We go in and out of what I call 'eternal focus,' and sometimes it manifests as an inability to formulate and speak words. We can develop a type of temporary aphasia. You may have heard it's not uncommon for researchers, or even those haunted, to encounter ghosts who are sometimes loquacious and other times mute?"

"Yeah?"

"Typically, if you experience that with a ghost it means they are going through a transition either as a walk-in to another body, or they are in the midst of moving to a different dimension."

"The albino raven...you call it a 'ghost bird.' What does that mean?"

"The reasons some cultures so revere the white animal are varied, but one reason is there are ghost animals who are vessels for the spirits of others. Most of the time, ghost animals are albino. What makes them ghost animals is their bodies are always inhabited by the souls of the dead, or another way of putting it that you might better identify with, they are possessed. The spirit in the white bird decided to move on, and I took its place so it would be easier for you and I to commune."

"Will you ever appear as a ghost again?"

"When the albino dies, my spirit will be set free. I can move on or stay."

"That brings me to another question. Why do ghosts stick around? Some leave right away while others 'haunt' places or people for decades, or even hundreds of years."

"I can't speak for others, but I can tell you this. Although my human body is now ashes, I'm not ready to move into the light, cross the rainbow bridge, meet the great goddess. I'm still here for a specific purpose, and that is to help you."

"With what?"

"I wish I knew, but I..."

"You *don't* know?"

"Even though I'm in the spirit world it does not mean I have all the answers. I received a message, or more of a plea, to look after you, to be here for you because something terrible—and I don't know for sure what, dear friend—is going to happen."

"Who gave you the message?"

"Your mother."

"Sally, you realize my mom's been dead for years, don't you? Are you saying you two talk in 'Ghost World?'"

"Because of you, she and I share a bond that transcends our other worldly experience."

——

The next morning, Maggie found Jake seated on the back deck in a lawn chair with his bare legs crossed. She pulled a deck chair next to him. "You don't look bad in those plaid shorts. I thought when we bought them you would look flat out nerdy, but I've been obviously mistaken." Maggie patted Jake's thigh. He responded by covering her hand with his and giving her fingers a squeeze, but neither said anything more for a moment.

They sat together taking in the light of Sunday dawn, as they did most weeks. Mornings were always Maggie's favorite time, and Jake's too. "Each new day holds endless possibilities," he told her. "We never know what's going to happen, what surprises are in store for us. Morning is the keeper of promises."

"You're such a sentimental goober," Maggie said. Nonetheless, she felt the exact same way. Every morning, a new start, a promise of a better day, but this one only held the promise of heat. As the sun's rays crested the San Padrino peaks, the sky turned scalding pink and fiery apricot.

Jake held his hand to his eyes to shield against the early light. "It's going to be another hot one."

"I've got something to tell you."

Jake released her hand. "Spill it."

Maggie let out a long breath. "Here goes. You'll be happy to know I finally believe in ghosts."

"You? Ha!" Jake poured French roast from a carafe on the side table and handed Maggie a mug full. She held it in both hands and took a sip. "You make great coffee."

"Glad you like it. So, ghosts, eh? What made you decide to shelve your skepticism?"

"Sally."

"You've seen Sally's ghost since we moved here?"

"Several times. I thought I'd hallucinated her because I missed her so much, or I'd had a little too much Jameson, and that might have been it, but besides as a specter who shows up now and again to scare the shit out of me, more recently she came to me as a raven."

"No kidding?"

"She's the ghost raven, the albino we see, and she says she's here to look after me and says something terrible is going to happen."

"Like what?"

"She doesn't know exactly. She says my mom asked her to stick around and both want me to keep strong on the trail of our killer."

"All right then, you best get to it since you're the Pukkukwerek. Do your job, Monster Killer. I gotta get back to my book." Jake kissed her. "I love you, Maggie."

"I know."

—

That afternoon as Jake worked on his novel, Maggie got online and input, "Native American Monsters, Myths, and Lore." She already knew the monster she'd killed in Wicklow had been a cannibalistic child-murdering Manitou. She'd several times encountered the killer in his natural state as she flew with the ravens. As a man, he hardly resembled the monster within, but he'd been a monster nonetheless. After he tried to strangle her and threatened to kill her grandnieces, she'd dispatched him without remorse or regret. She couldn't know if this murderer might be possessed by a Native monster, but she didn't discount the possibility. "I will turn over every fucking rock until I find this worm."

"What other cannibalistic beasts can we find, Chester?" With her foot, she stroked the sleepy bloodhound resting under her desk. He raised his head to look at her and thumped his heavy rope of a tail against the wood floor. "I don't know how I can fit my legs and feet under here with your huge old body. You're getting chubby."

The dog thumped his tail again, then rested his muzzle on her thigh.

About a half an hour into scrolling, sipping beer, and scrolling more, Maggie refined her search. "Cannibalistic monsters among American Indians." She got a hit.

The Chenoo—the legend of a cannibal demon with an icy heart, who ate the livers of his victims while they were yet alive.

CHAPTER 17

MAGGIE GREW TO both like and respect León, but she missed Diego who would be back in only a few days, and because of that, even with the late hour, she felt like celebrating. The last customers departed, and Maggie turned the sign to CLOSED. León, always the hard worker, scrubbed the floor and had refilled a bucket with clean hot water and Pine Sol. "I do believe these walls have never been washed even once since you bought the tavern, Ms. Maggie."

"You're right, but León, go home. You can wash walls another night. I kinda want to hang out here by myself for a little while, if you don't mind. And, again, you can simply call me Maggie."

"Out of respect, I shall call you 'Ms. Maggie,' if you do not mind." He dumped the water, dried his hands, and removed his apron. "I will be here tomorrow."

"Thanks, León. Have a relaxing evening. You deserve it."

Maggie pulled down a chilled bottle of Veuve Clicquot, her favorite champagne, and popped the cork. She snatched a beer mug off a hook behind the bar and poured the champagne. "Damn I wish Sally were here to share this with me so we..." A tapping sound on the window pane caught her attention. The white raven. "Sally!" Maggie motioned for the bird to come around to the front. She unlocked the door and opened it. The raven flew in and settled on the bar, then scratched behind her ear. "Champagne? What's the occasion?"

Maggie marveled that she understood Sally so well, because generally, unless in raven form herself, she did not understand the raven language. *It could be because this raven is unlike the others. Or, perhaps it's because Sally speaks in English as well as Raven, and the others do not?* "Nothing going on special. Jake is asleep by now, and I didn't feel like going home. Diego is coming back next week, and I'm super happy about that, so I thought it a good time to crack open the bubbly. I wish you could join me."

"I wish I could, too, my friend." She scratched behind her ear again. "But alcohol isn't good for birds anyway."

"Hey, you don't have mites or something, do you? I mean...the health inspector..."

"Oh, shut up! I keep myself clean."

"I don't want you shitting in my pub."

"For the love of the Goddess, Maggie. I can control my...you're a raven, too, you know."

"Only part-time. Are you sure you don't want a thimble of champagne?"

"No thanks."

"Great. More for me." Maggie took a swallow. "By the way, I'd been thinking about you before you showed up at the window."

"That's why I'm here. I have been thinking about you, too, and I'd hoped you'd still be around."

"Let's hope no one else comes by. If they look through the window and see me talking to a fucking bird, they'll summon the loony wagon and have me hauled off in a damned straight jacket."

"Watch who you call a 'fucking bird,' girlfriend. I see you still can't control what comes out of your mouth, can you?"

"Sorry." Maggie drained the beer mug and poured more champagne. "So, no other reason you dropped—I mean 'flew' by?"

"Knock off the snark, Mag. As it happens, I did sense something, but can't say for sure what it is, and I thought I should check in on you."

"Sally, I know you don't have all the answers, but I'm a stuck on this case. Our killer might be Native. I've researched cannibalistic..."

"I don't think so, Mag, not a full Native. But while you are investigating the case, I will stick around to keep an eye on things."

"Well, thanks. You didn't have to c..." The front door swung wide open, slamming against a chair near the wall, and in walked Hank.

"Shit. I forgot to lock the door after I let you in." Maggie said to Sally.

The raven lifted from the bar and flew to a safe distance.

"Hank, two things. Where the hell have you been? And what are you doing here? If you're here to drink, I'm sorry, guy, but we closed half an hour ago."

The big man came close, too close. "I have business with you, lady. I've waited for weeks to get you alone."

"You know you're a suspect in the Aunt Lorrie's Salt murders, right? You need to stay where we can reach you." Maggie put up a restraining hand. *Damn, I wish Diego, Tom, or Jake were here tonight.* "Back away from me. Now."

Hank took a step away. "You understand Rosie isn't coming back?"

"I'm sorry to hear it."

"You know why?"

"Let me guess. Because you beat the shit out of her?"

"No. Because of you." He stepped toward her again and thrust a finger in her face. "You did this. You have been harassing me, accusing me of murdering people. I didn't do any of it, but because of you, Rosie thinks I'm a criminal. Now she won't have anything to do with me."

"I said back away, Hank. I mean it."

"Rosie is all I have in the world, and she's filed for divorce, and now she's got a restraining order. Did you know that?" He grinned. "Of course, you did, and it's all on you, too, because you helped her. You told her to do it, didn't you?"

Maggie eyed the cubby where she kept the Glock. *Easy arm's reach.* "Back. Off. Now."

In one fluid movement, Hank pulled a handgun from his belt behind his back. He grabbed Maggie with one hand, and with the other, he held the muzzle of the gun to her throat. "You took Rosie from me, and when you did, you ended my life. Now, I'm gonna end yours, bitch!" As he prepared to fire into Maggie's neck, Sally flew from her perch into his face.

"What the fuck?" Still holding the gun, Hank let loose his grasp on Maggie, and flailed at the raven, hitting Sally and giving Maggie enough time to grab her Glock. She aimed and blew Hank's lungs out through his back. Blood spattered her face.

"Thanks, Sally. You saved my life."

"That's what friends are for."

Maggie dropped to the floor and checked Hank for a pulse. None. She pulled her cell from her pocket, dialed, spoke to the dispatcher, and waited.

—

Jake was the first to burst through the pub door with the sheriff on his heels. "God, Maggie! What the hell happened?" He grabbed her in his arms and held tight.

She wriggled free. "Let's say I eliminated one suspect," Maggie said with a smile in her voice and on her face. Mack and other assorted deputies combed the tavern. When the Medical Examiner showed up and squatted on the floor next to Hank, Maggie let out a guffaw. She laughed so hard, she doubled up. "I have no idea why the fuck I'm laughing. I can't stop. Hahahaaaa. I can't help it, my Jesus, I can't...hahaha."

Jake put his hand on Maggie's arm and looked her in the eye. "You realized you killed a man. Remember? This isn't funny, and you also know there will be an investigation by FID, and although I'm pretty sure the investigation is going to conclude in your favor, there's a chance you may not be cleared."

Maggie wiped her eyes. She'd laughed so hard, tears had spilled down her cheeks and mixed with blood. She looked like someone had smeared pink paint over her cheeks. Maggie recovered from her laughing long enough to reach for the tankard of champagne. As she brought the glass to her lips, she saw tiny blood splatters spreading into golden liquid. She slammed the mug on the bar counter and pushed it away. "Jake, I'm not sorry I shot that wife-beating, piece of criminal shit-swizzling trash, and he tried to shoot me in the throat. That guy needed killing. I know it's inappropriate for me to laugh, but there's something about this—do you know Sally saved my life?"

Maggie scanned the pub. "She must have flown outside when you all came in. Jake, she sensed something wrong, and that's why she came by. She perched on the ledge, there." Maggie pointed at the window. "She tapped like the Edgar Allen Poe raven, and after I let her in, she said she'd had a feeling, and then, Hank. I'm telling you, had she not flown in that fucker's face, he would have killed me for sure. Where is she?"

Dawn had broken before Jake and Maggie left O'Malley's. Maggie did not look forward to a tedious investigation, and a million hours of paperwork, and said so to Jake.

"The kill was good, Maggie. I know we're in for a ride with the investigating team and review board, but although I don't know for certain, I bet you'll be cleared even before the official report. Don't worry too much. This is an obvious case of self-defense, and it happened on your property, too."

"Right now, I'm too exhausted to think about it. We're going to have to hire a crew to clean this place...damn, that blood is going to be difficult to get off those planks. I'll have to close for a few days. I'm leaving my truck here. Take me home, Jake. I wanna go home, see my dog and my cat, and have a drink. I don't know how we're going to get all this blood up. It's every fucking where. I wonder where Sally is?"

"You're babbling, Mag. You might be in shock. Let me look at your eyes." He pulled his flashlight out and examined one pupil, then the other. "Yup. Let's get you to the hospital and have you looked at."

Ordinarily, she'd push back. Not tonight. She leaned on Jake who put his arm around her for support and walked her out to the parking lot where she almost stepped on a white raven, splayed across the gravel, the bird's eyes open, and dull.

—

Maggie knelt and picked the dead raven from the gravel. She rocked it in her arms as though cradling a newborn infant. "Sally, I'm so sorry." She looked to the sky and wailed. Jake reached to comfort her, but she pulled away. "Twice. I've killed my best friend, twice. Once in Wicklow because the killer thought she was me, and now here."

"You didn't kill Sally either time."

"Yes, I did—it's my fault she died. I fucked everything up. If it were not for me, she'd still be making coffee at Mama Winter's, we'd be sharing a bottle of wine tonight, she'd be the one I'd run to during my crazy times, she'd be...it's my fault she's dead."

"I know this sounds trite, but you can't blame yourself for Sally's death. I'm not even sure what happened here, or why she died, but it's *not* your fault."

"When she...Hank hit her. He hit her hard, but she seemed okay after. I even thanked her for saving my life, but she must have suffered from some internal injury. I should have known. I should have had her checked out by a doctor."

"A veterinarian?"

"Jake, shut the fuck up. She wasn't an animal."

—

At first light, Maggie held a funeral of sorts. She wrapped the albino raven in a silk scarf before placing her in a box lined with a plush towel. In an alpine meadow in the San Padrinos, beneath an incense cedar, with a garden spade, Jake dug a grave. Maggie knelt and lowered the box into the hole. With both hands she pushed dirt over it, mounding the soil and tamping it down. "Jake, let's get some rocks and pile them so a coyote can't dig her up."

In the branches of the tree, hundreds of ravens sat in respectful silence. Once Jake had smothered the grave in rocks, Maggie placed on top a dragonfly pin Sally years before had given her as a birthday gift. "Bye, my dear friend. It breaks my heart to have lost you twice." The ravens in the tree raised from the branches and flew on quiet wings into the early morning sky.

"Let's go home. I'm desperate for a bath, and some sleep. It's been a hell of a night." Maggie knew she would not be sleeping. Not today. Not tonight. Probably not for a long while.

CHAPTER 18

FOR THE THIRD night in a row, Maggie could not sleep. She rolled onto one side, then onto the other, flipped her pillow, stretched her legs, turned on her back. She tried deep breathing exercises the way her psychologist taught her to do after Sally's murder in Wicklow when Maggie experienced the worst insomnia of her life. At three a.m., she pulled herself out of bed. The moonlight filtering into the room through the blinds illuminated a sleeping Jake with Samantha curled on his chest. The cat's body heaved with each of Jake's breaths.

Chester at her heels, Maggie tip-toed out of the room, and closed the door, leaving man and cat to their slumber. "C'mon, Boy. Let's get you outside for a pee, shall we?"

As she walked through the French Doors onto the deck, Maggie pulled her robe around her against the blackness and chill of the pre-dawn air. Chester bounded through the dewy grass and lifted his leg against the trunk of a laurel tree, finished his business, and trotted back. Maggie was about to open the door to the house when a rustling of leaves in a fruitless Mulberry tree caught her attention. She flicked on the porch light and saw perched in the tree's branches hundreds of ravens, silent as ghosts, all facing her.

"Are you here to tell me you miss Sally?" Maggie plopped down on an Adirondack chair, put her head in her hands, and sobbed.

—

Maggie learned to bring layers when she had to be at the sheriff's department. Today, it was blasting cold. Maggie gestured to the wall thermostat. "Can't you shut off that thing for five minutes so I can thaw?"

"Sorry, Maggie. Can't do." Mack indicated the computer room

with his thumb, then handed Maggie a jacket.

"I brought my own. It's in the truck. Thanks."

When she returned with her wool coat buttoned to her throat, the sheriff had already assembled the team. She didn't care if she'd held up the meeting. One of the men bit into a jelly donut, squirting raspberry goo all over his shirt. He grabbed a napkin and rubbed at the stain on his uniform. To Maggie, it looked like a blood splatter. Another deputy held his coffee mug in both hands and blew on the surface to cool the steaming liquid. Jake leaned back in his chair, and when he made eye-contact with Maggie, he smiled at her. She didn't return his smile. All she wanted to do was swallow four ibuprofen, drive home, and sit in the dark.

The sheriff spoke. Maggie didn't hear what he said, but she was up next, so when he sat, she stood. "Thank you, Sheriff Mack." The men mumbled to one another, so she thumped the wall to command their attention. "Okay, gentlemen. What have we got?"

"Not much," said the deputy with the raspberry stain. "Most of us thought it was Hank."

"It still could be," said the deputy with the coffee. "No more bodies have shown up since...since Hank was..."

"Shot?" Said Maggie. "As in Maggie Tall Bear Sloan blew his lungs out? Yes, I shot him. He's dead. I killed him. Can we agree to call it what it is and not worry about my feelings here?"

The deputy apologized.

"No need to be sorry. I just don't want any of you to think you have to pussyfoot around me. That's all. So, back to the business at hand. Hank could be our killer, sure, but if he's not, who else are we looking at?"

"This guy has to be exceptionally strong, or he's not working alone. But, damn. I wish we had something substantial to sink our teeth into." Jake combed his fingers through his hair. "We aren't getting anywhere with this case."

"Could it be we've been searching in the wrong places or haven't caught the clues right under our noses. The killer, or killers, have to leave us something to work with." Maggie backed up to a whiteboard and picked up a marker. "Let's go over one more time what we know."

She drew bullet points:

Consistent M.O.

Missing livers, legs, and thumbs

Evidence of cannibalism

Aunt Lorrie's Salt

Possible multiple killers

"If Hank isn't our guy, who is? The butcher? Maybe we've got a Sweeny Todd thing going on," Maggie said.

"You think Bond could be our guy?" Jake asked.

"We can't completely rule him out," Maggie said, "but if it were him, it'd be easy for us to figure it out because he'd leave obvious and messy clues. What else do we know about our guy or guys?"

"He targets obese people," said Sheriff Mack. "So far, all the vics are well overweight."

"Right," said Maggie. "What does that say about our killer?" She waited for a response, and when none came, she continued. "We're looking for someone with a psychological or mental problem with obesity. Perhaps our killer had an abusive obese parent, or as a child or adolescent, our killer was ridiculed or bullied by someone who was grossly overweight."

"Anyone who is overweight fits the killer's profile for selecting vics, then?" The deputy with the coffee asked.

"Or has something going on we haven't yet figured out against specific obese people," Maggie said.

"That's the general conclusion," Jake said. "I guess we all better put down the donuts and get to the gym."

The deputy with the raspberry stain had selected a maple bar and was about to bite into it. Instead, he looked it over and slid it back into the box.

"There's something else," one deputy said. "In doing background checks on all our victims, we discovered each has a criminal record.

That might be another selection criterion the killer uses."

"E-mail that info to me," Maggie said. "I want to see the types of crimes, when committed, and if there were any repeats. We could be dealing with a Dexter type vigilante who thinks of himself as holy savior so uses his victims' criminal history as justification for murdering them. Our job is to connect how obesity and criminal records factor in these murders."

The problem Maggie had was Graciela Ramirez, who by all accounts led a clean life as a single mother, and of course, what about the dentist's wife and son? What could they have done wrong to deserve a horrible death? What about the vic who had worked at a food bank? "It seems to me these people are good citizens. This does not add up," she said later to Jake.

"Why not read the report and maybe you'll find out they aren't such model citizens after all."

Jake was right. Every one of the vics had a criminal record and some serious. Turns out the nice food bank lady had been arrested for pedophilia as a school teacher when she had an affair with her fourteen-year-old student, who later hung himself in his parent's garage. She spent some time behind bars, but was not implicated in the child's suicide because the Court established he'd been a distraught boy before the affair. The boy's parents and older siblings were convinced she'd pushed the kid over the edge. So, she did her time, changed her name, and once released from prison, moved to Hemacinto where she got involved with all kinds of local volunteerism.

The others, too, had committed grievous crimes, including the dentist who had almost lost his license when he killed a young mother of three by giving her the wrong anesthesia. A cagey judge acquitted him, but by all accounts, the dentist was guilty as hell and got off with no more than a smack on the hand.

Graciela had a record, too, nothing too awful, but still a record nonetheless. As a teenager, a violent gang recruited her, and during her tenure as a gang banger, cops arrested her on drug possession charge and carrying a concealed weapon without a license. She did a little time in juvenile hall, then after her release, she spent a year in community service.

"That's not enough to make a killer want to wipe her from the Earth," Maggie said to Jake, "and unlike the dentist, she paid for her crime."

"Could be more to it."

"I'll talk to Diego and see what he has to say."

—

The following night at closing, Maggie cornered Diego in the kitchen. "I so much hate to do this, but I have to ask you a few questions about your sister."

The cook untied his apron and followed her to a bistro table, where they both pulled up chairs. They'd already turned off the outside lights and had locked the door. Maggie wanted to make sure there'd be no hopeful drunks looking for a late-night whiskey walking in on their conversation.

"I need to ask you about your sister's gang activity and her arrest."

"Why? She's dead. There can't be any reason to dredge up this ancient shit now, is there? My mother will never be the same, my little *sobrinas* are without their mother, but you want to talk about this ugly history, and drag my dead sister's name through the crap now? Seriously?" Although his voice rose in tension and volume, his face remained neutral, but Maggie noticed he balled both of his fists so tightly she thought he'd cut off circulation to his knuckles. *God, is he ever pissed off at me.*

"I'm not supposed to discuss the case with you, but I will tell you I am working my ass off to find her killer, and I need to establish motive. I know you loved Graciela, and this is hard for you, but I need your help on this, Diego."

"She was with a bad gang, got caught with drugs and a gun and paid for it, and in more than one way. Her criminal record is exactly why her favorite *sobrino*, León, turned away from her. Is that what you want to hear?"

"I thought you said you didn't know why León had turned against Graciela."

"Because it's not something I wanted to share, okay? I have to protect my family. Are we done?"

"Nope. Get us a Guinness, and we'll talk more because I'm not quite finished."

Diego got up from the bistro table a little too brusquely, and when he returned with the pair of full mugs, he put them on the table with a little too much force, causing Guinness to splash over the edges of both.

"I have to ask this, Diego. Is there more to the story than I know?"

"What do you mean?" The nervous speed in which he responded coupled with the twitchiness in his eyes told Maggie there was indeed more to the story.

"Look. I have to know. If you want me to catch the son-of-a-bitch who did this to your sister, you need to tell me everything about her gang association and related crimes, and I mean everything."

The way Diego hung his head, Maggie thought he'd break into tears, but he maintained a measure of composure Maggie admired. "Yeah, there's more." He looked away then back. "She killed someone."

"Well, now, that's an important detail left out of the report."

"She was never caught. There was a battle, and she pulled her gun and shot at a rival gang member, but an innocent boy, only sixteen, flying by on the sidewalk on his skateboard got between Graciela and the gang banger, her intended target, just at the right time to catch her bullet in his neck. She panicked, ran, threw her gun into the Diamonte Reservoir. The cops caught her later with cocaine and another gun, but she was never a real suspect in the shooting."

"And you kept her secret. Your entire family knew and kept the secret all these years. What about the other gang members? They would have seen something."

"They saw the boy killed, but since they were never sure whose bullet hit the kid, and none of them wanted to go down for murder, they kept their mouths shut. Graciela knew it was her bullet, though, and knowing she'd shot an innocent boy tore her to pieces. That's why she got out of the gang. After her arrest, she did her time in juvey, and completed her community service, got married had her babies, got a divorce because the loser wouldn't renounce his gang shit, and was a drug-addicted asshole. She moved in before her divorce was final with her kids to my mom's, and you got the rest. At one time, I thought her ex had done this to her out of revenge for her leaving him, the *cabron*, but as bad as he was, I knew he would never hurt her or those kids. Now that she's dead, I guess it doesn't matter that you know."

"This is huge in helping us find the murderer, and you also helped with an unsolved killing."

"Aww, no way. Do you have to report this? My mom has been through so much as it is. This will kill her."

"I'm sorry, Diego. I do have to report it, and if you were the boy's parents, even after all these years, wouldn't you want closure?"

"I guess they deserve to know what happened to their boy." That is when Diego did cry, big tears ran down his cheeks and dropped onto the table. Maggie reached across and put a comforting hand over his. "Are you going to be okay?"

"I don't want my mother hurt any more. Are you sure you can't keep this quiet?"

"I am sorry, but no."

Maggie drove home with an unkindness of ravens following the entire way.

———

The next night, Maggie was hungry, so hungry, she thought she could eat an entire jumbo-sized all-meat pizza on her own. Around dinner time, she sought out Jake and found him in his writing space printing pages of a chapter.

"What are you up to?" Maggie had hoped he might take her to dinner.

"I've got my critique group in an hour. What about you?"

"I was hoping you and I could do something, but if you have your group, then..."

"I can skip one meeting if you need a night out."

"It's okay. You go. I'll see if Nola has some free time." She picked up her cell and dialed.

Nola answered on the first ring. "Sure, hon. Let's go for Mexican. I'll let James know he's on his own tonight. You know he hurt himself?"

"Oh?"

"He said he skidded on something in a parking lot, did the splits, and ended up crushing his penis and testicles against a rock, or something. I took him to Urgent Care, and the doc says his injury is consistent with a good kick to the balls, but James swears that didn't happen. You ought to see his pecker. It looks like an eggplant. We had to apply ice-packs to reduce the swelling, and now he can't even pull on his boxers without doubling over in pain. It's so bad."

Maggie suppressed a laugh. "James had better be more careful. By the way, I have a question."

"Shoot."

"It's about James."

"What about him?"

"Did he ever mention to you that as a kid someone might have bullied him or shamed him in some way?"

"No. Like I said before, no one ever bullied him because of his size and muscle mass. Even as a boy he was cut and buff, hon."

"What kind of relationship did he have with his parents?"

"I don't know all the details because James doesn't talk too much about his folks. He got along okay with his dad, but his mom was a piece of work. She was a real shrew."

"Was she abusive to James?"

"At least, she was verbally abusive, but she was that way with a lot of people."

"Was she overweight? Obese?"

"Yes. I believe her obesity contributed to her fatal stroke."

"That big?"

"She was so big she would have made me look thin when I was at my heaviest. In fact, James seems to like full-hipped, rounder women, and I thought that might have something to do with his mother's weight, kind of an Oedipus thing. I'm surprised he worked with me so long to help me get the figure I have now. When I was overweight, he couldn't keep his hands off me. Now, well...we have sex only once in a great while, and it's okay when we do, but sometimes I wonder if he'd prefer I'd kept more meat on my frame. He seems to have lost interest in intimacy with me. Why are you asking about James' mother and her weight?"

"It's nothing."

"This isn't part of the investigation, is it? James couldn't be a suspect."

"Not at this point."

"Hahaaaaa. My James is a big galumph, but he wouldn't hurt a fly."

CHAPTER 19

HAD IT NOT been for her family, Maggie would have stayed forever by the river and would have never moved to this dried husk of a town. She loved everything about her precious Wicklow, the rural mountain community where she was born and would forever hold her spirit. She missed her A-Frame with a deck over the water. She missed her chickens and her massive garden. She missed the blue spruce, the grey pines, the Douglas fir, and the white and pink dogwood and redbud bush blooms in spring.

What she didn't miss about Wicklow were the restaurants. There were hardly any, and other than the Italian joint, Nito's, The Silverado Pub, and The Dandelion Cafe, she rarely patronized any of Wicklow's eateries. "The worst in Wicklow is La Cantina, a faux Mexican food place owned by the same Thai couple that also owns 'The Golden Pagoda,' the most horrible Chinese restaurant on the planet," she once told Nola.

Mexican food was Maggie's favorite, but whenever she tried La Cantina, she found she couldn't stomach the Cheese Whiz on the tacos, the canned pinto beans, and the syrupy sweet margaritas made with a dollar store mix. She emerged from the restaurant every time disappointed rather than sated until she stopped going altogether. When Nola said, "Let's go for Mexican," Maggie was ecstatic. "Can we meet at El Coyote? Best chili Verde I've ever eaten, and damn the flan. Thinking about it makes my mouth water."

Maggie arrived at the restaurant early, but Nola was already seated. She waived, and Maggie made her way through the other diners and scooted into a booth seat opposite Nola. "Let's order a pitcher of top-shelf margaritas," Maggie said. "They make them from scratch."

"No, hon. Too much sugar. I'll have a glass of dry red wine."

The waitress showed up with a basket of warm tortilla chips

and a miniature molcajete of homemade salsa. "Would you like anything besides water?"

Maggie leaned toward Nola. "Are you sure you won't share a pitcher of margaritas with me?"

Nola shook her head, patted her steel-hard abdomen, and smiled at the server. "I'll have a glass of whatever your house red wine is."

"Even though you own a gym, you are allowed to enjoy a margarita now and again," Maggie said. "Give yourself a break."

"I have to stay away from sugar and, no offense, but I've not seen you in McCabe's for a long time, and looks like you would do well to stay away from sugar, too."

"No way I'll come here and not have a top shelf." Maggie turned to the waitress. "And make it the 32-ounce glass."

"One house cab, one jumbo top shelf it is. I'll be back in a moment to take your order." The server departed.

Maggie leaned back. "So, you think I'm putting on weight?"

"Not so much. I'm more thinking you need to *stay* in shape. You have a stressful job and..."

"...and that's exactly why we don't get to the gym every day. The Aunt Lorrie's Salt case is a time suck, but I'm also running a business, you know."

"What I know is you need to make your health a priority."

"We do our best. Tell me about my nephew? We paid for a year's membership, but I don't see he's losing much weight."

Nola's face darkened. "I'm a bit worried about Jimmy. He's bordering on obese, and he struggles on the machines. I dare not let him go more than fifteen minutes on the treadmill. I'm going to ask him to get a medical clearance from his doctor if he's to continue in the gym because he could have a stroke or heart attack."

"God no. If you tell him he has to get a doctor's release, Nola, he'll never go to your gym."

"He's got to also care enough about himself to alter his nutritional plan. He'd do well on a low carb program. I have the number of a good nutritionist if he'd be willing to see her."

"He's three-quarters Native American. His mother makes all the traditional native foods like fry bread, rice, maize, beans, acorns—all fatty and carby foods. It will be difficult for him to change those life-long eating habits."

Nola's face tightened. "If he cares enough about himself, he—bottom line is I did it. He can, too. I'm sorry, hon, but excuses don't sit well with me. There is plenty in life we can't control, but we can control what we put in our mouths and how we care for our bodies. I'm worried about your nephew, and you should be as well. You ought to see him struggle after only a few minutes on an exercycle. Sometimes I'm afraid he's going to collapse, and I'm not kidding."

"Fair enough. I'll talk to Jimmy about cutting back on the fry bread."

The server showed up with the drinks. "Ready to order?"

"Give me a second." Maggie picked up the menu and read through to the salads. She had entered the restaurant with her heart set on a platter of chili verde with rice and refries, flour tortillas, a side of cheese enchiladas smothered in ranchero sauce, and flan for dessert. "I'll have the chicken taco salad. No sour cream. No guacamole."

"Would you like another margarita? I'll put the order in with the bartender, and it'll be ready when your salad is out."

"No thanks. Ice water with a slice of lemon, please."

"Atta girl," said Nola. "By the way, any closer to catching the salt murderer?"

"A little, but I don't even want to think about it right now."

"Fair enough. Is there anything you can tell me, though, about the investigation?"

"No. Sorry."

—

The morning came too fast for Maggie. "Can't I sleep a little while longer?"

"Nope. We have a busy day ahead of us." Jake had brought her the customary French Roast. She sat up in bed so she could take the mug. "Thanks. Can you hand me my cell?"

"Sure."

She took a sip of coffee, set the mug on the bedside table, took the phone from Jake and pushed the buttons.

"Jimmy, can we meet for coffee, or a beer?"

"How you doin', Aunt Mag? Good to hear from you."

She got out of bed careful not to spill her coffee or drop her cell phone, walked to the living room, plopped down on the sofa, and stroked Chester's back with her bare foot. It wasn't even 8 a.m., and the climate scalded her lungs already. The air conditioning, although full blast, didn't quite do the job. Sweat trickled down her neck and ran in a thin stream into her cleavage. Although stretched across the cold oak floor, Chester panted and now and again, in slow motion, thumped his log of a tail against the floor. Samantha was nowhere to be found.

"I'd love to Aunt Maggie, but with a start-up business, and the kids it's hard to get away, even on the weekend. And, aren't you busy with the Aunt Lorrie's Salt Killer case?"

"I need to talk to you about something. I promised Nola."

"Nola? Why doesn't she talk to me herself?"

"It's nothing urgent. But I..."

"How 'bout I come by the pub after work tomorrow? It will be late, say, around nine? I can get Mom and Dad to watch the girls."

"Great! Shepherd's pie and ale on me." Jake walked into the room. Maggie held out her now empty coffee mug, and mouthed, "one more." He took the cup from her, but not before depositing a bundle of paper in her lap, the latest chapters of his new book, *The Monster Killer.*

—

Ravens roosted in the laurel tree in the front yard. There must have been fifty or sixty of the sleeping birds, and Maggie automatically looked for a white one among them. She knew there would be no white raven tonight, or any night, but she searched the branches from the bottom to the top. "Dammit it, Sally. I can't believe I've lost you again. I'll never be okay with it." She staunched her tears, went in and dressed, and headed for the pub. *At least I get to see Jimmy. I'm worried sick about him.*

It was already dark as she turned onto the street headed toward work; she checked her rearview mirror and noticed headlights close behind. *Damn, I hate tailgaters.* She tapped her breaks, and the car behind her slowed but tucked in close behind her again. *No front license plate, tinted windows, damaged front-end, dark late model sedan. Who the hell is this?* She took a sharp turn down an unfamiliar street, turned down another road onto a deserted residential area under construction, building pads and framed houses, long abandoned and weedy. It looked like an okay street otherwise, safe enough, but she couldn't be sure. *I hope this isn't a fucking cul-de-sac.* It was. She reached for her cell phone. *Dammit! I left it on the counter.* The mysterious car kept pace, never speeding or slowing, and once at the point where she had no choice but to stop or turn around, she hit the brakes, popped the latch on the glove box, and pulled out her Glock.

CHAPTER 20

"TOM?" MAGGIE LOWERED her sidearm the second she recognized the tall man stepping out of the sedan. "I could have blown your face off."

"I was on the way to the mechanic to drop off my oldest daughter's car for repairs, and I saw your truck headed toward the pub. Given what's been going on lately, and with what that prick butcher tried on you, I wanted to make sure you got to work okay."

"Where are the front plates? This isn't even yours, and I'd recognize that Seahawks Blue truck anywhere. What's up?" She circled the vehicle taking it in. "Looks like the front is pretty munged up. Accident?"

"The daughter rear-ended someone, messed up the front of her car, and the plate dropped off somewhere. She's in a shitload of trouble because even though she denies it, that girl might have been texting and driving, and she damned well knows better."

Maggie stowed her Glock back in the truck and walked toward the sedan. "I'm glad it's you, and not some murdering asshole."

It was early evening, but the heat off the asphalt, where weedy things did their best to take purchase in the numerous cracks, sweltered under her feet. Maggie's new blouse dampened where sweat worked its way through her pores, soaking her from skin to bone in the few minutes since she'd left her truck. Even her bra was wet and sticky. The late sky was blinding white, not blue, not bright, but white with heat. She'd be late to the pub, and none of this persistent heat, or her anxiety over being late to relieve Diego, did anything to improve her surly mood. "Dammit," she said under her breath. Yet, she couldn't help but feel grateful for Tom. His size alone would act as a deterrent to any asshole stupid enough to threaten her. He had been there for her front and center when James Bond attempted to assault her, and she'd not forget it. Sure, she could take care of herself, and always had, but two good guys, Jake and Tom, watching her back in this crap town where too many men loved to hurt women was not a bad thing at all.

"God, there are so many crows around here. Noisy things, aren't they?" Tom looked to the trees where the ravens had settled into their clicking, bitching, and grousing. He turned back to her. "I'm glad it was me following you, too." He smiled, and as he did, he reached for Maggie, who hesitated a second before giving him a hearty "thank you" hug.

She was about to break the embrace when she noticed from the corner of her eye a second vehicle, and a second man standing nearby. How she had not heard the auto approach, or anyone exiting a car and closing the door was beyond her. *Perhaps the ambient traffic from East Florida, or the noisy ravens in the mesquite with their incessant knocking, krawing, and cawing — so damned loud I can't hear myself think some days.*

"What's going on here?" Jake asked.

"The question is, what the hell are you doing?" Maggie said. "I thought you were on the way to your writers' group."

"I saw someone following you a little too closely, so I veered off to see if you were okay. Don't you answer your cell at all anymore? Is is off?"

"I left the damn thing on the kitchen counter. Sorry."

"Hi," Tom said to Jake.

"What are you and Maggie up to, Tom, out here in a deserted spot hugging? Either of you got anything to tell me?" Jake set his jaw in an angry knot of tendon and muscle.

Maggie crossed her arms. Her back stiffened into an unyielding slat. "I've got to say you're being a jerk."

Jake looked from Maggie to Tom, then back to Maggie. "I knew something was up between you the second I first saw you two flirting at the pub."

"Flirting? Really? What the shit-hell is wrong with you?" Maggie's neck and cheeks flushed with rage. "I told you already nothing is going on between us. If you don't believe me, fuck the fuck off!"

"Hey! What about those Seahawks, you two? I'm betting they'll have a great season and make it to the Superbowl." In a loud enough voice to catch both Jake and Maggie off-guard, Tom kept talking. "Locket is gonna end up on the MVP list again this year. Either one of you care to place a bet on that?"

Maggie swung around to him. "You, too, fuck the fuck off."

Tom wheeled about, got back in the sedan, and sped out of the cul-de-sac.

"Jake, the way you drool over Nola you have no damned right to accuse me of anything with Tom. You'd dive headfirst into her panties if you thought you could get away with it, so back off you jealous adolescent turd."

"Jesus Christ, Maggie." He scoffed. "Did you ever catch me embracing her in a deserted cul-de-sac perchance?"

"Why don't you ask me what's going on rather than assuming some bull crap? I gave him a hug because the reason he showed up there to begin with was to protect me."

"How, by following you into a remote area and fondling you?"

"Grow up!" Maggie ran to her truck, jumped in, slammed the door, and peeled out toward the pub. She hadn't gone a mile when she noticed another vehicle behind her, close, too close. This time she recognized the car.

⸺

When she got to O'Malley's, she found Diego pacing and mumbling under his breath. "Where were you, *Jefa*? I've been waitin' over a half an hour for you, and I thought something terrible happened. You're never late."

A strand of hair had escaped his net. Maggie reached up and pushed it under. He kept still and let her. "You're like my abuela sometimes, you know that?"

Maggie snickered. "I know I'm fifty, but I'm no one's grandma. Diego, I've had a crappy afternoon. Let me decompress a little, okay? I'm sorry I'm late; get out of here and let me explain later because I gotta make a private phone call before it gets busy." When she saw the pained look on his face, she attempted to comfort him in her own way. "I'm all right, and keep your hair under the net while you're here, okay? The Health Department will be all over my ass if they pull a surprise inspection."

He reached up and patted his hairline to secure any loose ends. "Are you sure you're all right?"

"I'm sure." *Okay, so three guys have my back. Not too shabby.* "Thanks for worrying."

Diego had already removed his apron and tossed it in the laundry. He pulled off the net, and his dark hair tumbled out from beneath it to his shoulders. He waved at Maggie as he exited the pub, and as soon as the door closed, she picked up the land line phone next to the register. "Jake?"

"You still pissed off at me?" he asked.

"Most definitely, but we'll talk about it later. Something happened you need to know about, and we may have to put a call into Sheriff Mack."

"What's up?"

Maggie didn't care one wit about his frosty tone. *I don't have time for this.* "James Bond is what's up."

"Can you elaborate, please?"

"After you and Tom left, I headed back to work, and behind me was James' car."

"What? He followed you?"

"Seems to be the day for it. First Tom, then you, then that dickwad. I feel like I'm leading a 4th of July parade or something with all the clown cars lined up behind."

"Just tell me what happened."

"What happened is I let him follow me to the pub, got out of my truck with my Glock drawn, and the second he stepped out of his car, I aimed at his pretty boy face."

"Wow. Okay. So, why did Bond follow you?"

"It went like this. When I pulled the Glock, he backed up with his hands in the air until his ass hit the side of his car and there was nowhere else for him to go. 'I don't mean any harm, pretty lady. I thought I'd come in for a drink and to try to smooth things over with you. Can you put down your gun?' I said, 'No way, you miscreant fucktard.'"

Jake guffawed. "Miscreant fucktard. I'll be using that in a book."

"So, I said, 'You step foot in my pub, and I will shoot your ass. Get away from me and stay away. Get the hell off my property.' He left, but I have a creepy feeling that he was lying about why he was there. Jake, we need to up his number as a suspect. I don't believe that guy had any good on his mind."

"I'm calling Mack." Jake hung up without saying goodbye.

Maggie poured a double shot of Jameson and downed it to settle her nerves, and that's when she heard Sally's voice.

CHAPTER 21

"YOU'RE BACK? WHERE are you?" Maggie almost gave herself whiplash trying to figure out where in the bar Sally's ghost manifested. Then she saw her friend appear at a bistro table holding a transparent mug of transparent coffee. Maggie expected to feel anger or doubt, but what she felt was joy. "I am so glad to see you because I thought you were gone forever. I was sure I'd killed you a second time."

Sally sipped her translucent coffee. "Mmmm. Good brew. What makes you think you killed me? What happened in Wicklow was not your fault. What happened here was not your fault. Get over yourself."

"Get over myself? What the hell does that even mean?" Maggie pulled up a chair opposite Sally.

"What I am saying is you are making my death, or rather deaths, about you. You didn't do anything to get me killed. In both cases, I ended up in the wrong place at the wrong time. So, it's not you, all right? You're taking on guilt that isn't your right to own, and by the way, it's no picnic being a raven, is it? How do you manage it?"

Maggie felt tears well in her eyes. *Jeezus, I don't want to cry. I don't want to cry. I don't want to cry.* She missed Sally so much she ached with the pain of it, the loss of her best friend in the world next to Jake at times overwhelmed her.

"Well, are you going to say something?" When Sally put the mug on the table, it made the same sound as it would have had anyone living placed a half-full mug of coffee on a wooden surface.

"How come your ghost mug makes a sound when you put it on the table?"

"You can hear *me*, can't you? Answer my question. How do you deal with the raven thing?"

Maggie put her elbows on the table and looked into Sally's eyes. They were still the crisp blue she'd always remembered, but somehow, she could see through them and behind them. It was as though looking through those eyes gave her all the knowledge in the world, but she couldn't articulate or comprehend it. Sally's eyes held the universe, and the sight of that infinite cosmos overcame Maggie like a tsunami overcame the shore. She couldn't breathe from the fear of drowning in all that knowing washing over her at once. She found herself inhaling hard and holding it, then her lungs let loose the air, and her breath came out in a rush, choking her. "Sally..." She gasped for oxygen.

"You okay, Mag? Why in the Goddess name were you holding your breath? Do you need some water or something?"

"I'm okay. I don't know." She sat up and put her hands in her lap so Sally couldn't see them trembling, then composed herself. "So, the raven thing. Okay. How do I manage? Sometimes it's actually fun, especially with the freedom that comes from flying unfettered through the skies and over the mountains, lakes, and towns, but mostly it's because I was born that way. I am half raven and I..."

"Wait." Sally laughed. "Are you actually admitting out loud you're a shapeshifter? I never expected to hear that from your mouth."

"Shut up, will ya?"

The ghost threw back her head and laughed even harder. Her hair, tangled into loose curls, fell across her collar bones. It looked so real, so soft, it was all Maggie could do not to reach across the table and take a fist full and experience its lushness.

Sally picked up her mug again and took a swallow of the invisible coffee. "I knew you'd come around. First, you finally believe in otherworldly things and even admitted so to Jake. Now you understand the truth about your own nature and admit it to me. It's about damned time."

"Well, there's still a lot of shit I don't know. So, let's not dig too much into the depths of my psyche, Ms. Armchair Shrink. Just because you're dead doesn't mean you know everything. You told me so yourself, smarty pants." Still, Maggie wondered if Sally didn't know everything. *What I saw in those eyes, I do not understand.* "Why are you back?"

"I've told you before. I'm here for you because you'll need me. How many times do I need to say it?"

"I don't get it."

"I know you don't. Not everything is meant for your understanding. All you need to know is I love you, and I am here for you because you will need me. Everything else will come to light in it's time."

Sally's image, coffee mug and all, dissolved into nothingness, and the air in the pub grew dense and quiet. The fragrance of jasmine dissipated, gradually replaced by the scent of old wood, roasted peanuts, and beer. For a fraction of a moment, Maggie again wondered if she'd imagined the whole thing, but she knew she hadn't. "Sally, thank you for being here," although she realized her friend had gone, for now anyway.

—

Maggie arrived home late once again. The house was cool, and the darkness suited her. Jake and Samantha were fast asleep, but Chester, who had greeted her at the door, hopped up next to her on the couch the minute she sat down with her gin and tonic. With a swizzle stick, Maggie swirled the ice in the glass, rattling the cubes against the sides like bones. She took a good taste of her drink, put the glass on the coffee table, and closed her eyes. She scratched Chester's back. "You're getting gray, old man." The hound looked at her with soft brown eyes, making Maggie's heart swell a little. "I love you, you mangy beast."

"So, you tell the dog you love him, but you won't say that to me?" Jake had come out in his boxer shorts, his hair a matted mess, sweat on his forehead glistening.

"I didn't want to wake you. Sorry."

"It's okay. I was waiting for you, but couldn't keep my eyes open. Your niece called, Flower. She says it's important that she talk to you about something, and she says it's private. And by the way, Sheriff Mack says they found another body charred over a spit in The San Padrinos. Same MO as the previous. Our sick murderer is still out there, Mag. We have to go into the sheriff's office first thing in the morning."

"Dammit. It's Sunday tomorrow. I need a break."

"I guess neither of us is getting a break." Jake plopped down on the couch leaving Chester between Maggie and him.

Maggie took a sip, rattling the ice bones again. "Want one?"

"No thanks. It's almost three a.m. How can you even stand gin at this hour?"

Maggie responded by taking another long drink from her glass, then tipped her head back and drained it. "Flower said it's important? When did she call?"

"About ten."

"She never calls, especially that late. I wonder what's up? And you didn't ring me at the pub?"

"If you ever left your damned cell on, you'd know I tried to. What's up with you leaving your phone off?"

"I don't always. I sometimes shut it off when I'm working, or trying to get some rest, and I sometimes forget. So what?"

"You're on an investigation. For shitsake, Maggie. Mack and I have to be able to reach you."

"Okay. Okay. I'm exhausted. Quit badgering me, and can you get me another gin and tonic? Never mind. I'll do it myself." Maggie rose from the couch and headed for the liquor cabinet. "I'll call Flower after we get back from the station."

"Ah, I didn't mean to downplay the urgency. Flower seems awfully upset. You might want to call her now."

"At three in the morning?"

"That's a good idea."

Maggie picked up her cell and dialed. On the first ring, Flower picked up. "Auntie Mag?

I'm so glad you called." The child was breathless and excited. "I kept my phone next to me all night, waiting for you."

The fear in the little girl's voice startled Maggie. "Honey, what's up? Tell me."

"This is kind of embarrassing, and I don't understand it."

"I don't care. You can tell me anything." Maggie leaned back into the couch.

"Remember our 10th birthdays?"

"How could I forget it? What I would like to forget is how fast you and Bird are growing up." The brief silence after worried Maggie. "Did you hear me, Flower?"

"It's kind of about that."

"What's up?"

"I got my period, Aunt Maggie, and I haven't told anyone but Grandma Cathy and Bird. Don't tell Grandpa or Daddy. It's private."

"Ten? That's a little early, but since I started mine at eleven, I guess that's okay. I promise I won't tell Grandpa. Do you have questions?"

"No. I've got pads and everything. I know what to do. It's something else."

"What is it?"

"I don't know how to explain, but that night after everyone else fell asleep I dreamed I turned into a big black bird and flew out the window. I could see all of Hemacinto, and I flew and flew."

"God no," Maggie whispered.

"What, Auntie?"

"Nothing. Go on."

"The thing is, I'm scared because I don't think it was a dream. It was like I was an actual bird."

Maggie dropped the cell in her lap and covered her mouth with her hand.

"What is it, Maggie." Jake stood. "Tell me. What is it?"

"It has begun," and with that, Maggie sunk back into the couch cushions, put her hands in her lap as though in an attitude of prayer or meditation, and didn't move.

CHAPTER 22

MAGGIE RECALLED IN detail when Sally came to her as the white raven and told her to watch Flower. "Christ. I don't want this for her," she told Jake. "I cannot help but wonder how Flower knew to call me."

"She trusts you, and didn't you tell her what you are? As for her being a shapeshifter, I don't think you can stop it. What you can do is support her, guide her, let her know what to expect, and give her some coping mechanisms. She is what she was meant to be, just as you are what you're meant to be, so even if you didn't tell her you're a Pukkukwerek she could have tuned into some universal intuitional thing."

"Don't get sappy new agey on me, Jake. Not now. Please."

"I'm telling you, you're fooling yourself if you think you can stop or control this."

Maggie brought the back of her hand to her mouth and yawned. She picked up a book from the coffee table and thumbed through the pages.

"Am I boring you?"

"No. It's the white raven, I mean Sally, told me the same thing, and something in me doesn't want to hear it. I'm not prepared for this, ya know? Plus, we've got an investigation that's sucking up our energy big time."

"You will have to deal with it at some point. Maybe after the conclusion of the case, if it doesn't take years. Flower needs you, and family comes first."

"When this bullshit is over, and we've either killed or put away that psycho, can we take a trip? Just you and me? I haven't enjoyed anything resembling a vacation for over twenty years, and I'm fuckin' exhausted to the point of feeling like I can't do it anymore."

"Where to?"

"Ireland."

———

The latest victim turned out to be a middle-aged woman who worked as a teacher's aide. "That woman never hurt anyone, or so I thought," Sheriff Mack said. "She was in Weight Watchers with my wife, and from all accounts, she was a nice lady who did a lot of good for our community, but when we investigated, we found a record. Apparently, thirty years ago she killed her husband and got away with it. The jury found her not guilty, but she'd been an expert with guns, even entered and won some shooting competitions, and she shot him precisely through the heart. There are plenty who think it was pre-meditated, rather than an accident that happened as she cleaned her rifle. Damned shame. Anything more on James Bond?"

Maggie shook her head. "We don't have enough to go on to bring him in, but we are keeping an eye on him. My cook made a big portable barbeque with a spit for him a few years ago."

"And?" Mack leaned back in his chair.

Jake leaned back in his chair, too. "The barbeque alone isn't enough. From what we can tell, there's not much out of place. The butcher is at his shop at the same time every day and closes at the same time every night. He rarely leaves except to make deliveries when León can't. He takes his wife out on Saturday nights, works out at McCabe's, and stays home in his underwear on Sunday. We can't find a damned thing."

The sheriff snickered. "How do you know he's in his underwear all day?"

"Because he's a crude son-of-a-bitch who goes outside in his hash marked stained tighty whites, and even mows his lawn in his skivvies," Maggie said. "I wish we could find something on that creep other than the barbeque. I'd like to cuff him and bring his sorry ass in myself. If his house wasn't set back from the street where every kindergartener walking to school couldn't see him, we could get him on indecent exposure. But as stupid as he is, I guess he is at least smart enough to figure he can't parade his disgusting muscle-bound Sasquatch body in front of little kids, the depraved cockwomble spunkmuffin maggot."

Both Sheriff Mack and Jake laughed until tears came. Jake abruptly turned serious. "We should investigate that Tom Anselmo guy. There's something about him that's not quite right." Jake shuffled in his seat like a schoolboy who, after having stolen the family car for a late-night joy ride, got caught and now sat in dread of his daddy and mommy's wrath. And wrath is what he got.

Maggie leaped to her feet and got in his face. "What the fuck is wrong with you? Are you so damned jealous because I'm on friendly terms with Tom that you'd go out of your way to discredit him? What a dick move." By then, her voice had reached a shrill, strident, pitch. Mack motioned for her to sit. She gave him her best 'shut your trap, or I'll stick you' look and then plopped down in her chair with a hard, definitive thump. The heat from her fury alone was enough to warm the frigid sheriff's office. With her hands gripping the sides of her chair, she spoke through her teeth to Jake. "Great. You waste time investigating an innocent man. Good for you. However, since everyone is a suspect, I'll spend time investigating your girlfriend, Nola. How does that sound?"

"It sounds crazy. And, vindictive. Tom is at O'Malley's more than most regulars, he's followed you, we don't know much about him, and..."

"And Nola is married to someone who appears to be our Number One suspect. I'll handle the investigation into her myself." Maggie instantly regretted her commitment to investigate the only woman friend she had in Hemacinto. She set her face to neutral to conceal her embarrassment from—yet one more time—a complete idiotic lack of control.

"I thought Nola was your friend."

"Yeah, Jake, but as you have pointed out a thousand times, I'm a lousy judge of character, remember? So, who says she can't be a murderer?" Maggie's gut burned with shame. *I'm only doing this thing about Nola to spite Jake. Jesus, what is wrong with me to even think of investigating my only living female friend? Fuck me.*

"We don't have time for personal vendettas and lover's fights, you two. Settle this between you at home, and unless you both have solid evidence against either Tom Anselmo or Nola Bond, no go on these investigations, and Maggie, finish your documentation and get it in. We found one more citizen dead, and I need you both focused so we can catch this killer." Sheriff Mack chided the couple like they were errant school kids—his disappointment in them evident in his tone.

"Sorry. We deserved that," Jake lowered his eyes to his lap.

Maggie stood. "Are we done here for today, fellas? I've got things to do at home."

———

After an icy silent ride home, Maggie pulled over to the curb in the front of the house. "Got your house keys?"

"Yeah, why? Where are *you* going?"

"I need to be by myself for a while, Jake. I'll be back before dark."

He exited the truck, but before closing the door, he stuck his head back into the cab. "Have you got your cell phone with you, and actually turned on?"

"Don't bug me about my damned cell phone, or anything right now, okay? I'm in a crappy mood."

"I reserve the right to worry about you. With everything going on, you need to be able to call me if you get into trouble." He hesitated for a half second. "I love you, you know."

"Yes, I know. Thanks." She smiled for the first time in days.

Jake exited the truck, and Maggie watched him walk to the front door and put the key in the lock. "I'd be so screwed without you, Jake Lubbock." she whispered, then she took off toward the reservoir.

———

Even though there was much she hated about Hemacinto, there were things Maggie loved, too. She liked the people, most of whom were good salt-of-the-earth blue-collar family types who loved their kids and wanted nothing more than to enjoy their weekend barbeques and softball games. Her pub regulars were great. They drank a lot, ate a lot, listened to tunes on the juke, came in on weekends for the live Celtic music, or to watch football, or to play darts, and the money came in steady. She had made a new friend, someone she genuinely liked, and Jake and she had a pretty good life overall. She thought O'Malley's an excellent pub, and with Diego running things, she felt confident enough to spend more time away.

She had her family close by, too. She didn't have to haul fire wood or shovel snow. A huge bonus. But, the one thing she loved most was the scent of the desert air. Sage. Wild lavender. The blossoms on the few remaining apricot trees from orchards long abandoned. The tiny yellow, purple, and white wildflowers released their perfume in the early spring, and although she couldn't smell them, the random and scattered clumps of California poppies, wild mustard, and blue lupin that sprang up through the impossibly hard clay delighted her.

She idled the truck so she could leave the air conditioner running, slipped a Celtic Women CD into the player, rolled the window down a crack so she could inhale the fragrance of the afternoon desert. She leaned back, closed her eyes, and let her mind wander from Hemacinto to her beloved Wicklow and her life there, then back to Hemacinto and her life here.

After a while, she rolled up the window, holstered her Glock, grabbed her cell, a too-warm bottled water, stashed those things in her backpack, and stepped out from the cab of the truck. "Time for a walk," she said to no one. She started out on the path around the Diamonte reservoir. Families enjoyed picnics on the shore. Rental pontoons on the lake ferried lazy fisherman from one shore to the other, where they'd stop here and there to drop line and open a cold brew. There were sounds. From somewhere the strains of mariachi music. From somewhere else, the dull thunks and thwaks of a soccer ball a group of teenaged boys kicked to one another on a grassy patch. Tiny lizards and jackrabbits scuttled between the chaparral. A baby king snake crossed her path, and a pale cream-colored butterfly no larger than her thumbnail landed for a brief second on her shoulder. Maggie drew the air into her lungs and felt the worries of the world exit on the breath of each exhale. It was now early Autumn, but still, the sun blazed as though no one had bothered to tell it the seasons had changed. Gold, red and russet colors had begun to overtake the tree leaves, and the wildflowers had started their shift from lupin to wild mustard.

Now and again, a lone hiker or a couple holding hands would approach from the opposite direction and greet her. "Great afternoon," one might say. "Yes, it is," She'd say in return. Maggie opened a rusted gate, leading to one of the dirt trails, and when she walked far enough to be certain she'd be at last alone, she found a flat boulder perfect for sitting, and climbed it. There were ravens. Always ravens. "Sorry, guys. I don't have any corn today." They settled in the branches of a nearby Palo Brea tree nestling themselves in the lime green leaves and watched her. "Can I get a moment's peace all by myself?" But she was glad to see them. She spent an hour, followed by another, buried in her thoughts. She imagined what it would be like to visit Ireland with Jake.

"I don't know why I can't tell you everything I feel for you. You've proposed to me at least six times. Are you gonna give up on me, Jake?" She hated it that they'd fought earlier, and in front of the sheriff, too. "Damn. Why can't I keep my mouth shut?"

She thought about the people she'd killed and the people whose lives she'd saved. She thought about the case. "Who in shit's name is our killer? We don't have to make a big deal out of it, or even tell Mack, but it might not be a terrible idea to investigate Tom and Nola because besides the shithead butcher, who I still think is too stupid to have done it, we're comin' up empty. If nothing else, we can rule them out, and they might provide us unwittingly with some clue. Who knows? I'm going to talk to Jake when I get home."

Then she thought about her friends. "I'm damned fifty, and in my entire life I've known three, or maybe four, women I could ever let my hair down with, and only two of them true friends." But even her casual friends meant so much to her. Lacy from the FBI she'd met at Quantico and played pool with on weekends was a casual gal pal. She'd never gotten too close to Lacy, but close enough. "What happened to you? Where'd you end up, eh Lacy?" Dawn, the youngster with the orange and green hair, and as many piercings as her eyebrows could hold, who had bought Mama's in Wicklow, and rented Maggie's A-Frame by the river. "I need to give Dawn a call. We haven't chatted in a long time."

Maggie noticed a small figure in the distance walking toward her down the trail. She shielded her eyes with one hand and squinted in hopes she might recognize who approached. A girl. A very young girl. Slender, long-legged, her hair tucked under a green duck-billed cap. The girl sat in the rough tan gravel, right in the middle of the path, and put her head in her hands. *Resting? Crying?* Maggie couldn't tell. *Should I help?* But it looked all the world to Maggie as though the girl wanted to be by herself. *Leave her alone.*

She returned to her mental meanderings. She thought about Nola, who in so many ways reminded her of Sally. Maggie had been so delighted to finally meet a kindred soul in Nola, but still her new friend could never replace Sally who had twice died yet remained with her. Beautiful, petite, blonde, sassy witch, Sally. She felt tears brim her eyes. "Sally, I'm so damned sorry about..."

"Who are you talking to?"

"What the fu...the hell...I mean the heck?" Maggie slid off the rock and embraced her tearful grandniece, Flower. She held the little girl as she sobbed into Maggie's chest.

"Are you okay, honey? What's wrong? How did you know I was out here?"

"I rode my bike to your house because today is your day off, so you wouldn't be at the pub, and Jake answered and said you'd come up here by yourself. Your truck was in the parking lot, and I saw one of those big black birds like the kind you and I turn into."

"Raven."

"Raven? Well, anyway, he flew down and almost landed on me, but then he ended up on the ground. He kept making noises and jumping up and down. I thought he was hurt, and when I went to touch him to see if he was okay, he let me. I was so surprised because he didn't try to bite me or anything. But there was nothing wrong with his wings or his feet, so I walked toward a path, but do you know there are three paths, and I didn't know where to go? The raven bird kept jumping around, though, and then he got up and flew in front of me, and then he looked like he might even try to peck me because he got so close to my face, but I wasn't scared or nothing. He'd fly a little tiny ways, then come back, and do it again. I didn't know what he wanted, and then I figured out he was trying to show me something, and he did."

"What did he show you?"

"Where you were. He showed me the right way to go, and that's how I found you."

"Smart girl. So that you know, when the ravens come to us, we're supposed to pay attention. Sometimes they want corn, but mostly they have something important to tell us, so we have to listen to try to understand even if we don't speak their language. They are our friends."

———

Out of nowhere, they appeared like a storm cloud, concealing the sun. Ravens. Hundreds upon hundreds of ravens silent in their flight, casting an enormous shadow on the desert floor as though celestial beings or dark angels from the netherworld had taken to the air and spread their wings wide enough to cover the earth.

"Why are you here, Flower?"

CHAPTER 23

"AUNTIE. I TURNED into a bird again last night, and what is that Pukkukwerek thing?"

"An old Yurok legend tells of a woman who shapeshifts into a green-eyed raven, known as the Pukkukwerek, a monster killer whose destiny is to protect our people. I am supposed to be one of those."

"No kidding? You?"

"The Yurok revere the Pukkukwerek, Flower. Being one means you are destined to rid the world of monsters and demons to protect your people."

"My people?"

"The Yurok, but anyone else you love, too."

"I'm a Pukkukwerek?"

"You may be." Maggie felt as though she would throw up, sick with worry about her little grandniece. Being a shapeshifter meant much more than she wanted the child to ever know—misery, fear, and danger. *Goddamn it.*

"But what I saw...," the little girl burst into tears.

Maggie folded the child into her arms. She stroked the girl's head and let her cry until Flower, at last, pulled away and wiped her eyes with her bare arm.

"Tell me what happened, Flower."

"Well, first I saw feathers come out of my arms, like the first time. It didn't hurt or nothin', but it was kinda creepy, and then it all happened that I was a girl one minute and a big black bird pecking at the window to get out."

"How did you get out? Did you wake Bird or Grandpa?"

"No. It was cracked open already because Grandma says we have to have fresh air in our room to be healthy even when it's super cold, so she always opens it a little at night when she puts us to bed.

I used my nose, I mean my beak, and pushed and pushed until it got open enough for me to squeeze through, and then I flew up and up. It was fun at first. I wasn't cold, and the moon was out, and it was cool being a bird."

"Yes, it is cool being a bird."

"Then I went to the mountains, and I could see bears walking around and everything. I flew down to see better, and they even looked up and talked to me, and I understood. I understood bears!"

"What did they say?"

"They said 'Be careful Pukkukwerek.' So, I felt a little nervous, and I wondered if I should go home, but then I saw a fire and thought it might be campers or hikers, and I wanted to see them, so I flew down close." The little girl held herself as though to stave off a chill, or to protect herself. Tears spilled out of her eyes again, and she wiped them away. "That's when I saw..." She burst into tears, and Maggie had to once again comfort the child. She held her and spoke to her in a near whisper. "You're safe now. It's okay to tell me what you saw."

The little girl stayed on Maggie's lap, her long legs folded under. Maggie's thighs burned from the child's weight. Ten-year-old girls can be heavy, but she didn't care. "Tell me."

"There were people, and they were hurting a man, a big man. They cut him... Auntie. It was awful."

"I'm here. No one can hurt you."

"They made him take off all his clothes, and then held him down. There was blood everywhere, and the man was screaming and screaming. He wouldn't stop. It was so terrible."

No, no, no. She's too young. Please. Maggie had no idea who she pleaded to or prayed to, she only wanted Flower not to have seen what she had. She held her little niece closer. "I'm here, sweetie."

"And then, and then..." The little girl cried, sputtered, and coughed.

Maggie pulled out the water bottle she'd tucked in her pack and opened it. "Drink some of this, sweetie."

Flower took a gulp of the water and handed the bottle back to Maggie. "And then, Aunt Maggie, this is so horrible, one of the people, the one..."

"Which one?"

"A grown-up man. I don't know. Anyway, he took a big knife like Grandma uses to cut up a deer side to make jerky, and the man on the ground, bleeding so hard and screaming...It was awful. The same guy cut something out of the poor man, right from his body, maybe his stomach, and...I can't say...It was too terrible to watch, but I looked anyway."

"It's all right, Flower. What did you see?"

"The poor man didn't stop screaming, and the guy with the knife picked up this bloody thing he cut out and, and, and..."

"And what?"

"He put salt on it like the kind Grandma uses when she makes acorn stew, you know, the kind in the brown plastic container..."

"Aunt Lorrie's?"

"Yes. He put salt on the bloody thing and took a bite, then handed the bloody stomach or whatever to the other man, and that man took a bite and he was laughing after, and there was blood all over their faces, and he handed the part back to the first man, and he bit it again, too. It was tough or something because the people chewed a long, long time before they swallowed. And then the man on the ground got quiet and still. He was dead wasn't he?"

"I imagine so."

"But that's not everything. The two men did something even worse. They used a big saw and cut off the man's legs, and even though the man wasn't screaming anymore, it was awful. Then the most awful—they put the dead, naked man on a kinda sideways pole. They stuck it through his rump and they pushed and pushed until it came out of his mouth. I thought I was going to throw up."

Jesus H. Christ. Why did she have to witness that? Why? "Go on, sweetie. Take a deep breath and tell me what happened next."

"They lifted him and put him over the fire and with a big handle, one of the men turned and turned the dead guy over the fire. He was kind of fat, and it took both of the people to get him on the pole before they put him over the fire. And, and, and they cooked him like grandpa makes a turkey over the fire pit. Auntie, it was so terrible. And then something else happened."

"What?"

"One of the men took out another big knife, and sawed at the man's legs they'd cut off earlier into pieces, and he put the leg pieces on a big plastic sheet or something, and cut it into even littler pieces, then put those into another bag, like a big black bag that Daddy uses to put leaves in when he does yard work. And the dead man on the pole turned all black, and I tried to scream but what came out—only caws and other bird sounds, and that made one man grow and look at me."

"Grow? Tell me more."

"He got taller and bigger until he was as big as the tree I was sitting in, and he talked to me. I wanted to fly away, but I was too scared to even move. He looked me right in the eye and told me he would kill me, too, if I didn't watch out. He had big hands, and his finger was so long he almost poked me with it, and he called me 'little Pukkukwerek,' and said one day he'd kill me anyway, even if I did watch out, and you too, Auntie, and cook us over the fire and eat us. The other man shouted up at him and told him, no, he said that the other man wasn't allowed to hurt me. His voice was low and growling like a dog does when it's going to bite. But the other man, the bigger one, told him to shut up and he did."

"You know, this raven stuff might only be scary dreams." She hoped to convince the little girl.

"No! It is real."

"Can you tell me what the people looked like?"

"They were in regalia, but I don't know what kind, and I haven't seen it before. Not Wintu. Not Modoc. Not Yurok. One man was big and the other small."

"They were Native?"

"They were dressed like dancers at a pow-wow, but they had stuff on their faces like designs, and I couldn't tell what they looked like or if they were Native or white people. But, Auntie, one looked like...well they looked like people I know kinda, and I couldn't believe it."

"Well, you shouldn't believe it. With all that on their faces, you couldn't see them, right? So, there's no way you could know who they were. Is there anything else you can tell me?

"When they talked together I almost could tell who they were, even with their growly sounds."

"You recognized their voices?"

"They sounded like...like people I know, but they weren't the same, exactly. So probably not."

"Who did they sound like?"

"I can't, I can't, I don't know." The child broke into deep sobs again. "Then one of the men picked up the bag with the raw leg pieces, and the two of them walked away somewhere."

"Did you see where?"

"To the left."

"South?"

"I don't know. Wherever left is."

"Can you take me back there and show me?"

"I don't know if I can find it again, Auntie. It was far in the mountains that way."

Flower pointed in the general direction of the San Padrinos. "They did something weird, too."

"Weird?"

"Well, one man took the whole container of the Aunt Lorrie's, you know the big ones like we get at Costco, the same one the guy used to salt the bloody stomach thing?"

"Yes."

"He cut off something from the dead man's hand. It looked like his cooked-up thumb, and the one killer guy put it in his pocket. Then he put the whole container of Aunt Lorrie's right on the burned man's body, but not until after the evil guys cut off a piece of the man's arms and, it was terrible, ate the chunks right there, burned and all. It was so gross, and that's when I was able to fly home. But even when I came through the window, and turned back into a girl, I couldn't sleep all night. I was so scared I hid under the covers until Grandma got me up for breakfast."

The unkindness of ravens nearby set off a cacophony of clicks, knocks, and caws so loud their calls drowned the world. Maggie knew for Flower nothing could ever be the same. Her childhood had ended. Maggie bit the inside of her cheeks to stop her own tears, but she couldn't. She held the little girl against her chest, and as Maggie rocked the child, the two cried together.

CHAPTER 24

MAGGIE PACKED FLOWER'S bike in the back of the truck, and once the little girl had settled into the passenger seat, Maggie started the engine, but instead of putting it in drive, she idled. "Do you know why we aren't going right now to Baskin Robbins for an ice-cream?

"Ice cream? Yahoo! Can I get a strawberry shake for Bird?"

"No."

"Why not?" An 'ah ha' look lit up on the little girl's face. "We aren't going because I didn't buckle my seat belt?"

"BINGO. Right answer, skeeter."

The girl scrambled to get her seat belt on.

"Thatta girl."

"Can we get ice cream now?"

"Yes, but I have one more question."

Flower rolled her eyes. "If I answer this one can we go? It's hot in this truck, and I want mint chocolate chip."

"Deal. Once Jake told you where I was, why didn't one of you call me?"

"We tried. Jake said you always leave the ringer off or forget to turn it back on." The little girl's eyes widened. "Shoot. I promised Jake when I found you, I'd tell you to turn your phone on and call him. I forgot. I'm sorry, Auntie. Can we still have ice-cream, please?"

"I wanted to ask you this the time you called when you first turned into a raven. Do you remember? But, here's my question: how did you know I turn into a bird like the kind you turn into?"

"Two more questions. No fair because you promised only one."

Maggie gave the little girl a look that meant business. That's all it took.

Flower averted her eyes to avoid her aunt's cool stare. "I remember it was only a little while ago at the pow wow, and I know because when I asked Daddy what you said about the bird thing, he told me you'd understand about my being a bird because you turn into one, too. Can we go now?" The little girl rolled down the window and stuck her head out. "I'm going to die if you can't turn on the air-conditioner." She panted like a hound and pretended to wipe a gallon of sweat off her face with her hand.

Maggie laughed. "Quit being such a drama llama. Roll up the window, and we'll go but let's call Jake first like you promised." Maggie fished her cell out of her bag and, yep, turned off. *Damn. Why do I do that?* She turned it on and pushed the buttons.

"Where are you? Is Flower with you? She was supposed to call the minute she found you? Is she okay?"

"Don't sound so panicked. She found me, we're talking, and Jake?"

"Yeah?"

"We have a witness to the last killing."

"Great. Who is it?"

"I'll tell you later when I get home. We're headed off to Baskin Robbins, then I'm dropping Flower home, and I want a word with Jimmy. I'll be home around four unless I get hung up at Danny and Cathy's."

"Should I call Mack?"

"Later. We probably should convene the investigating team, but I need to talk to you before we do so because this one is tricky."

"Define 'tricky'?"

"You'll know when we talk."

———

When Maggie and Flower pulled into the driveway, Danny, Cathy, and Jimmy were on the front porch waiting. Flower ran to her father, and he embraced her. "I was getting a little worried," Jimmy said to Maggie. "It's almost dark, and she's got school tomorrow."

Cathy clucked her tongue. "Come in with me, Flower. Bird is in doing her homework, and you need to get something in your belly and join her at the table with your books. You've got at least an hour just on math to get done."

"Okay, Grandma. Are you mad at me, or something? Am I in trouble?"

"Nope. We all know you needed to talk to Aunt Maggie." Cathy passed through the screen door letting it slam behind her. Danny followed her in. "Maggie, we'll see you later, okay? And about that raven thing, Flower is going to need you."

Maggie felt her neck stiffen. "Can I talk to you for a couple of seconds?" She said to Jimmy.

Jimmy jumped to his feet and walked around the side of the house. "Over here, Aunt Maggie."

The side yard was a small citrus orchard with blood oranges, key limes, ruby grapefruit, and Meyer lemon trees. Maggie loved them, the glossy green leaves, the heady scent of the flowers when the citrus trees were in bloom, the cool shade. Today, right now, she was too angry to even see the trees or the ravens roosting among the branches. "Why did you tell Flower I'm a Pukkukwerek? She's way too young to know these things, let alone understand what's happening to her."

"Yeah, and that's exactly why I wanted her to know. She needs you right now; otherwise, she's going to be scared and confused. Besides, you don't remember us talking about it at the pow-wow?"

Maggie detected his annoyance and countered with irritation of her own. "I told her I'd tell her about it later. She's too young, and shapeshifting is not what I want for her, and you goddamn well know it."

"I understand full well what you want, Aunt Maggie. You want to ignore the truth once again so you can deny your heritage."

"Bullcrap. I only think...like I said, she's too young, Jimmy, and as long as she believes what she's experiencing are nightmares, maybe she can still be a little girl for a while longer."

"She *is* a little girl, *my* little girl, and I aim to protect her. She needs you to help her navigate through all this."

"I don't think I'm qualified. A tribal elder, or..."

"You. You need to be there for her, not some stranger. You."

"Okay, Jimmy, I'll do my best, but I can't promise. I gather the entire family knows about Bird, Danny? Cathy?"

"Everyone but Bird, and we are going to figure out the best way to tell her so she can understand what's going on with her sister. We may need you to help with that, too."

"I don't know, Jimmy. I don't know if I can. I want to help, but I...why for fucksakes did you feel like you had to tell the world?"

"You mean at the very public pow-wow with Bird and Flower next to me? Flower had questions after that Yurok dancer called you a Pukkukwerek, Maggie, so would you have preferred I lie to her? And, Mom and Dad needed to know, too. They are our family. Truth be told they're both proud you are a Pukkukwerek, and Cathy especially hopes this might help you return to your Native roots, especially since she and Dad are going back up north. Can you at least help us with Flower, or is it too much to ask?"

With her forefinger and thumb, Maggie pinched the skin between her eyes. "Okay. Okay. I'll see what I can do." A raven flew from a branch of a Meyer lemon tree and landed on her shoulder. Instead of being startled by its presence and its weight, Maggie experienced a sense of comfort. "Hey, fella. How you doin'? I'll see you later, okay?" She stroked his head, and the bird leaned into her for additional head scritches and cuddles, then without so much as a nod, he sprung from her shoulder and flew into the sky. Maggie and Jimmy watched as the raven flew out of site, cawing and knocking on his way.

"He looked pleased," Jimmy said. "I bet he's telling you he's happy I know who you and Flower are."

—

Maggie and Jake sat together in Adirondack chairs on the back deck, gin and tonics in-hand. The night sky had turned from purple to black, brilliant with stars, and other things in the night sky. They enjoyed counting the "shooters" and "travelers," so they named the comets and satellites. Samantha curled herself on Maggie's lap and revved up her kitty motor, her purr so loud Maggie thought she could not hear anything else. Chester tucked himself under Jake's chair and fell asleep.

"Did you see that?" Jake said. "Double shooter and a traveler all at once."

"Jake, I'm going to try something tonight." She'd told him about Flower, her witnessing the last murder and Maggie's argument with Jimmy. "I don't know why he thinks I'd be a great guardian for the girls. He doesn't even like me."

Jake snickered. "He loves you, Maggie, and he knows you love the girls, but you said you're going to try something tonight. What is it?"

"If it works, I'll tell you. Let's go inside and watch a movie or something, plus I want another gin."

"Of *course* you do."

—

Once Jake had tucked himself into bed, Maggie opened a side window, and directed her thoughts. Before she knew it, her fingers had curled into raven claws, feathers sprouted from her limbs, and wings sprung from her shoulders. She flew out the window and soared over the San Padrinos, stopping to talk to an old stag who had seen a good many autumns in the mountains. He reminded her of an old bull elk she'd befriended in the forests outside of Wicklow. She had perched on a low hanging branch and watched as the stag stood guard over his sleeping harem. "You have quite a family," she said to him.

"That I do." He shook his rack of antlers.

One antler hung by a thin thread of sinewy material. "What happened there? How'd your antler break?"

"I don't have much longer," the stag said. "The youngsters are challenging me for my herd, and even though I can fight them off for now, I'm getting old. My eyesight isn't so great, and I'm slower than I used to be. He held up a foreleg and showed her a scar that ran down from his haunch to almost his hoof. "I got this from a cougar a few years ago, and now every time the weather changes the entire leg hurts. If a young stag doesn't finish me, another lion or a hunter will. It's only a matter of time."

In human form, Maggie might have cried. She loved the old stag, having talked to him a few times during her flights through the forest. But there was something else, something that brought her satisfaction. She had never been able to will herself to shapeshift. She'd done it. "I can control this, then. I can shift in and out of raven whenever I choose. I had no idea."

CHAPTER 25

THE SHERIFF'S DEPARTMENT was sometimes so cold that Maggie could see her breath. Today, it sweltered. Maggie had turned all the fans on full blast. They rattled and banged with high speed, and the one in the center of the room thumped as though it were trying to batter itself to death.

Even for an autumn day, the heat blistered everything it touched, outside and inside. Sweat bloomed like grotesque roses on the deputies' shirts. Maggie kept ice water nearby, and took big gulps to keep herself hydrated. She took a long pull from her bottle, grabbed a black marker and stood at the whiteboard. "Let's go over what we have as of today about our latest victim."

The men were uncomfortable in the stuffy room, and clearly had no interest in being there.

"These killings are almost ritualistic. I want you," she pointed to a large man in the front, "to research any Native lore and mythology that might have a bearing on the case. It's possible that our guy is a local tribal member."

"Why me?"

"That's obvious, isn't it?"

"I'm Luiseno Indian, and that automatically means I know all about Native lore and mythology?" The big deputy smirked.

"It means you have access to elders on the rez who may know something about local myths and lore. Do it, okay?"

Jake raised his voice, "You know Maggie is half Yurok."

The deputy looked sideways at Maggie. "She looks white to me. But all right, then, if she's Yurok why doesn't Maggie do the research then?"

Maggie tightened her jaw. "I'm not a local, but beyond that, I told *you* to do it."

He shrugged. "Okay. Good enough for me. I'll get on it."

"All right, gentlemen. We've got how many bodies now? Five, right? And, in only the last twenty-five months, meaning each killing occurs about two to three months apart. I don't know if the timeline has any bearing on the case, but if so, we've got about three months total to catch this asshole or assholes before someone else roasts on a spit. Are we clear?"

The sheriff stepped forward, "Plus, we need to get this done because the fucking media is on my back. And it's a matter of time before the FBI tries to take over. We solve this ourselves and fast, or we get the FBI."

"The FBI doesn't know anything about our local issues, so they could cause more problems then they'll solve. Maggie and I have had some shitty experiences with the FBI while up north," Jake said.

"That's right," Maggie said, "The killings are in this county alone, and we aren't getting any hits from the database about similar murders anywhere else. Therefore, once again it makes sense because our killer operates locally that we need to handle this locally. And, there's a high likelihood there are multiple killers, possibly a gang or cult, although most serial killers work alone, so who knows? By the way, you in front." She pointed to a thin older deputy with thick glasses. *How did he ever pass the fitness test? He's gotta be blind.* "I want you to investigate any cults operating in the area. My guess is this murderer or murderers are popular townspeople, folks we work with, do business with, and go to Church with. But I'm not ruling out something more organized with more than one perp involved. No matter, we've definitely got us a serial killer or, killers, on our hands."

What was clear to Maggie, is the deputies, all male, all long-time residents of the city did not like her, but at least they showed respect for the most part, paid attention, and followed orders even if now and again one pushed against her authority. They took care of business and did their jobs well—that's all Maggie cared about. There was one youngster, a new guy, she had to coach about the protocol of a homicide investigation, and she suspected he was a bit slow, but other than that, the investigation team had proven themselves.

"Have there always been serial killers?" The young deputy asked.

One of the others snickered. "Ever heard of Jack the Ripper?"

"Yes, there have always been mass murderers and serial killers, but the term 'serial killer' was coined by investigators in the Ted Bundy case, and that was in the late 1970s, so the term is relatively new," Maggie said.

"Do you think the killer or killers chose Hemacinto on purpose, then? It's more than just random chance they are operating here and nowhere else, right?" The youngster asked.

"Exactly," Maggie said. "I want you to investigate all the residents who moved here the year before the first killing. Focus on business owners, religious leaders, teachers, anyone involved in the community."

The young man nodded and settled back into his chair.

"Now. Start now, Kiddo. Go." She waved him out with both hands.

The young deputy closed his laptop and left the room.

"Okay, so where are we? Let's reiterate. From what we know so far, we're not talking transients or someone coming from the outside for the sole purpose of killing and eating our town's residents, but someone may have chosen Hemacinto deliberately. We also know the victims have dire criminal records, and most are living here under assumed names. Are we all on the same page?"

The men shuffled in their seats. One raised his hand. "This one witness you talk about, who is it?"

"My grandniece. She was, uh, hiking in the evening, by herself. She's in plenty of trouble for that because she's only ten and was supposed to be home in bed." Maggie laughed. "Kids. You know how it is. I guess she, uh, snuck out the window and decided to go on a little unauthorized adventure, and, uh, somehow ended up where the last murder took place and, she, uh..." Maggie paused. "She hid but could see everything."

The same deputy spoke. "The killing took place pretty deep into the mountains. Are you telling us a ten-year-old girl managed to get that far in by herself at night?"

"Yep. That's what I'm telling you." Maggie felt beads of sweat forming on her brow, not because of the heat, but because of her nervousness. "Let's get back to business, shall we? We can talk about my niece later."

A few of the men nodded.

"Good enough. We've got Kiddo working on researching residents and transplants who moved here before our first incident occurred. I need two volunteers to investigate all new businesses in town in the past two or so years and look for businesses that have transferred title during that timeframe."

One deputy, the same who had walked out on her and Jake when Sheriff Mack first introduced them to the team, raised a hand. "I'll do it."

"Great. Take Kiddo with you."

"You have him on online research."

"Take him anyway. He needs field experience. The rest of you, continue knocking on doors, and making calls."

Mack, who'd been standing at the back, clapped his hands once. "Okay, team. You've got your marching orders. Let's get this sonofabitch."

———

Maggie and Jake arrived home late. "I don't feel like making dinner," Maggie said.

"Should we go out?"

"Let's order a pizza, but don't tell Nola." Maggie patted her stomach. Several ravens lit on the window sill and tapped against the glass to get her attention.

"Yeah, yeah," Maggie said. "You heard the pizza thing, and you're worried you won't get any, right? There will be plenty of pizza bones to go around, you winged pigs."

"You talk to those ravens as if they understand you."

"What makes you think they don't? On another note, why do you think the investigating team is more open to me, now? I know they don't like me, but I'm feeling less hostility off these guys, and getting more cooperation."

"I know why exactly. They're afraid of you, Maggie. You are a formidable presence, and they want to avoid your wrath. These guys finally realized they better not fuck with you, so I guess they're smarter than you originally gave them credit for."

This pleased Maggie. "Hemacinto is not accustomed to strong women, is that it?"

"Not in the sheriff's department, that's for sure." Jake looked off into the distance and knit his brow. "You know? I'm going to have to put something about this in the book somewhere."

CHAPTER 26

MAGGIE TOOK A liking to the youngster, the least jaded of the bunch. She didn't allow herself to get too close, though, because the last young deputy she'd developed a friendship with back in Wicklow turned out to be something entirely different than she could have ever imagined. She avoided using his name unless in a professional capacity, preferring to call him 'Kiddo' and never asked anything about his personal life. She may have liked him, and she wanted to help him, but she had no intention of ever getting to know him all that well.

She took him aside one day right after lunch to grill him on the procedures. "Look, Kiddo, I need you to understand how to do your job if you want to keep it. The sheriff is grumbling about trimming the team because of budgetary concerns, and I want you with us."

"I could lose my job?" The young deputy grew silent. "I suppose I could work at the firehouse with my Uncle Tom. He's a fire captain in town, you know."

"Your uncle is Tom Anselmo? I'll be damned."

"Why? Do you know him?"

"He comes into my pub." Maggie rubbed her hands together "Let's get cracking. Tell me the steps of a routine homicide investigation by memory. Let's start with what happens when the first officer arrives at the scene."

"All right. The first step is to arrive safely and observe all the activity and people, and take note of anything they see, hear, or smell, the time of day, the light, weather, what is there vs. what is missing but should be there, who is at the scene, who is leaving the scene. Everything."

Maggie nodded her approval. "Go on."

He continued to explain the procedures up until the first on the scene checks the body.

"Wait. What comes before checking the body?"

"Oh, yeah. The officer must ensure the safety of any who might be there, too. He or she must defuse potentially dangerous situations between possible suspects, and there might be unattended weapons or an agitated crowd present. Fights or assaults may have broken out."

"Right, Kiddo."

"Why do you call me 'Kiddo'? I'm almost twenty-five. I'm married and I..."

"You're a Kiddo. Now, what's next? You've done a good job so far, but there's a key component missing, the most important element of any investigation is..."

"Documentation," Sheriff Mack's voice tore through the room. He had walked in unnoticed and stood with his hands in his pockets. "Maggie, you know that better than anyone and yet, you don't have all yours in, do you? Get on it right away."

"Damn. Okay, Kiddo, we'll finish this later. Get out of here." Maggie flipped open her laptop.

—

By the time Maggie submitted her paperwork and stepped into the parking lot, the late afternoon had turned breezy and balmy, and the sunset lit the sky in colors of summer fruit, peach skins, lemon juice, and mango flesh. She took a deep breath almost expecting to smell the tropics but inhaled the scent of white sage instead. She wanted to go back to the lake, walk the paths to clear her head, but Jake awaited her.

When she arrived home the day had turned to dusk, and already she could see Venus hanging low in the sky, and the NorthStar shown as if competing with the planet for the best light award.

"You worked a little later than I thought you might."

"I had to get in my fucking documentation."

"Are you saying Sheriff Mack got on your ass again?" Jake couldn't conceal his mirth, probably because she'd been so snappish with him when he'd earlier pressed her to get in her documentation. "You want a drink?"

Maggie gave him her famous stink eye. "What do you think? Yes, I want a drink."

"Have you interviewed Nola yet?"

Maggie felt a pang of remorse. *I wish I'd kept my goddamn mouth shut, now I'm on the hook to investigate her, and for murder no less.* "I'll get to it. I'm not bringing her to the station. I'm going to invite her to share a bottle of wine, and I'll ask her informal questions to rule her out as a suspect."

"But you will bring her in if she does turn out to be a suspect, won't you?"

"Ah...what did you say? If you are in any way implying because of my friendship with Nola, I won't do my job go fuck yourself with a four-foot broom handle. Besides, aren't you too busy attempting to discredit Tom Anselmo to grill me on my investigation because you're a jealous little bitch?" Maggie felt flames building in her gut, and she was afraid to say more lest she spit fire at Jake. "Can you just fix us a drink, and stop with the damned questions?"

"Wow. You are in a special kind of mood tonight, aren't you?" Jake turned his attention away from her and focused on the contents of the booze cabinet.

"Jake, I'm sorry. I am acting like a twat, but it's Nola, my friend, and I'm a complete shit for questioning her."

"That thing with Diego building a traveling spit barbeque for James Bond is somewhat incriminating, but we already have Bond on our radar. Let's see what Nola has to say. As we discussed earlier, she might give us some unmined intel about him. And, Maggie? I understand how hard this is for you."

"It is. It's harder than dried dog turds that have been in the sun for so many months they turned white."

Jake handed a whiskey soda to Maggie. She rattled the ice bones, took a long drink, and picked up her cell.

"Who are you calling?"

"Nola. There's no time like the goddamn present."

Nola didn't pick up until after the fifth ring. Maggie prepared to leave a voice message, click the 'call ended' button, and get back to her whiskey.

"You're there."

Nola seemed out of breath. "Hi. What's up? I'm in the kitchen prepping pulled pork. We got in a good lot of meat from León, and James butchered it this morning. León will deliver it to O'Malley's tomorrow afternoon. I think he's on the schedule to work with Diego in the kitchen on Wednesday night anyway, and when he gets off here, he can bring it by."

"Can you make the delivery instead, and then stick around for a visit? I'll buy the wine."

———

Seven p.m. and Nola was due any time at the pub. Diego had gone home early, and with the bar nearly empty, on his own León handled the kitchen, the bar, and the service with ease.

"If it gets busy, I'll jump in to help, but Nola's coming by this evening to share a bottle of wine with me." Maggie pointed to a private corner booth with high wooden backed benches and plush seats. "We'll be sitting there. Set up a bottle of Pinot Noir and two glasses, please." At the mention of Nola's name, León's eyes widened, and keenly observant Maggie noticed. "Anything wrong?"

"No, of course not. I will make certain the two of you enjoy the best Pinot Noir we have. Do you care for anything else?"

"I'll let you know."

Tom Anselmo, her only customer, sat at the bar in his usual corner seat with his Stella watching sports commentary on the television. Maggie had chatted with him earlier. "Hey, Tom, what's up?" She'd asked him. He told her all the grisly details of the auto accident that took the lives of four teenagers. "I wish I could have filmed the aftermath of the crash and the mangled kids to show my daughters, so they know what happens besides fender benders when someone texts and drives."

"You're a good dad. And, for that, and because I'm in a crappy mood about something I have to take care of but can't discuss, I am going to do something to feel better about myself by making one person happy today at least. Your next Stella is on the house."

Nola burst through the door like a movie star in a pale pink dress so tight anyone could see her panty lines. She swept her long blonde hair behind her ears. Tom gave an appreciative glance at Nola, but that was it. He turned back to his beer and his televised program.

Maggie greeted the other woman with a hug, and the two sat at the booth facing one another. León appeared with a bottle of Hass and two glasses. He made eye contact with Nola but held it a little too long, and she returned his attention.

I thought those two were done with each other. A stab of disappointment sliced through Maggie. "León, please bring us a pitcher of ice water and two glasses, and then we are good for now." León disappeared.

"It sure is warm in here," Nola poured herself and Maggie glasses of the red. "It's been too long since we had a girl's night. What's going on with you, hon?"

"The investigation is kicking my ass, and this place keeps me busy, so nothing much other than Jake is busy with his book and his writing group. We're working on a plan to get into McCabe's more often and work out beginning next week, so I'll see you more there, I suppose." Maggie checked the thermostat on the wall above her head. "It's not even seventy degrees in here. Do you want to freeze my customers?"

"Of course not. I don't want these guys to get too cold, their testicles might shrink." Nola chuckled and leaned forward to

Maggie. "Tell me how the investigation is going. Got any solid leads or suspects?"

"I can tell you we are making some progress, but as I've said a few times before, I can't say more because it's an active homicide investigation."

"Glad you're making progress. What if this guy quits and you can't find him?"

"My experience with serial killers is they don't quit unless caught."

"Let's drink to you catching him, then." Nola and Maggie held up their glasses, and the women toasted.

Maggie shifted in her seat. "I've a question for you."

"I'm all ears." Nola played with a strand of her hair, letting it fall across her breast.

"I have to say you have the best hair ever. I wish I were a blonde."

Nola whispered. "It's not mine."

"It's a wig? It looks natural."

"It's not a wig. That's not what I meant, hon. I've bleached it for decades. My hair is black."

"Black? I would have never guessed. Looks damned great."

"Thanks, but that's not what you wanted to ask me about, is it?"

"I'm a little uncomfortable asking, but you and León aren't still..."

Nola's face tightened. "No." The look in her eyes could have instantly brought the temperature in the pub down by another ten degrees.

Maggie shook her head. "I'm only wondering. No need to get defensive."

"What you ought to be wondering about is Tom Anselmo."

Maggie turned in her seat to look at him. "Why the hell should I be wondering about him? He's a regular. He's a friend, and he's never caused any problems. What are you getting at?"

"For a cop who is supposed to be observant, you can't see he has the hots for you?"

"Oh, for fucksakes. He does not. He's in love with his gorgeous real blonde wife. He's one of those affable guys who talks to everyone, so what in goddamn shit makes you think he's got any feelings for me?"

"I see the way he looks at you, and I know men. I also see that sometimes he seems to follow you if that makes sense. He shows up where you are. You haven't noticed?"

Maggie thought about Tom following her to work that one time, and stopping in the cul-de-sac, and how he'd conveniently showed up when she needed help. "No, I haven't noticed."

"I'm telling you, he's got the hots for you and there's something else not quite right about him, and why isn't he with his wife instead of you after his shift? You know, he could be one of your suspects."

"What do you mean there's something not right about him? He's a good customer, has never behaved like anything other than a gentleman. As for his wife, he loves her, but she goes out of town on business, so she's working in New York, or Denver, or somewhere else. I don't know, okay? But I don't buy for one minute he's interested in me, besides I'm at least a decade older than he is. He adores his kids." Still, Maggie wondered if Nola was right. For the first time, she thought it might be a good idea that Jake investigated Tom. "I've got another question."

"Sure." Nola drained her glass and refilled it. "Next bottle is on me."

"I'm buying tonight. Don't worry about it."

"Your other question?"

"Diego tells me he built a large barbecue with a spit for you when you first arrived in town. And, by the way, when did you guys settle in Hemacinto and why here? This place is pretty run down and ratty, lots of gangs, miserable summers, violence, and now we have our own serial killer. Why for shitsakes here out of all the places you could have chosen?"

Nola laughed so loud Tom swiveled in his bar stool and smiled at the women, then finished his beer, and stood. "I'll see you later, Mag."

She waved in return. Nola, who loved attention from men, and was a big flirt, didn't acknowledge him at all.

"So, what about my question?" Maggie asked.

Nola laughed again. "*One* question? Priceless." She laughed a third time. "That's more like a dozen you threw my way. If I didn't know better, I'd think you were investigating me."

Maggie's cheeks flushed. She was glad the light in the pub was low enough so Nola couldn't see it. "I'm curious, nothing more."

"I don't mind telling you. Yes, Diego built us a large barbecue with a spit because we'd thought about opening a western style joint and wanted it portable for catering events and parties. Once I opened the gym, I decided not to join him in restaurant ownership, or a catering business. Way too much work and way too many hours. I take care of McCabe's, and he takes care of Bond's."

"You don't use the barbecue, then?" Maggie twisted her wine glass by its stem.

"We've used it a time or two. We are thinking about selling it. I'll make you a good deal if you want it." She tilted her head and smiled with the familiar warmth Maggie appreciated. The sincerity. The kindness. The humor. All there in that smile.

"No thanks. Diego is already busy building us one of our own. I wish I'd known about yours before he started work on it."

Four times since the women sat, León poked his head out of the kitchen and stared full-on at Nola.

"Hey, León, can you bring us another bottle?" Maggie asked. *He still has it bad for Nola. Poor kid.* "And you're in Hemacinto, why Nola?"

"We needed a change. It's so damned cold, winters are long where we lived, and we wanted less snow, although I have to tell you I hate the heat. I so wish we could find a place that isn't so oppressive with the damned hellish temperatures."

"You didn't check before you moved here?" Maggie had noticed that even in the chillier nights, Nola never wore so much as a light sweater, and she kept her gym colder than an iceberg, much like the habitat of the Chenoo?

"We did. James and I both wanted to move to California as the natural conclusion to a romantic dream, but I so miss my mountains and the snow. The heat makes me so sick I have to stay in my office most of the day with the air conditioning on full tilt, even in winter."

"Me, too. I'd go back in a split second to Wicklow if I could." *One more way Nola and I are on the same life page. She loves the mountains, and so do I. She's so so so much like Sally.*

"Besides, he has..." Nola paused, "Or rather had an old friend here."

"Hank or Paul or whatever name he went by?"

"Yeah, that's him. James is still upset, since the two men went way back, but we both understand why you had to shoot him. I am sorry for Rosie though. Even though things were not good between them, and she'd left Hank, she lost her lover and her husband in awful ways. It all has to be so hard on her. We never socialized with them, but saw them around town now and again, and it's just an awful thing for any woman to have to deal with."

"I imagine so. Tell me, when did you two move here?"

"Let me think." Nola tapped her long hot pink fingernails on the table. "Two and a half—no—closer to three years back."

———

Later as Nola was about to leave, León appeared from the kitchen, wiped his hands clean on a bar rag, and still wearing his apron, started out the door after Nola. Maggie stopped him.

"León, let's get this place cleaned up so we can get out before dawn. Okay with you?"

The look of frustration and disappointment in his eyes wilted Maggie. But once they got down to business, his tension eased. They worked in tandem to clean the kitchen, wipe down the bar and tabletops, and mop the floor.

"Is it all right with you if I leave?" León removed his apron, folded it into a perfect square before putting it, not throwing it, *placing it* in the laundry.

He's such a neat freak. "Go ahead. I'll lock up."

Maggie had locked the door when she heard a faint scraping noise behind her. At first, she assumed there might be a rat or mouse. "Fuck, I'll have to get an exterminator." But when the scraping noise grew louder, the hair stood up on the back of her neck, and she turned to search the pub. She thought it might be one of the ghosts from the old speakeasy. There were several, but most were harmless. Some dressed in flapper dresses with feathers in their hair, some were dapper drunks in pork pie hats and bow ties.

One dressed as an early 20th-century policeman, a headless man, turned out to be a malicious son-of-a-bitch. Maggie thought for sure had to be Murphy, the one Diego had told her about, the crooked cop on the take who had extorted money from the O'Malley's until someone found his body in an orchard, sans his noggin. He would at times pull nasty pranks, like the time he opened some of her top shelf liquor bottles and poured the contents onto the bar. Or another time when he tipped over the cash register. Sometimes, she'd be closing, and an ale mug would come flying at her from nowhere like a missile, sometimes coming so close she felt the breeze of it pass her head. "Knock off that shit, Murphy." She'd seen him enough to know if it were him, she'd find him standing in the entrance to the converted storage room, usually leaning against the door frame as though he owned the place. She'd confronted him many times, "Get the hell out of my pub and go haunt someone else," but he never heard her, or if he did, he never responded. *It's not him anyway.* No headless specter stood in the doorway. "One of the others?" But no mysterious figures floated across the ceiling, no one rattled the pots in the kitchen, no jazz age music, or the sound of clinking glasses and bawdy laughter coming from the storage room, so she knew it couldn't be any of the O'Malley ghosts.

"Who is it? Dammit, Sally. Is it you?"

"Yes, it's me." Sally manifested in front of Maggie as if emerging from a dark mist or a cloud of smoke. The acrid smell combined with the jasmine hit Maggie full on. She thought for a moment she might vomit, and then the smoke and smells disappeared.

"You're making dramatic entrances, now, or are you purposely trying to scare me, or what?"

"Not on purpose. I don't know why we sometimes pop in on a cloud thing." Sally scratched her chin. "I wonder if my coming in on dark smoke has anything to do with my dark mood."

"What's got your panties in a wad?"

"You."

"Do you mind explaining that?" *Damn, she's mightily pissed off at me.*

"I don't like one bit what I saw here tonight."

Maggie wondered if Sally was referring to León, Nola, Tom Anselmo, or even Diego. "Are you saying one of the people in the pub is our killer? I'm not buying it. Who?"

"You're leading the investigation. You figure it out, girlfriend." A rush of smoky substance appeared, along with the same acrid smell from before; Sally stepped into it and she, along with the cloud and the odor, vanished.

—

On her drive home, Maggie noticed a familiar sedan on the side of the road less than a block from the pub. She craned her neck to look. "Is that Tom's daughter? What is she doing here?" But in the car sat a man with the headlights off and cab lights on. She looked again to see Tom Anselmo with a cell phone in his hand.

CHAPTER 27

MAGGIE MADE A U-turn and pulled her truck behind Tom and switched off the ignition. She got out, tucked her Glock in her waistband, and rapped on the sedan's driver side window.

Tom looked up, his expression startled and confused, while he fumbled with the cell phone dropping it on the floor. He rolled down the window, "Hi, Maggie. What's this about?"

"I saw your daughter's car here, and thought she might need help, since it's late and dark, and..."

"I'm getting new tires and wheels on my truck, so I borrowed her car to get to work."

"It's pretty late, Tom."

"I don't work a nine-to-five job. What's this about?" He repeated.

"I thought the fire department was on San Jacinto Drive, not Florida. What takes you out this way?"

Tom leaned over to retrieve his cell from the floor, and when he did, Maggie reflexively grabbed the handle of the Glock. He fished around between his feet and brought up his cell. "I need to call Aimee. I pulled over because we were texting; she's in Houston on business, and we like to keep in touch when she's gone. I didn't even hear or see you pull up behind me, and you scared the crap out of me. Right about now, she's probably wondering why I didn't respond to her last message."

Maggie took her hand off the Glock. "I'm curious about what you're doing out here at this hour on this street, and so close to the pub."

"Not that it's any of your business," Tom stopped short. "I forget. You're a cop, so I guess you're curious about everything."

"Pretty much, especially anything out of the ordinary, and finding you parked on this street, this close to O'Malley's, this late, and in a car that is not yours is a bit out of the ordinary."

Tom didn't immediately respond. *There's something he doesn't want to tell me. Shit.* She liked him and didn't want to think he'd lie to her, or that Jake might be right and Tom could be their killer.

He shifted in his seat as though he was looking for a way out. "Okay, Maggie. You got me. Any night I work late on my way home I drive by the pub to make sure you're okay. After that incident with the butcher, and Hank, and knowing how dangerous this town is, and knowing you often close up by yourself late…" His voice trailed off into the opened window and disappeared in the crisp night air.

Maggie didn't know if she should be annoyed because he was checking up on her, or grateful that he did, and decided on the latter. "Thanks. I appreciate it. You better get back to texting Aimee, and when you're finished on the cell phone, take it easy driving home."

She climbed back into the cab of her truck and dialed Jake. When he answered, she knew he was not a happy man.

"I am getting worried. It's late, Maggie, and I was about to head out to the pub and make sure nothing happened to you. Can you please call when you're not coming home when I expect you, so I don't sit here scared some murdering gangbanging meth head asshole hasn't put a bullet in you?"

Maggie told him about seeing Tom on the side of the road and questioning him.

"I don't know how I'm supposed to feel about this, Maggie. It's not his job to look after you."

"What you need to feel, you jealous turd, is grateful there is another man scared some murdering gangbanging meth head asshole might put a bullet in me and has my back. You ought to thank him."

———

The Native officer reported to Maggie the results of the interviews he'd conducted with elders on the Soboba reservation.

Maggie went home and sat down to her laptop. Chester tucked in under the desk, as always, and she removed her shoes and stroked his back with the toes of one foot. The big dog yawned, and before long he rested his head on her other foot and fell into a deep, rhythmic snore. "Why in hell can't I fall asleep like that?"

Maggie knew about the Wendigo and had even won a battle against one in Wicklow. She read the accounts anyway. "A Windigo or Manitou is a cannibalistic monster who roams the northeast parts of the United States, especially around the Great Lakes region, as well as Canada, and is one of the most powerful, vicious, and deadly monsters in the Native American pantheon. Having been human at one time, once a person eats human flesh, he turns into a raging monster with an insatiable appetite for 'people meat.'"

Maggie scrolled down further and found the story of Comazotz, the Mayan "Death Bat," "Comazotz, demands routine and regular human sacrifices."

I wonder if the burned victims are actually human sacrifices to Comazotz? She dislodged her foot from under the sleeping hound, rose from her desk and stretched. The dog, now awake and most likely annoyed at the disturbance, panted.

"Sorry, Boy. I'll make it up to you later when we go out back for a play date and a beer break later, k?" She grabbed an ice water, thought better of it, and poured two fingers of Scotch into the full glass, spilling a little over the edge. She licked the scotch off the rim of the glass. "No use wasting good booze." She sat down and returned to her research, but before inputting new keywords, she picked up her cell and dialed her sister-in-law, Cathy. She didn't often call Cathy to ask about things Native, because every time she did, Cathy guilted her about not paying adequate attention to her Yurok culture. "You can't turn your back on your people, especially since you are a Pukkukwerek. You are destined to protect the Yurok, and others you love, you know."

"Yeah, yeah. I know. I need a favor."

"I'm listenin.'"

"Cathy, what do you know about cannibalistic monsters in indigenous lore and mythology?"

"Some. I can tell you about the real bad ones my grandpa told me about when I was a little girl."

"Wintu?"

"We have scary stories in our tribe, but some Natives have scarier ones like the Iroquois. Do you know the stories about Kanontsistonties, or The Flying Heads they're known as?"

"I'm not familiar with that one."

"They are real evil demons and can be giants or small, and fly around to kill people. The Kanonstonties hate anything hot, like summer or fire because heat makes 'em weak and kills 'em real fast."

As Cathy spoke, Maggie took notes the old-fashioned way with a pad and pen. She had written the names of everyone they'd investigated related to the Aunt Lorrie's Salt Killer case, even Tom and Nola. Next to each name, she penciled in a demon or monster from Native lore for comparison. For the Flying Heads, she wrote "Nola." *She hates the heat, but that's not enough to suspect her of anything. Lots of people hate the heat. Besides, she's white. She does have black hair, though, so could be part indigenous. I don't think it's her. I'm a Quantico-trained profiler. She. Does. Not. Fit. The. Profile.*

"If you want another story about monsters who hate hot things, I will tell you about The Chenoo."

"I know about that one but tell me anyway."

"The Chenoo is from the northern tribes and is an ice monster because he has a cold heart and kills every human he meets. The gods turned him that way because he did something terrible and had to be punished by walking the earth as a man-eating monster."

"Cathy, are Chenoo always male?"

"Nope. The females are real mean and show no mercy to anybody."

Maggie's insides knotted. *The Chenoo. That's got to be it.* She wrote "Chenoo" next to Nola's name.

"You heard about that Water-Panther from the Cree, and

Shawnee and some of them other northern tribes like Ojibwe? And you know about them Skinwalkers, the Yee Naaldlooshii of the Navajo people?"

"I've heard of them, yes." Maggie compared her notes from the deputy to Cathy's stories, looking not so much for similarities but differences. Anything could be a clue.

"I notice parallels between these myths."

"There is a reason. All the people want to teach their children to be good and not to eat other people, so when you tell a child he will turn into a terrible beast if he does not obey, the child is afraid and won't do the terrible thing. It's like when white folks tell all them scary Bible stories and how their God will punish people if they don't follow what their God tells 'em to do, but tellin' these monster stories is the Native way."

"Makes sense, and do you have other monster legends?"

"There are hundreds. Do you want to know about any in particular?"

"Any that involve cannibalism, or only the scariest ones."

"I told you most of the scary ones I know except the legend of Owl Woman who comes out at night and eats children. Or Skudakumooch, The Ghost-Witch. That one is real bad, too."

The liver thing is what nails it for me. Our killer could be a Chenoo. But who do I know outside of my own family who could be Native? Nola? It was then she thought of the child killer in Wicklow, the one who threatened her then six-year-old nieces, the one who terrorized the county, and how in the end he turned out to be indigenous. She had no idea that he was Native until the day he tried to kill her and she returned the favor by emptying her Glock into him. *Could be anyone.*

Maggie and Cathy said their goodbyes, and then Maggie got down to searching for clues within the story of The Chenoo. What she discovered about the monster gave her nightmares filled with fire and blood, but Nola wasn't in any of them.

CHAPTER 28

MAGGIE NEVER DID take Chester out to the patio for the promised play date and beer break. After her talk with Cathy, she got online and read story after story about the Chenoo from different tribal accounts, and before she knew it was dusk, and then the dusk turned into dark. She'd finished her scotch and water hours before but was so absorbed in her research she forgot both the time and a refill. Chester had long meandered off to sleep on the couch with Samantha. Even though Maggie was so focused on the Chenoo she forgot to turn on the lights, she remembered something else. *I promised to make dinner tonight for Jake. Damn.*

She closed her laptop, flipped on the lamp, and ambled stiff-legged into the kitchen. She stretched and when she did, her shoulders and upper back cracked and popped. *I'm getting too old for this shit.* Once in the kitchen, she snapped on the light and glanced at the microwave clock. *Crap; he'll be home in less than an hour.*

When she heard ravens calling to her from the back fence, she opened the French door and threw a handful of corn out onto the deck. "Sorry, fellas. No time to talk tonight." She brought out a bag of split peas, and an onion from the pantry then retrieved a wrapped ham slice from the refrigerator. The dog and cat appeared hopefully in the kitchen. "Split pea soup and cornbread tonight. It's all I've got time for, and you two hate split peas." She hesitated. "Wait, it's not the peas, it's the ham you want." She sliced two slivers of ham, one for the dog, one for the cat, and tossed them on the floor before chopping the remaining slices into small pieces.

She'd begun frying the onions in oil when she experienced a definite creepy feeling, and the hair on her arms stiffened as though she'd rubbed a balloon against her skin and had generated static electricity. She stopped stirring to listen and heard nothing but the ticking of the 96-year-old clock in the living room. She looked around. No cell phone nearby. No Glock. But she did have access to a big enough knife. She inched toward the knife block, and as she did, she saw it. The apparition, and with it the scent of Jasmine. Sally stood life-like in the kitchen with a worried look.

"You scared the ever-living crap out of me, Sally. Jesus! Can you at least give me some warning or something before you pop into existence?"

"Sorry. I can't always control my appearances. I'm learning, though."

"All right, so you're here for a reason? Not that I'm unhappy to see you, but you didn't turn up for casual chit-chat, did you?"

"God, those onions smell good. You better turn down the heat under them, or they'll burn."

"You can smell things?"

"It's more of a memory than an actual smell. The other thing I remember is the two of us making split pea soup and cornbread in your a-frame on the river in Wicklow, and our glasses of pinot noir out on the deck. Sometimes I miss being alive."

"I miss you being alive, too. But you aren't here to reminisce, are you?"

"No. I'm here to tell you something important."

Maggie turned to fill the pot with broth, and she poured in the peas and added the chopped ham. "I'm listening."

"You're wrong."

"I'm wrong about what?"

"You aren't as close to finding the Salt Killer as you think. You're off-base."

Maggie felt angry bile rising in her esophagus. Exhausted after spending hours in research and finding frightening things, late getting dinner going, she wasn't in the mood for cryptic games. "How the hell do you know? You told me yourself even though you are dead you don't know everything. I'm working this case, and my gut tells me I'm getting somewhere, and you show up, scare the crap out of me so you can say you remember how fried onions smell and to tell me I'm wrong? What the fuck, Sally?"

"This is something I do know. You're wrong and being wrong this time can cost you your life."

———

Jake showed up at the appointed hour right as Maggie removed the cast iron frying pan with the cornbread cooked until golden and crispy on the top, the way Jake liked it best. He put on kitchen mitts and took the pan and set it on the stove. "You make better cornbread than my Arkansas grandma."

"Thanks. Can you set the table and get us out a couple of cold beers?"

"Sally was here, wasn't she?"

Maggie stopped in her tracks. "What makes you think that?"

"I smell jasmine."

"You can smell her perfume?"

"I smell it sometimes. Unless you have a jasmine candle lit somewhere, that's all it can be."

"How do you know it's her? What if I bought a bottle of the stuff for myself?"

"It's Sally. Remember, I grew up with you two. I know what perfume she always wore, exactly like I know you don't wear perfume ever."

"Do you see her?" Maggie ladled soup into wide-rimmed bowls, and cut the cornbread into triangles, leaving it in the frying pan to keep it warm.

"No, not really. Sometimes I sense her, like an essence, and sometimes I believe she wants to talk to me, but for some reason, I can't hear her. It's as though she's whispering to me, but her voice so low I'd have to be Chester to hear her."

"Dogs hear high pitched tones that we don't, not whispers."

"How do you know? What makes you an expert in dog communication?"

"Look, I don't care. Okay? Let's eat now, because if you want to bicker over what sounds Chester can hear, I'm taking my dinner out to the patio. I'm hungry, tired, and don't want to deal with any petty shit tonight, that is if you don't mind." Maggie sometimes hated herself for being short and snappish with Jake out of nowhere and for no reason, and this was one of those times.

But Maggie knew Jake. He had loved her almost his entire life and knew her better than she knew herself, and he appeared unfazed by her angry outburst.

"Fair enough, but Sally was here, wasn't she? And, only a few minutes before I got home, too."

"She was." Maggie opened the French Doors, put her hand in her pocket, and withdrew another palm full of corn to throw on the patio. "Those damned ravens have been begging all afternoon. This is the third time I've had to throw corn to get them to quit bugging the crap out of me."

"Did Sally have anything to tell you about the case?"

"Only to say I'm wrong, that we aren't anywhere near finding the killer or killers, that my research is useless, and that if I don't get it right, I'm going to die. Is that what you mean?"

"Interesting." With a church key, Jake popped the top off an icy bottle of Harp and handed it to Maggie.

"Interesting, you say? No shit, Sherlock." She took a long pull off the beer, then she and Jake carried their brews and food to the table.

Jake scooted his chair in and buttered a piece of cornbread. "Do you have any idea about what she meant?"

Maggie told him about her research into Native monster myths and told him the story of the Chenoo. "It has to be a Chenoo from everything I've read and heard. They cut off the limbs of their victims, they eat the livers while the vics are still alive, they cook their human meat, and some tribal legends say they like salt. It all adds up, don't you think?"

"Do you believe Sally was telling you that you are wrong about this killer being a monster from legend, or that you're wrong thinking it's a Chenoo? I can see how you might go in that direction after our experience in Wicklow with the Manitou, but it doesn't mean we're up against the same sort of thing here. What do you think she was talking about?"

"How in fucksakes do I know?" Maggie had not even gotten her first spoon of soup to her mouth when her cell phone buzzed. She threw her napkin on the table, and a bit of the fabric landed hard enough in the split peas to splatter them. "Dammit!" She answered the phone.

"Auntie Maggie? It's Flower. I turned into a raven again, and I'm scared. I have to tell you what happened. Can you come over right now?"

CHAPTER 29

MAGGIE WORRIED TOO much about her nieces. She had fallen in love with them both the moment they popped their little fuzzy haired heads into the world, but with their mother gone, they were left to fend for themselves when it came to understanding some things in life that their father, Jimmy, couldn't explain to his daughters. And there were dangers aplenty in the world. Maggie and Cathy did their best to fill in for the girls' long-gone mother, but Maggie took it upon herself to be the twins' constant protector, and they were a handful.

Bird made her appearance first via a standard vaginal path with no complications, but Flower decided to enter the world feet first, nearly ending her mother. The doctor prepared to take her via C-Section, when she finally made her full appearance, squalling so loud it rattled windows, her face livid purple, and her tiny eyes scrunched shut.

"Breech means she's gonna be her own person. She ain't never gonna do things like everyone else," Cathy had said. "I see already great determination in those eyes."

"You mean stubbornness," Jimmy said. "That one cries all night long, as well as every time she doesn't get exactly what she wants. Flower is going to be big trouble."

"Like her Aunt Maggie?" Grandpa Danny said.

Jimmy scoffed. "Exactly."

—

Maggie pulled her truck into Danny and Cathy's driveway. Cathy flipped on the porch light, but other than one small lit lamp in the living room, the house was dark. Danny's car was missing from the driveway where he always parked it, as was Jimmy's.

Cathy opened the door and gave Maggie a hug. "Come in. Flower has been waitin' to talk to you all night. She went Pukkukwerek again and is plenty scared about it, but she won't tell me what happened. She wants you."

"Where is she?"

"I put her in the bathtub with hot water and some sage and lavender to settle her down a bit. She'll be out soon."

"And Bird?"

"She's got a cold, and her chest is all filled up, so I gave her an aspirin, and I rubbed Vick's VapoRub on her. She's all tucked in and sleepin' like a kitten now."

Maggie searched the room, swiveling her head to one side then the other, as though expecting to see something or someone, even Sally's ghost. "What about Danny and Jimmy? Are they working late?"

"Danny is takin' care of stuff up north so we can move. The people who bought the property left a real mess, and Danny is cleanin' up everything so we can get moved and have a Bear Dance this year."

Cathy switched on the overhead lights of the kitchen, giving the space a golden and cozy feel that Maggie had come to love. The women sat at the yellow picnic table, and Cathy put on a kettle for tea. "We move maybe next month or the month after. Jimmy and the girls will be happy to get this house to themselves."

"Jimmy? Where's he?"

"He's on a date. Third one this week and we don't know why he don't bring her here to meet us. He goes once or twice or more each week out with her, and sometimes don't come home til' almost morning."

"He's in love. Good."

"Not if he don't bring her here to meet us, it ain't. The girls don't even know who she is."

"I'm sure he's only cautious. If he introduces the girls to her, and they love her, and it doesn't work out..."

"I know. Drink this tea down, all of it. It's got healthy herbs I gathered myself, and it's good for the blood."

"Do you have anything a bit stronger?"

"Nope. Danny and me are tryin' to slow down a little on the booze, so we don't keep much in the house anymore."

Disappointed, Maggie took the tea from Cathy and blew on the hot liquid to cool it. "Do you have any muffins or anything at all I can snack on? I left the dinner table to come here, and I haven't eaten."

"I got some chicken leftover." Cathy made a plate of cold chicken legs and already prepped potato salad and handed it to Maggie, who tucked in and ate every bite. It was then Flower appeared in her robe and slippers, a towel wrapped around her wet hair. She ran so fast to Maggie the towel unwound itself and tumbled from her head onto the wood slat floor.

"Honey, are you okay?" Maggie asked.

"No. I'm not." Although she was a lanky, tall ten-year-old, she climbed into Maggie's lap, buried her head in her aunt's chest, and sniffled. "I want it to stop. Make it stop, please."

"You want what to stop?"

The little girl pulled away and sat straight on Maggie's lap. "It's the raven thing. It's so much fun sometimes, but other times I see awful things." She looked over at Cathy and stopped talking altogether.

Cathy picked up the empty dish from in front of Maggie and deposited it in the sink. "I'll go in and check on Bird. You two need to talk." She exited the room, leaving great aunt and great niece alone together in the comforting silence and warmth of the kitchen.

Maggie patted the little girl's knee. "Tell me what happened."

Flower wiped her nose with a napkin from the table. "At first, I flew and flew, and I didn't feel cold or nothin'. It was like...well, it was better than the roller coaster at Six Flags. I went up and up, then went down fast, and back up."

"I agree. flying is fun."

"And I saw raccoons, and deer, and a mountain lion, too, and they could talk to me, and I could talk to them, and there were trees, and streams, and all kinds of cool things. And, then..." The little girl made her voice so quiet Maggie could barely hear her, "the terrible thing. I saw those terrible people again, two of them, and they had already killed and cut off someone's legs and were cooking him over that fire, but his eyes were even worse than the other man's."

"Whose eyes?"

"The man they killed. His eyes."

"What about them?"

"I got kinda close on a tree, and I could see the eyes, and they burned in the fire, and then they popped open like they all of a sudden broke." The little girl burst open her fingers wide on both hands to demonstrate the eyes exploding, "and icky grey stuff spilled out of them and when the stuff came out, it hit the fire and sizzled like when Grandma tests the pan with water drops to make frybread. I was so upset I wanted to cry. The man was all black from fire, and when his eyes popped it even made a noise."

"Where were the other people? The ones that did the awful thing?"

"They were there."

"Go on. Could you describe them to me? Were they in regalia?"

"Not this time, but it was the same guys. They kinda had something like a scarf on their face and those hoodies that covered their hair and everything, and big gloves. I couldn't see them, but, Auntie Maggie?"

"Yes?"

"I know them. I don't know who they are, the two bad guys, but they are someone I know, and like I said, when I saw the poor man's eyes break all open and stuff, I tried to scream, but all that came out was a 'kraa, kraa' noise. When I did that, one bad guy looked at me and said my name even. I couldn't tell who the voice was, but I know I've heard it before." "He called you Flower?"

"No, he called me Pukkukwerek."

CHAPTER 30

JAKE'S CRITIQUE GROUP met on Wednesday nights. He'd leave at 5:45 p.m. nervous as a tick out of worry the others wouldn't like his work and return home at 9:45 energized and confident. "They liked the scene about how you kicked Mingan's ass when he tried to assault you at your house in Wicklow. Of course, I changed his name, but it's him all right."

"Thanks a lot. I've done my best to forget that piece of ass-tainted crap, and you have to bring him up." She laughed.

"Well, they thought I handled the dialogue perfectly. The whole table agreed I can write the shit out of a riveting fight scene, but I have you as my subject matter expert, and you did such a good job of explaining things I almost feel like I'm plagiarizing. Sometimes I'm not sure I'm doing this writing thing the way I'm supposed to."

"Yours is a novel based on non-fiction events, so even with creative license, you have to tell it as it was; otherwise you'll lose credibility and the readers aren't going to believe your work. Look, Jake, I don't know why you're so goddamn insecure. You're a great writer, and you're doing a great job of telling a great story, and if you didn't have talent, you couldn't pull this off as well as you have. Quit worrying and finish the damned book."

He drew her into his chest and held her in both arms. "You and I make a great team. Are you sure you don't want to marry me?"

"I'm sure."

—

It was a Wednesday night, and Maggie looked forward to some time to herself with a hot bath and a hot toddy, and to eating Chinese delivery in her robe. When the cell rang, she smarted from a sharp pang of disappointment. "Better not be Mack wanting me to come to the station," she said to Samantha, who sat in her lap kneading Maggie's thighs. "Watch out for those claws, girlfriend. You're putting holes in me." She let the cell ring a few times and decided to at least check Caller ID to see who would be calling her at six thirty at night, interrupting her plans. Her nephew, Jimmy. She clicked on the phone. "Hey. We haven't talked in weeks. What's up?"

"Aunt Maggie, I know you're busy with the pub and the investigation, but I have something important I need to talk to you about."

"Is it the girls? Flower?"

"No. It's something..." his voice trailed off. "It's something personal no one else can know about, at least no one in the family."

"Sounds serious, Jimmy. Jake is at his critique group tonight and won't be home for a few hours. Come over, we'll have some beers, and I'll order in Chinese."

Jimmy showed up at her door a little while later with a six-pack of cold Singh Tao tucked under his arm. "You can't have Chinese food without Chinese beer, right?"

Maggie gave him a hug, took the six-pack and removed two, putting the others in the refrigerator. "I've got kung pao shrimp and noodles on the way."

The two sat side-by-side on the couch. "What could be so serious that you need to talk to me," Maggie said.

"There are two things, Aunt Maggie, and both are sensitive. I don't want Mom, Dad, or the girls to know, all right?" His eyes were watery and swollen.

"I promise not to say anything. What is it, Jimmy?"

"I hope you don't get too upset."

"Try me." She patted his arm.

"Okay." He cleared his throat and faced her full on. "I'll spit it out then." He inhaled hard as if to brace himself. "I've got a serious gambling problem."

"What? You? I can't believe it because it's not something I'd..."

His face contorted with disappointment. "I knew you'd not

understand, and I should have never come over." He stood and turned to the door, but Maggie grabbed his arm and pulled him back next to her on the couch. "Sit down. I'm not judging you, but I am a little surprised because you're so responsible and this is out of character."

He cleared his throat again. "It's more than that."

"Let me guess. You got yourself in trouble with gambling debt, and you need money?"

His eyes widened. "How'd you know?"

"Tell me how much."

"It's a lot."

"Exactly how much?"

"60,000 dollars exactly."

"Jesus W. H. Z. Cristo, Jimmy. Are you into a loan shark"?

"Sort of. And, what's worse is I did something terrible." His shame was so palpable it hurt Maggie to see it.

"What could you have done that is so awful." She smiled. "I'm on your side, you know. You can tell me anything."

"Can I tell you I put Dad and Mom's house up as collateral on the loan, and the shark tells me if I don't pay him the 60k cash by tomorrow noon, he's going to call in his marker and take their home?"

She thought for a moment during which an uncomfortable, heavy silence fell between them. "This is what I'm going to do. I'll transfer money into your account so you can pay off this reprehensible dickwad, but you get yourself into Gamblers Anonymous first thing in the morning and stay the fuck away from the Soboba Casino. Let me know you understand."

Jimmy flung his arms around his aunt. "I...I don't know what to say. Thank you. You saved my life." He pulled away, and his voice hardened, "You *will* keep your promise and not tell Mom and Dad? They're stressed out about leaving us and the move, and..."

"Haven't I always kept my promises?"

His smile warmed the room. "I love you, Aunt Maggie."

"And I, you, so this is a big thing you told me, but I'm glad you trusted me enough to…"

"That's not all."

"Good God, what else?"

The delivery man knocked on the door. Maggie answered, paid him, and brought in the bag filled with the white cardboard boxes of Chinese food, soy sauce packets, and wooden chopsticks. Maggie went to the kitchen for paper plates and put them on the coffee table, then sat. "Oops. I forgot something. Do you mind getting us another beer?" She asked Jimmy, "but before you even touch one goddamned egg roll, tell me what else you came here to say or I'll give your share to Chester. Understood?"

He went to the kitchen and appeared with two more bottles from the refrigerator, popped them open, handed one to Maggie, and plopped back down. "The food smells so good, and I'm starving."

"Tell me what you need to, and we'll dig in. Fair enough?"

"It's about the person I'm dating. Aunt Maggie, I am in love, so much so it makes me crazy to even think about it. I'm walking into walls because I can't focus on anything; it's that bad."

"It's wonderful. You haven't had a woman in your life since the girls' mother left you, and that was well over nine years ago. You deserve to have someone to care about who loves you in return."

When he looked away from her, she tilted her head to one side. "But there's something wrong. Isn't there? You aren't entirely happy about this. Why? Is she married or something?"

"Aunt Maggie, I'm not sure how to say this—the person I'm in love with is not a woman. I'm gay."

CHAPTER 31

MAGGIE THOUGHT SHE'D be more shocked at Jimmy's coming out, but the more she thought it over, the more everything made sense, especially his years of showing little interest in women, always ostensibly because of his little girls. "Getting into a relationship with a woman would take me away from my daughters. They need my full attention while they are young," he'd always say when asked why he didn't date. "They have to come before my love life."

Jimmy always tended toward the chunky side, but he was handsome, and women threw themselves at his feet. When he spurned their attention, even the most smitten among them assumed he was only a great father, and sooner or later he'd come around if they were patient enough. Some even tried to get to him through his girls, bringing them candy and little gifts, or goo-goo talking to them, but Flower and Bird, even though young, were smart enough to know when they were being played and would have none of it. "I don't like that lady," one or the other would say when a woman would flatter them excessively, saying things like, "Aren't you two just the cutest things? You're both so adorable, and you have the prettiest hair I've ever seen," or some such inauthentic nonsense, or when another woman would cozy up to them and ask questions like, "So, is your poor daddy all alone? Is he seeing anyone? Wouldn't you like a mommy to take care of you?" Once, Flower, who'd been raised as had Bird to respect her elders, got her fill of one of these needy women lusting after her father, forgot her manners. "Find a boyfriend and leave us and our daddy alone, you phony. Go away!"

Maggie was delighted for Jimmy and honored he felt safe enough to confide in her. "Love is love, and I'm happy for you," she said to him. "When do I get to meet your special guy?"

"Not yet, since I haven't even come out to Mom and Dad, and

I have to figure out the best way to tell the girls. I'll let them know soon, and when I do, I'll bring him over to Mom and Dad's so everyone can meet him at the same time."

Maggie embraced her nephew in both arms and hugged him so tightly he almost lost his breath. "Hey, take it easy. You're hurting my ribs," but she knew she wasn't hurting him in the least. She searched his eyes for a sign of relief and saw in them more softness and joy than she'd seen in a long while. The tension he'd come into her house with had evaporated, his shoulders relaxed, and Maggie knew he'd get a good night's sleep tonight, the best he'd had in a long while.

"I owe you, Aunt Maggie."

"No, you don't. We're family. I only want you to be happy, and if you've found love with the person who is right for you, that is repayment enough right there. Keep in mind whatever is good for you will be good for Flower and Bird, too. I hope you figure out how to tell them soon because I know they will accept this man and love him once they meet him and see how happy he makes you."

"My turn to ask you a question," Jimmy said.

"Fire away."

"How is the investigation going? I hope you find this murderer soon because from what I read in the papers, he must be pretty smart to have evaded all of you for so long."

"I can't tell you much, Jimmy. You know that. Let's Maybe say we are getting closer, though."

"That's a good thing for the community, because he could get to anyone, and the girls are scared. How many killed now?"

"Too many."

"Do you think it's someone local? I can't imagine anyone around here would be a serial killer, so it has to be someone from the outside."

"I can't say anything more, Jimmy. Please don't ask."

—

Maggie knew she had to call the sheriff after what Flower had told her about the latest murder. There'd been no missing persons report, and no one in town appeared to be looking for a friend or relative, but that wasn't the issue. Her biggest problem was figuring out how she'd report to the sheriff another body roasted over a fire somewhere in the mountains.

"How can I tell Mack for the second time my ten-year-old great niece happened to stumble across the murder scene when she was hiking by herself, at night, in a remote and rugged area of The San Padrinos in a place even the most experienced adult hikers avoid?" She said to Jake.

"I hear ya. The first time, you got away with saying Flower was a witness, but that was even a little dicey, and I don't know for sure Mack or the deputies 100% believed you then. The second time, no chance in bloody hell they'll believe you. Don't even try."

"I can say I got an anonymous tip from someone calling on an untraceable burner phone, but whatever—I have to report it now. I should have called it in immediately, but I had to figure out how to report it without coming off like an inmate in an insane asylum. I'll call Mack before I go into work my shift at O'Malley's."

She didn't have to call. When she and Jake heard the sirens on their way to the San Padrinos, they guessed someone found the body, but what they had not counted on was the fire, the one started by the killers accidentally when they set the blaze to cook their victim. They had left the body unattended, roasting over the blaze, and a gust of wind blew a spark into a dry Grey Pine, igniting a forest fire. Tom Anselmo and his crew squelched the flames in short order, but not before they came across what was remaining of the murder scene. Tom called it in, so Maggie was off the hook.

The cell rang, but before she even checked, she knew it was Sheriff Mack. "You actually have your phone on? What a surprise. Good thing I also have Jake's cell number because you hardly ever answer yours these days."

Maggie held back the snarky response she wanted to deliver. "I'm trying to be more conscious about turning it back on. What's up?"

The Fire Captain, Tom Anselmo, says one of his crew discovered another body while putting out a fire in the San Padrinos way the hell back into the most inaccessible part of the range. We're lucky the firefighters were able to get up there at all with their equipment." He paused to blow his nose, and the sound blasted like a Canadian goose call. Maggie held the receiver away from her ear until he got back on. "Sorry about that. I'm working on a cold." He said. "Could it be our suspect is getting more desperate for us not to find these bodies for some reason? Maybe he hopes coyotes would get to this one before we can make a positive ID."

"Could be," said Maggie, "But that would not match the killer's MO. He sets the scene so nicely for us and seems to be getting a royal kick out of baiting and taunting us with his damned Aunt Lorrie's Salt containers. I believe he does want us to find those bodies."

"We have to interview Tom."

"Why? Is he a suspect?"

"No, but he said as they were going in to fight the fire, they saw your kitchen guy walking out on foot."

"Diego?"

"The other one. León."

"What? That makes no sense. I'm going into the pub tonight, and he'll be there. Before we bring him to the station, let me talk to León on my own."

"That's not a good idea because you could tip him off and he might flee. Bring him and Tom both in."

"Let me get a hold of them, and we'll do that." Maggie had no intention of "doing that," though. She'd talk to León tonight, and if Tom is in the pub, she'll ask him a few questions. *Neither of those men is in this; I know it, and besides that, Flower says she somehow recognized the murderers, but doesn't know Tom, and I don't think she's ever met León, and if she did, she probably won't even remember him.*

When she got to O'Malley's, there were plenty of customers bellied up for beer, but Tom was not among them. Salvador handled the bar.

"Have you seen Tom?" She asked him.

"Nope."

León, however, worked full steam in the kitchen with Diego, chopping carrots with the biggest baddest butcher knife they had, and he worked with precision at a furious speed. She addressed the kitchen boss, Diego, "I hate to interrupt with so many customers, but I need five minutes with your nephew."

"León? We're backed up here, and I can't afford to let him slow down right now."

"I only need to ask a few questions, and I'll get him back to you. I'm working tonight, too, so we'll get caught up on those orders."

Diego whistled to get León's attention and gave him an order in Spanish. León wiped the blade of the butcher knife as though he might handle a priceless antique, and carefully put it back in the block. "This is a German-crafted knife, and one of the best money can purchase," he said. "We must take special care of this one."

"Let's go outside and talk," Maggie said.

"It is my pleasure to engage in conversation with you, Ms. Maggie." He removed his apron and folded it like a grandmother might fold a hand crochet coverlet, and rather than hanging it on the hooks provided for that use, he placed it methodically and with great care on a clean space on the counter.

Out the back door of the pub, Maggie had put a bistro set with two chairs so employees could take their breaks outside if they wished. The first thing Maggie noticed was the ravens. She had gotten used to the idea that they, like Sally's ghost, might appear at any time, and would always follow her everywhere. But tonight was different. There were many of them and by their frantic "kraas, croaks, kraas," she knew something was up. "What are you guys bitching about? I don't have any corn with me if that's what you're after."

León and Maggie sat, and the young man scooted his chair in

and folded his hands on the table like an obedient little boy. "What questions have you for me, Ms. Maggie?"

"What do you do for fun when you aren't working? You have your delivery job with Bond's and are apprenticing to be a butcher. You work here, and I understand you provide some meats to the shop from that organic farm in El Centro, which seems like a third job to me. You must not have too much free time."

"Since I left USC, I have more time than you might imagine because I am no longer spending hours in research, reading, class time, and writing term papers, and all the other activities related to the academic life. I now have far more time for personal endeavors."

"Such as?"

"I garden. I work out at McCabe's regularly, and I enjoy the outdoors."

"The outdoors? Do you camp, boat, hike?"

"I often hike by myself in the San Padrinos to get fresh air and to clear my mind."

"Were you hiking the day the fire started in the mountains?"

"Why, yes, I was as a matter of fact. As soon as I saw the smoke, I headed out. I could not call because there is no cell phone reception where I go, and I thought it would be best to get out safely, then report the smoke."

"Did you see anyone while hiking?"

"Yes. I encountered the fire crew on their way in to fight the fire, and even said hello to Captain Tom, who seemed nonplussed to run into me."

"Why do you think that was?"

"There are not too many hikers on their own in that part of the mountains. The trails are rough or non-existent, but I generally enjoy a good adventure and prefer the paths less traveled."

"Did you see or hear anything at all unusual?"

He looked away and scratched his chin as though thinking with care. "Nothing in the least unusual. No."

I've one last question. "Are you dating anyone? Is there someone special in your life?"

León tensed and shifted uncomfortably in his seat. "Why do you ask, Ms. Maggie? If you think Nola and I are seeing one another, I assure you we are not, but yes, there is someone special in my life, but not a local, so we seldom see one another. Do you have additional questions?"

The young man lost his crisp demeanor, and the way he fidgeted in his chair, Maggie wondered if he might be lying, and was still seeing Nola on the sly, but decided not to press the issue until she could talk to Nola about it first.

"Thanks, León. We better get inside and help Diego, or he'll kick both our asses." At that, the knocking, clicking, and calling of the ravens grew shrill and raised to a cacophony so loud Maggie put her hands over her ears as protection. "Let's go in before these damned screaming birds bust our eardrums. They're royally pissed off at me for not bringing out bread scraps or corn, the little shits."

CHAPTER 32

THE MORE MAGGIE thought about Nola and the Chenoo, the more the disparate pieces of the investigation began to come together and form a cohesive picture, one that unsettled her. "It all fits. Nola hates the heat, has a thing about overweight people, has naturally black hair so she could be Native even if she claims no indigenous heritage, and she comes from the north where the legend of the Chenoo is widely accepted among the tribes," she told Jake. But, despite the evidence, she still didn't want to believe the killer could be Nola. "For sure it can't be her," she said.

"Why can't it be?" Jake said.

"For one thing, besides that she doesn't exactly fit the profile of our killer, even as strong as she is, she could never on her own handle mounting a 285 to 360-pound body on a spit and hoisting the entire package four feet over a cooking fire, even with the legs sawn off."

"You don't think with her, uh, charms, she couldn't get help?"

"Right, Jake." Maggie spoke through clenched teeth. "You think she's so hot men will kill for her? You're watching too many shlocky made-for-t.v. movies, you horny bastard."

"I wouldn't rule it out so fast. Her husband may even be complicit, as in the Sweeny Todd thing we talked about earlier, but it looks to me like you can't own up to the fact that Nola is your friend and may also be a serial killer."

"And you're full of shit. You've got such a big boner for Nola you can't deal with it honestly, so you're projecting."

The hurt look on Jake's face staggered her. "Why do you have to be like this, Maggie?"

Maggie prepared to barf out another invective, to tell him to fuck off yet again, but she caught herself. *I'm upset, and maybe a little bit jealous of how Jake looks at Nola, but I have to quit ragging on him.* It was at that moment she realized she could lose Jake one day if she didn't treat him with a little more kindness. "Okay. I'll try harder."

"Try harder at what?" Jake asked.

"I'm thinking out loud," she said. "Pay no attention to me. How about we go out for dinner, or to a movie, or both? We haven't been on a date for a long time, and we can use a break."

His smile in response was all she needed. *Yes, I will try harder.*

———

Maggie felt sick to her stomach when she called Mack. "We've got a strong suspect," she told him. "Jake and I will bring her in."

"A woman? A woman can't do this, at least not alone."

"Jake and I believe she could very well have used her sexuality and her looks to get men to help her."

"You must be talking about the butcher's wife, then, what's her name, Nola, and you were to bring her in for an interview anyway. Why haven't you?"

———

Nola was more baffled than angry when Maggie asked her to come into the station, but Maggie could tell right away from her stiff posture when she showed up, and her lack of a smile, Nola was indeed pissed off big time.

"What's this about, hon? You don't think I had anything to do with those murders, do you?"

"It won't take long. I have a few routine questions, and you'll be out in a minute."

"I don't get it, Maggie. How can we be friends yet I'm on your suspect list? Did someone say something to implicate me in this awful mess?"

"I only need a few minutes of your time."

"I guess this is serious," Nola said.

"This is work, and it's no easier for me than it is for you. Where were you on…" Maggie listed the dates of the murders.

"I can barely remember what I ate for dinner last night let alone what I was doing on all those particular dates. If the murders occurred during the day, or even some nights and weekends, you know I'm at McCabe's. Call Skye if you don't believe me, but I never take time off."

"What about when you are helping James?"

"Well, then I'm at Bond's helping to prep your damned pulled pork, aren't I?"

The more annoyed Nola became, the more suspicious Maggie grew. "Why are you so upset?"

"Oh, let me see." Nola looked to the ceiling as though pondering a lengthy response. "My friend, who I also thought was a *real* friend, calls me into the sheriff's office for an interrogation…"

"An interview."

"No. An *interrogation*, and in a serial killer investigation, too, and I'm supposed to not be upset?"

"Jake or the sheriff could have asked the questions, Nola, but I…"

"And if it had been Jake or the sheriff in here instead of you, I may, or may not, have felt less hurt. But, I'm disappointed in your betrayal because you, as my friend, are supposed to have my back."

"I'm asking you questions related to an ongoing investigation I'm leading. I'm doing my job, and that's hardly a betrayal."

"I honestly don't get it, Maggie. Why am I here?"

"I don't want to be a hard ass, but I need you to answer the questions. I'll get you out of here in a few minutes, and then we'll set up another date for wine, but this is business. Do you understand?"

Nola stiffened. "I understand all right, but I doubt it."

"Doubt what? If you answer my questions, I will get you out soon as promised."

"That's not what I'm talking about. What I meant was I doubt we'll be sharing wine again. Ever."

It devastated Maggie to hear Nola say that. *I should have let*

Mack handle this interview. If she's not guilty, I've lost a friend. If she is guilty, I've lost a friend. Either way, I lose. Dammit all to hell.

"So, what other questions do you have?" Nola tapped the table impatiently. "Let's get on with it because I've got a business to run, and I have to be there for my clients if you don't mind." Nola's voice was so cold and hard Maggie thought for sure her friend was indeed the Chenoo with the heart of ice.

"I need to ask you one more time about León. You don't see one another any longer, is that correct?"

"Are you kidding me?" Nola chewed the tip of one of her acrylic nails. "I spend a fortune on these because I used to chew my nails to the quick, and I'm so upset I'm tearing up a brand new eighty-dollar manicure."

She's evading the question. "Can you answer?"

"You mean your last question, which was? I forgot. Can you please repeat it?" Her voice was pure saccharine snark.

Bullshit. She doesn't want to answer. "I asked if you and León still saw one another."

"I have told you how many times? Two? Three? More? León and I had sex one time in my office a long while ago. There is nothing between us. Skye is as happy as a hummingbird because she thinks she has a chance with him now since I've cooled on him, and besides, he spends more time at the butcher shop than he ever does in the gym. I tell you, if I didn't know better, the way he follows James around, I'd think the guy is in love with my husband." For the first time since entering the interview room, Nola laughed. "Besides, when we last were in the pub together, didn't you ask all these questions? Were you interrogating me, then, too? Stupid me. I thought we were friends."

"Did you say your natural hair color is black?"

"Yes, I did say that. Because I bleach my hair does that make me a cannibalistic serial killer?"

"It could mean you're part Native American. Are you?"

"Not that my ethnicity has anything to do with why I'm here, but, yes. I'm part Choctaw on my paternal grandmother's side. What of it?"

Maggie didn't blame Nola for being angry, but she wanted to get this interview over with and get home to Jake, Samantha, and Chester, drink until stumbling into bed and sleeping forever.

——

By the time Maggie arrived home, her head felt like it would split open on its own and her brains would fall out. Worst. Migraine. Ever. On top of that, her heart hurt from the loss of her friend.

Jake brought her a cold compress along with a cold beer.

"Thanks. I need to get to bed and be in the dark for a while, or I'll be in pain for days. And, Jake?"

"Yeah?"

"Seriously. When this is over, we're off to the Emerald Isle, just you and me, okay?"

"You bet. I hear Dublin is a great city, and I'm already looking into air flights and B & Bs for us."

"Really?" Maggie would have sung her delight, had she been able to sing, but her voice was worse than that of a wounded cur dog so her singing would come out as suffering rather than joy. "When I get over this goddamn headache, I want to see what you found in Ireland. It'll be fun. Right now, though I gotta hit the hay and turn out the lights." She gave Jake a peck on the cheek, was about to head off down the hall with her compress and beer when Jake's cell phone rang. She halted mid-step to find out who called. Jake had already begun his walk toward Maggie and had pressed the button for speakerphone mode. Sheriff Mack.

"I need you two down here. We've found another body."

"Anyone we know?" Maggie asked.

"The butcher."

CHAPTER 33

ALL MAGGIE COULD think about is what Nola would be going through. After her friend had been cleared as a suspect, Maggie hoped the two of them would renew their gal pal relationship, but no. Right now, though, Nola was hurting, and Maggie wanted so much to comfort her.

When Jake and she arrived at the sheriff's office, the team had already assembled for the brief. Jake and Maggie took a seat at the back, but Maggie hardly heard a word Mack spoke, other than "The M.O. on this one is different, so we don't think it's the work of our serial killer."

"In what way?" Maggie asked.

"His wife discovered his body at the shop, so not on a spit in the mountains. Our killer removed Bond's heart, not the liver. Although the killer had severed the thumb as in the others and left his calling card with the seasoned salt container, the legs were intact. It's odd."

—

The second she and Jake left the office and headed for home, Maggie told Jake she'd drop him off so she could find Nola. "If there was ever a time when she needs a friend, it's right now."

"I'll go with you. Something could happen out there."

"Like what? I've got my Glock, and I'll be fine. Nola will need another woman to cry with, and besides, I've got an escort." She pointed her thumb to the outside of her truck window at the dozens of ravens flying overhead. "They'll take care of me."

The hardened skeptic, Maggie had been forced over the years and through many unexplained experiences, to reluctantly accept the unacceptable, to rely on her unscientific senses, and to gradually welcome her true nature. But some things eluded her such as why the ravens were around sometimes, and at other times when she thought they'd make an appearance, there were none in sight. They'd come when she was in danger, they'd come for corn handouts, they'd come to teach her things, to give her direction, and sometimes to harass her the way birds tease dogs, but for whatever reason they were around she was always pleased to see ravens nearby. Clearly, there were times when they watched out for her, such as when she was about to leap out of her truck to confront the man behind her who had honked at her, and she almost gave into road rage.

She pulled in front of the house to let Jake out but stayed to talk for a moment. "Who knows what I would have done to that guy had ravens not prevented me from getting in his face?" She said to Jake.

"Did you consider he could be a whacko with a gun of his own and might have shot you in the face? Those birds may have saved your life. Or, it could be that asshole driver is a mentally unhinged stalker who would have made your life miserable had you challenged him. After my interactions with them, I can tell you those ravens know things we don't, and they're here for you, Maggie, and always have been."

"I know." She stuck her head out the driver side window. "Thanks, guys, for everything, but if you shit on my truck, I'll be baking blackbirds in a pie."

Maggie kissed Jake before he exited the truck, and with her hands white-knuckled on the wheel, and the escort of ravens following above, she paid little heed to traffic signs or laws as she sped around Hemacinto in search of a friend who she knew would be crippled with pain and needed her. She first headed to McCabe's, arriving in time to greet Skye as she posted a note on the door of the locked gym. "Closed temporarily due to a death. Please call for reopening date."

"Do you know where Nola is?"

"She's not at the hospital or morgue because I drove her and after she identified her husband's body, I dropped her back at

Bond's. She might still be there."

"You didn't stay with her?"

"She needed me to come back here and close up. She's in terrible shape, and I don't think she should be alone. I'm glad you're around right now."

When Maggie arrived at Bond's, she met León at the door.

"Hello, Ms. Maggie. Nola asked for me to take care of the shop until she figures out what she wants to do with the business."

"Do you know where she is?"

"I drove her home approximately two hours ago. Most likely, she is there."

"I need her address."

"I do not know if I can give it to you without her permission."

"Give me her address, León."

Maggie input Nola's address into her GPS and the directions routed her through one of two rare affluent parts of town where actual leafy trees lined wide clean sidewalks instead of the normal trash and tumbleweed-littered cracked asphalt streets bordered by sand, cactus, and sage. Most of the houses were faux Spanish Colonial pretentious affairs with wrought iron fences festooned with curly goo-gaws and hand forged doo-dads, all set on vast expanses of excessively groomed and excessively greened lawns, all locked behind gates set far back from the street as though to block the hoi polloi and riff-raff. Maggie sucked breath through her teeth. "Jayzus. I guess the butcher and gym businesses are damned lucrative."

When she pulled up to Nola's gate, the first thing Maggie thought was, "The house isn't painted pink?" She could see Nola's Lexus in the driveway leading to the four-car garage, but there were no lights in the windows, no warmth, only the heavy quietness that wraps itself around an abandoned house. Maggie tried for the ninth or tenth time to call Nola on her cell and left her ninth or tenth message. "Nola, call me right away. I'm worried."

She sat in the cab of her truck for a few minutes, hoping she'd see movement on the grounds, or even get a glimpse of Nola somewhere. When the darkness and quiet got to her, Maggie called Jake. "Nola isn't home, or she might be, but if so she's in the dark by herself, and she's not answering my calls."

"What do you want to do?"

"I want to break in to make sure she's okay."

"Do you think she hurt herself?"

"Jeeze. I didn't think about that. It doesn't seem like suicide is something Nola would do, but maybe. It's hard for me to believe how she could be so madly in love with that syphilitic toad sucker, but she is, and with his unexpected death she might...well, I don't know. I need to make sure she's okay."

"We can call Mack, and he can get a judge..."

"Nope. If she's inside the house and is hurt, it will take too long to do this through legal channels. I have to get in there now because I've already let too much time pass, and if she did anything to herself—I only hope it's not too fucking late."

"Maggie, don't. Wait for me and I'll..."

Maggie clicked off her phone without saying goodbye.

It had grown so dark even with the street lights, it was difficult to make out much other than the reflective glow of the ravens' eyes, the birds perched like black uniformed sentinels on the wrought iron fence, silent but watching. Maggie grabbed her flashlight, flipped it on, and holstered her Glock in preparation to walk the perimeter in hopes of finding a way over the fence. She didn't get too far around the side of the house before she heard what sounded like a dog whining in pain. She aimed the beam of her flashlight at Nola.

Maggie didn't bother to ask Nola to open the gate for her. She climbed the fence and found her friend crumpled on the perfect green grass in complete darkness, leaning against a wall. She held her head in both hands, still and quiet until she made the sound again, the whining, not crying, not sobbing, but an anguished keening, filled with so much pain that normal human crying could not express it adequately. As Nola lifted her head and looked into the sky, perhaps preparing to raise her whine to a howl, she saw

Maggie and stopped herself short. She stammered rather than spoke. "Wh...wh...what are you do...doing here? How did you... find me?"

Her long blonde hair hung in wet ropey strands over her face, and her eye makeup, usually so precise, ran down her cheeks in thick black smears that looked like she'd rubbed twin smudges of soot on her face. Her eyelids were nearly swollen shut from crying, the color drained from her lips, and her mouth distorted by agony morphed into a grimace that made the beautiful Nola look like an unwashed lunatic. Maggie had never beheld such grief in any other woman. She squatted on her heels next to Nola, and said nothing, but held out her arms. Nola crawled into Maggie's embrace and whined and whined and whined.

CHAPTER 34

FOR THE MONTHS going into winter and then transforming into early spring following the butcher's death, all of Hemacinto went quiet. There were fewer crimes reported, Sally made fewer appearances, and when she did, she was warm and friendly. Best of all, Flower had not shifted for some time giving the little girl a much-needed break.

Busy nights at O'Malley's and visits with her family, especially Jimmy and the girls, kept Maggie busy. Jake finished the first draft of The Monster Killer and had read from cover-to-cover a book called, "How to Find a Good Literary Agent or Small Press: What to look for, and what to avoid."

Jake and Maggie spent hours on the internet pouring over Irish travel sites and checking out the B and B's around the Wild Atlantic Way and The Ring of Kerry. They even rented a DVD on Celtic culture, and Maggie stepped up her Gaelic lessons.

The investigation had taken its toll, leaving Maggie emotionally spent. "So many dead in this one little town, and no iron clad leads," she told Jake. "I'm getting goddamn sick of this job, this dead-end investigation, and the guys on the team hating me. It's getting old real fast."

"I thought you loved solving crimes and catching bad guys, Maggie. It's what you do best."

"I want it over. I have tried to retire twice now, and it's time."

"Take a break and get back to it when you're ready."

When not putting in a lackluster performance on the investigation, or working at the pub, Maggie spent as much time as she could with Flower doing all she could to help the child to understand how and why they'd both become the famous "monster killers" from Yurok legend. Maggie also spent hours purposely shifting into raven, now that she knew she could control it, and grew intent on teaching

Flower how to shift at will. Trying to work the raven thing out so she could support and mentor her grandniece was not easy, though, since Maggie had only in recent years even accepted her shapeshifting, and there was much she didn't understand herself, but she did her best with Flower. "It's kind of like this," she said to Flower. "You have to set your intention to fly."

"What is 'intention'?"

"A goal. It's something you want to achieve, but before you shapeshift on your own, you have to think it."

"Think it?"

"Think about being a raven. Imagine it. Then focus your mind completely on being a raven. Feel the wings coming out of your back, imagine your beak, and black feathers sprouting on your arms. Try it."

The little girl tried and failed and tried again. She'd begin her transformation and make it part way. The wings would grow from her back, inching their way through her flesh, and her hands would morph into talons, but no feathers appeared, making her look like a plucked chicken, and another time she'd be left with wings and claws but with a human head and legs. Or, everything would be precisely raven, but she still had a nose instead of a beak. Then she'd try again, and again. Eventually, she got it right.

"Yay, Auntie," she said in perfect raven. "I did it, and mostly by myself, too."

"You did a fine job. Good girl."

Sometimes, the two of them would shift together and soar into the night sky over Hemacinto. "It's pretty down there with all the lights," Flower said to her aunt.

"Hey, your raven is improving."

"My flying? I am getting better, so the other ravens tell me. I can almost dive down like a falcon, now, too."

"No. Your communication. Now we can honestly say you are bilingual because you speak English and Raven, and I bet not many girls your age can do that."

One thing disturbing to Maggie was her friend, Nola, who grew increasingly reclusive in her grief. She rarely returned phone calls, or answered, and when she did, she came across as confused sometimes, sad sometimes, angry at other times, and refused any offers of help or comfort. "I'm better alone right now, Maggie." Most days she left Skye to run the gym. She closed Bond's, meaning no deliveries of pulled pork to the chagrin of Maggie's customers, who were otherwise a happy bunch, but most notably the killings stopped which fueled all kinds of mild to wild speculation among townspeople and law enforcement alike.

Some thought the butcher had supernatural powers and could make himself invisible, or somehow magically duplicate himself so he could be at Bond's or at home and be out roasting his victims at the same time. So, in some people's minds, James Bond's superpowers were how he'd gotten away undetected with murder. Others worried about the meat they'd bought from Bond's, some making corny Donner Party jokes. Some said Nola killed her husband out of jealousy because of his outrageous flirtations with other women, and in doing so, she unwittingly killed the killer. Most of the time Maggie found all this nonsense amusing, but even Jake joined in on the speculation.

"It makes sense that James Bond is our guy," Jake said. "He dies, and no more murders. End of story, so pretty soon Mack can close this case."

"Who, then, killed Bond?"

"Could be a revenge killing, maybe one of the victim's family members or lovers."

"He was a prime suspect, but there's no telling for sure if he did do it," Maggie said. "Sometimes, serial killers go underground and live as model citizens for years, even decades, then resurface to kill again. It very well could be a coincidence the killings stopped after Bond died, so there is no reason yet to believe other townspeople won't end up in the San Padrinos on a spit."

"I guess then, we can't yet ratchet down the Sweeny Todd idea."

"We can't know until we find out who killed Bond, and maybe not even then. Let's hope the butcher wasn't involved, because if he is our killer, like others in our community, I would be concerned about the meat we bought from him."

"You're saying we have been eating human flesh since you started buying meat from Bond's?"

"That is what I'm saying." Maggie thought about the dream of the film with Sally and the macabre cartoon ravens. What was it that one had told her? "You are what you eat, Pukkukwerek," yes that was it, or something close. Regretting her recent heavy lunch, the knowledge of having served and consumed human meat made Maggie's stomach lurch until she thought she'd blow hamburger patty chunks, desiccated creamed spinach, and flat Harp ale all over Jake.

———

Everything in life seemed to run hot and cold for Maggie. Most people experienced ups and downs, but for Maggie, the extremes seemed more exaggerated. "Could I be bi-polar or something? she once asked Jake.

Some days, she was exuberant about life and optimistic; other times her mood and personality were cold, dark, and surly. No one ever said of Maggie that she was "sweet," or even "nice," and her volcanic temper was legendary, but when she was in a good mood, Maggie could be cordial, compassionate, and reasonable. This particular Monday morning was not one of those days. She walked into the sheriff's department with a chip as big as Montana on her shoulder and was prepared to give out shit the second she detected shit from anyone else.

Despite that late winter weather cooled the desert to a bearable temperature, once again either the air conditioner or the heater in the office was on the blink. Although often so cold if someone were to spill a pitcher of water on the linoleum the deputies could ice skate on it, today it was over eighty degrees inside. She'd had enough. "Can't you afford to do something about this?" She said to Mack. "It's fucking miserable in here for everyone. Icy cold or blistering hot. Always."

"Sorry," he said to her. "Nothing I can do right now, is there? Besides, we aren't here for vacation; we're trying to solve murders, as you might recall, that is if you aren't too busy complaining."

Maggie wanted to verbally punch the sheriff in the solar plexus in response to his tart reply, but she stopped herself from lashing out, and instead she turned on her heel and stomped off to the briefing room like a thirteen-year-old whose daddy had grounded her for skipping classes.

When she stepped into the room, the deputies and Jake were already seated. Sweat beaded on foreheads and saturated shirts, and each man looked as though he might be slowly suffocating. Although that alone may have generated sympathy in anyone else, seeing hot and tired men crowded into the small stuffy room soured Maggie's mood even more. She looked from team member to team member with murder in her eyes. "We're getting nowhere. I need you guys to quit jerking off and do your jobs."

Kiddo raised his hand.

"You aren't in kindergarten. If you've something to say don't raise your hand like you're asking permission to go potty; just say it."

"I've followed your orders exactly," he said. "What more can any of us do?"

"How about you use your own thinking?" With a forefinger, Maggie tapped her temple. "Why in shit's name can't any of you come up with anything about this case on your own?"

"Because we aren't supposed to?" The Luiseno deputy asked.

Maggie threw up her hands in complete, unmitigated aggravation. "You're fucking with me, right? You are *supposed* to think. You are *supposed* to come up with original ideas. What you aren't supposed to do is act on those ideas and thoughts without passing them by Jake, Sheriff Mack, or me, but yeah, thinking for yourself is, let's say, encouraged, that is if you want to ever advance. If all you want to do in your career is hand out traffic tickets and arrest hookers on Florida Street, then do exactly what you're told without ever taking any initiative to come up with an original thought of your own." She leaned forward to him and sneered. "Try that and see where it gets you."

The deputy said nothing, but the flush of rage on his face told Maggie all she needed to know; she'd made yet another enemy, and she'd better turn this around or he'd never cooperate with her now.

She softened her voice and managed a weak smile. "Look. I'm sorry everyone. I've had a horrible day, and, I'm not in a good place. So, let's take care of business, and I'll get us all out of here and into our air-conditioned cars as soon as I can."

Maggie took some time to explain in detail the different kinds of serial killers and worked out a more detailed profile of the murderer. "And we have disorganized and organized killers."

"Which one are we dealing with? And are there more than one?" Kiddo asked.

Maggie felt irritation welling up at the interruption but stopped herself short from spewing venom all over the young deputy—it would have proved an unwise move and she knew it. She took a breath to settle herself and kept her annoyance locked in her head. *Why in fuck can't they let me finish a sentence without bombarding me with damned questions?* She took another breath, then exhaled slowly through her nose to release the heat inside of her. "I was getting to that, Kiddo. We are working with an organized killer here. He likes doing the same thing in the same way in an orderly fashion. He may slightly detour, but he will always revert to his orderly MO. Everything with these guys has to be tidy. And, this perp or perps, too, not only targets obese people for some unknown reason, but we've found out more in our investigation about our killer's motive. Jake, do you care to expand on this?"

Jake stood. "Every single vic has a serious criminal record, pedophilia, domestic abuse, murder, gang activity, meth dealing, which tells us that's both his motivation and his justification, at least to himself, as warped as it might be."

"Are we hunting a Dexter type character, then?" One deputy asked.

"You watch too much old t.v. programs. Maybe that's why you're such a complete brainless twat," said another.

The room full of men broke into guffaws, and even though she didn't find the comment particularly funny, Maggie joined in with pretend enthusiasm, the purpose of which was to ease tensions between her and the men. To Maggie's relief, it worked.

—

Later that night, over gin and tonics in the comforting near darkness of their living room, Jake and Maggie discussed the investigation, and in particular, her relationship with the deputies. "Why were you so bristly today in the sheriff's office, Mag?"

She sighed, took a drink of her cocktail, and set the glass on the coffee table. "It's a combination of things. I don't mean to act like that, and I did apologize, but..."

"But you do act like that, and good you apologized, but apologies aside don't you understand when you behave that way it is not in your best interest, and is in fact, counterproductive?" He made a huffing noise and shrugged his shoulders in what might look to anyone like a white flag move, a surrender. "Never mind. You are who you are, and that isn't going to change, is it?"

"I'm trying. I woke up on the proverbial wrong side of the bed, and it happens to everyone now and again. We aren't getting anywhere with this case. We haven't made one inch of progress in over six months. Sally comes around, but not often anymore. I didn't tell you this, but she popped in a couple of days ago while I was at the pub. She was sweet as sweet can be compared to the last visit, but she told me once again that we are off-track and yet again gave absolutely not one fucking clue as to what she meant.

Nola's is so broken up, and she's still so pissed off at me for interviewing her she won't even talk to me, and we are no closer to finding her husband's killer than, well...I only want this over with, so we can properly retire and take a month's trip to Ireland. That's all I want right now, and if this case drags on for years like the last one did, we'll end up in a nursing home drooling on ourselves and shitting our diapers before we ever make it to Dublin or Galway."

"You're being a little dramatic, aren't you?"

Maggie narrowed her eyes and tensed her jaw. "You wanted to know why I do what I do. If you don't want to hear the answer, or if you're going to judge what I say rather than listen to the response, don't ask the question." She grabbed her three-quarter full glass of booze and downed it in one gulp, then slammed her glass down on the table. "I've had enough of this craptastic day. I'm headed to bed." She let Jake kiss her, then pulled away and started down the hall toward the bedroom with Chester and Samantha on her heels, leaving Jake on the couch. She hadn't gotten more than five feet when she smelled Jasmine and Sally materialized in her full glory in front of both Maggie and Jake.

Startled at the sudden appearance of the ghost, Jake dropped his gin and tonic, splashing the drink all over the floor and shattering the tumbler into brilliant shards.

"You and Maggie aren't wearing shoes," Sally said. "One of you two better clean up this broken glass before someone slices open their feet."

CHAPTER 35

"YOU CAN PICK your jaw off your chest any time now, Jake," Sally said. "You know I've been around, so you can't be too shocked to actually see me."

Unable to respond Jake kept still as his face turned ashen, and he continued with his mouth wide open, to stare.

Sally laughed so hard if she'd been alive, she would have turned red, and devolved into a coughing fit. "If you could only see what you look like. Anyone right now might think you'd seen a ghost." Amused at her own bad joke, her laughter renewed and this time, her belly laughs came so fast and spontaneous that Maggie, infected by her friend's exuberance and spontaneous mirth, lifted her head and laughed, too, so loud that the sound sent Chester scuttling behind the couch to escape it. Maggie rarely laughed in earnest, but when she did, the entire world knew she was so tickled by someone or something she'd been unable to contain herself.

Once Jake recovered from the shock of seeing Sally, and could finally breathe, he spoke. "I'm sorry, Sally. I am thrilled to see you, but I'm...you took me by surprise."

"It's been so long. If I were alive, I'd hug you until you ran out of air, old friend. How about a virtual hug, instead?" Sally opened her translucent arms wide as though to invite him into her embrace, then she dropped her arms to her sides, and sat on an easy chair across from the sofa. "Let's talk."

Maggie grabbed a broom and mop to take care of the broken glass. "You want another G and T?" she asked Jake.

"Yeah," He said with his eyes fixed on Sally's ghost. "I need it."

Maggie mixed them both a drink, then sat next to Jake. "I assume you're here for a reason other than getting your kicks scaring the shit out of poor Jake?" She said to Sally.

"I want to talk about your investigation."

"I suppose you'll be telling me once again without explanation that I'm wrong?" Maggie stirred her drink with her finger.

"Yes and no. I am here to tell you that you're still headed in the wrong direction, and this all will still end badly for you, Maggie, if that's what you mean, but give me a second to check in and make certain I'm okay to share something with you two that might help."

Sally's eyes went blank, then within less than half a second, they disappeared altogether until what remained were two hollow, vacant, black holes that went on forever, giving her face the quality of an apparition in a Grade B horror movie.

Jake flinched and gasped.

"No worries," Maggie said. "She's done this before. Her eyes will be back in her face soon enough. I can't say Chester will ever come out from behind the couch again, though, and I believe Samantha is hiding in the closet." She issued a chuckle that failed to materialize as a raucous laugh, most likely to Jake, Samantha, and Chester's relief.

Sally's eyes returned to fill the holes in her face, and she smiled. "This is what I know. The killer is not a legendary or mythological Native cannibalistic demon. There are more than one. They are both from the community, not outsiders. And both killers may or may not be part indigenous, not sure from what tribes, and I hope that helps because it's all I've got for you right now."

"That's a hell of a lot more than you've told me so far," Maggie said. "Thanks."

"What's this business about things not ending well for Maggie?" Jake asked. "Is she going to get hurt? Should I be worried?"

"I can only tell you she'll be hurt for certain, but there will not be much physical pain. Most will come from deep grief like she's never experienced. Someone very close to her will die."

Jake shuddered, and collapsed back into the comfort of the couch cushions. "Is it...me? Am I going to die?"

Sally shook her head. "I can't say. I'm sorry." She vanished.

—

The silence between Maggie and Jake was so loud all Maggie could hear was the blood pulsating through her ears. She held Jake and almost cried, but worse she almost slipped and told him she loved him, halting herself in time. *Because I'm afraid I might lose him does not mean I have to get mushy.*

"So, I am going to die." Jake smiled. "I guess a good agent better sign me so I can get published. That right there is my dying wish, to see "The Monster Killer" in print, that along with spending as much time with you as I can. I owe you a trip to the Emerald Isle, and I aim to keep that promise."

"She didn't say you were going to die, Jake. She said she couldn't say, so let's not jump head first into doom and gloom here, okay? Let's go to bed. I've had it." Still, the thought of possibly losing her best friend and only lover pained Maggie. She would not sleep that night, or for many nights after.

After Jake fell into a restless slumber, she transformed herself into a raven and flew over the city of Hemacinto, over the lake, over the San Padrinos, the entire time making a mournful noise that could have only been the sound of a raven crying. She didn't return home until dawn, exhausted, thirsty, emotionally worn, and still unable to fall asleep.

—

When her cell rang, Maggie had been tossing and turning in her bed, and relieved to have an excuse to get up, she sat and grabbed her phone. When she realized who was on the line, she couldn't click the answer button fast enough. "Nola?"

"Yes, it's me, hon. I wanted to call and apologize for being such a bitch after you interviewed me. I know you were only doing your job, but then what happened to James, I..." Nola became silent, then sniffled.

"It's okay, Nola. I do understand, and I'm glad you called. You know I do care about you very much."

"I do know, and you're the only friend I have here, so I don't want to do anything to ruin that, and I really need you right now..." and she broke into gut-busting tears Maggie could almost feel.

She waited for Nola to settle down. "Do you need me to come over? I can be there in ten minutes."

"No," she said swallowing her tears. "Not today. I'm sorry to get all blubbery on you, but it's so hard. I'm going through all of James' clothes to figure out what's going to The Goodwill, and what's going in the trash bin. It's something I have to do alone. I called only because I wanted to apologize. I'm sorry there was no funeral service, so it wasn't that I didn't invite you, there wasn't one, but I kinda wish we could have done something because I almost feel like I need it to say a proper goodbye. James and I decided long ago when we die, we'd rather just be gone, remembered for who we were at our best rather than bringing everyone down with heavy funeral stuff, or graves, and headstones."

"I'll tell you what. When you are up to it in a month or two, we'll have an old-fashioned Irish wake at O'Malley's, with music, tons of Irish food, and everything. That might help you with closure."

"Thanks, hon. I would like that. Right now, I can't even think of such things, though. Skye is covering for me at the gym, but she has other responsibilities, too. I must get back to work, and I've got insurance crap to deal with, but as it is, I can't make it an entire hour without breaking down. I need to process this alone for a time and work my way through the worst of it. After I got the news, I was such a mess that I didn't want to talk to anyone. I didn't even want anyone at the cremation. León wanted to be there. The poor guy seems almost as broken up about James as I am, but I asked him to stay away." She paused for a moment as if to think things over. "The Irish wake is a great idea. Do me one favor in the meantime."

"Anything. Just ask."

"Find the murderous asshole who did this and rip his goddamned head off."

———

Things were quiet over the next few days. On Wednesday morning, Jake left on his own for the sheriff's office so Maggie could stay home and get some rest. To Jake's relief, Diego, Salvador, and León covered the pub so she could take a little time off.

"Good," he said "You need to stick around home and get some sleep. It's been a few days since you've even been to bed and you look like you were dragged through a knothole backward and landed in someone's idea of Hell."

"Are you planning to come home before your critique group tonight?"

"I'll stop by to check on you and grab a sandwich before I go."

"On second thought, don't come home to check on me. Get yourself a hamburger or pizza. I need time alone."

"Okay, suit yourself." Jake put his arms out, and they embraced. He held her close to his chest and she returned his hug, feeling the warmth of his skin through his shirt. She took in the smell of his Old Spice and felt comforted and loved. She didn't want to let go. She didn't want to let go now. She didn't want to let go ever.

After he left, she settled into her office chair to go over her investigation notes, and Samantha leaped into her lap and snuggled in. Maggie grew sleepy and decided to rest her head for a moment. She didn't know how long she'd slept having fallen deep asleep at her desk, and with her head at an odd angle. "This is gonna hurt for a week," she said, rubbing her neck with one hand.

It might have been when Samantha jumped from her lap, or it might have been the cat's noisy chattering at a raven through the glass of the French doors leading out to the patio that woke Maggie. "Either way, I'm glad. I need to get into bed and get some proper shuteye," but sleep didn't happen because her cell phone, which Jake had made sure she'd turned on, rang. The caller ID said "Jimmy Sloan."

"Hi, my favorite nephew. We haven't talked in a few weeks. What's up?"

"Is Jake going to his writing group meeting tonight?"

"Yes, he is. He wouldn't miss it."

"Would you mind if I dropped by while he's out? I need to talk to someone; no, not someone, I need to talk to you."

"Is everything okay?"

"Not so much."

His voice broke, and Maggie was sure she heard him sob. "Jimmy, what's wrong?"

"I'll tell you when I get there."

———

When Jimmy showed up at her front door a few hours later, he looked haggard and drawn.

"When was the last time you took a shower?" Maggie asked. "Come in, and I'll fix you a drink."

Aunt and nephew embraced; he entered, and without saying a word, he sat and slumped down into his seat.

"Wow. You really *are* fucked up." Maggie handed him a whiskey neat, and he downed it in one swallow, silent as a corpse.

"Take your time to compose yourself, but you'll have to talk sometime and tell me what's going on. I haven't gotten any sleep lately, and I'm going to head for bed soon."

"Aunt Maggie?"

"I'm listening."

"It's about my lover."

"Don't tell me. Did he break up with you?"

"No. We still see each other, kind of, at least for business, but it's that I'm crazy in love with him, and he's..." Jimmy's voice broke, and he let a few tears slip from his eyes and down his face before brushing them away with his sleeve. "He's been in love with someone else for a long time, someone he knew he could never have, and now the other guy is dead, and my lover is inconsolable. I am trying everything I know to comfort him but it just..."

"Wait. Do I have this straight? He's shattered your heart, but now you are trying to make *him* feel better? What gives with that?"

"You have no idea how much I love this guy. I'd do anything for him."

"Who is this clown?"

Jimmy looked down. "You know him."

"Okay, fine. So, I know him. Who is he?" Maggie clicked through all her memories one at a time in quick succession to see if there might be anyone she knew who Jimmy would have been attracted to, anyone gay. A blank. *I have no idea who might be gay or not in this homophobic redneck dirtbag town.*

"I don't know if I should tell you."

"Why the goddamn—why did you come here, then? To blubber on my shoulder? I'm here for you, Jimmy, but if you don't trust me enough to even tell me who..."

"León."

A shock wave of disbelief shot through Maggie. "No! What? Can't be. He's got it bad for Nola, and he told me he has a girlfriend, so I hope you understand how this is spinning my head."

"Aunt Mag, he's good to me. Before I came to you about my gambling debt, I was about to get my legs broken because I'd gotten myself into trouble before with the same loan shark, and he's one nasty piece of work known to kill people just for cutting him off in traffic." He looked thoughtfully. "You cut him off once, actually, but I talked him out of hurting you. He carries a Glock like yours, and he always has it with him."

"The loan shark has killed people?" *Is the loan shark is our murderer, then? And, the shark guy had to be the dickhead who honked at me when the ravens prevented me from getting out of my truck and into his face. Thank you, ravens.*

"So, I've been told."

"Christ, Jimmy. This is bad. So, let me see if I've got this right.

León paid your debt, you are in love with him."

"Everything is all messed up, and you're the only person I can turn to."

"Can you at least tell me who he was in love with, or do you even know?"

"That last guy who got himself murdered. The butcher, James Bond."

Maggie reacted as though someone had sucker punched her in the face. "Bond? You've got to be shitting me. What about Nola? How can León be in love with Bond? I thought he was crazy in love with Bond's wife. They had sex, you know." She hit her forehead with the palm of her hand. "Dammit. Sorry, I shouldn't have told you. Nola shared with me in confidence. Fuck."

Jimmy patted her on the shoulder, and spoke in a near whisper. "You think I don't know? León is in love all right, but not with Nola. Never was, but she had the hots for him big time, and he decided to use her feelings for him to get closer to James."

"He was using her? What a conniving little prick. I didn't think he had it in him. So, James was gay? I know Nola—and again, I shouldn't say this so you can't breathe a fucking word—said her husband hadn't paid too much attention to her, as in they haven't danced the horizontal bop in some time, so James wasn't interested in Nola because he was fucking León?"

"Nola never knew James was bi-sexual, or that he had affairs. He fucked a lot of people, men, and women."

Maggie thought back at how hard James had come onto her, even in the interview room at the sheriff's office, the sex texts, and the episode in the pub after. "I suppose that makes sense, but poor Nola. She loses her husband in a horrible way, and now this. It's bound to come to light he was into men, and that's going to crush her to pieces."

"The thing is, León apparently wasn't Bond's type, and so he may have let León blow him once, but I don't think anything else happened between them. He liked León because he works hard for not much money, brought him good organic pork, and because he entertained Nola, keeping her out of his hair. But he didn't want a relationship with León, and James wasn't going to leave Nola for him. That's what he told León, anyway. You know what's truly pathetic, Aunt Maggie?"

"What?"

"Me. Like I said, when León came to me crying that James didn't love him and didn't want to be with him, I said and did everything I could think of to ease his suffering. He was so hurt and so pissed off, and I couldn't stand seeing him that way. In all honesty, I was glad Bond gave him the brush off. I hoped in my heart of hearts with James out of the way, León would finally turn to me."

"But, he didn't, and that's why you're here."

Jimmy let out a drawn-out moan. "The last time I had my heart broken was when my wife dumped me. I was more surprised than hurt about her, though."

"Right. Besides, it's probably for the best she did leave since you are not into women, and you are good with Flower and Bird on your own."

"Yet, I still loved her in my own way, and the girls..."

He broke into another sobbing fit, and Maggie put her arms around him and let him cry it out until he was ready to resume. "This special kind of hurt, this broken heart, this is real. León does not love me, and does not want me, and won't even have sex with me anymore. I am dying inside. I know this might be TMI, but I have had sex with other men, starting when I was only fourteen. It was mostly stuff in gas station bathrooms or, when I was older, once in a while a quickie out back of that gay bar, The Purple Gauntlet, in Redding when we lived in Wicklow, and once in high school under the bleachers after a Friday night game, but I've never been in love before. It hurts so bad."

Maggie he him until, at last, he broke away. "I don't know what to do, and the worst part is I still owe him a huge debt, so I have to see him and work for him in his meat delivery business until it's paid off."

"I know, sweetheart. I understand exactly how you feel. I'm glad it's meat deliveries you're doing for him to work off your debts, because if you're into something you shouldn't be, like selling meth for him, I might have to kick your fleshy butt the entire seven hundred plus miles back to Wicklow. I'd be one miserable harpy, and you won't like it."

He nodded. "Aunt Maggie?"

"Yup?"

"I've lived this lie for so long, and I don't know why I didn't come out sooner. I just couldn't. I wanted to, but I was so afraid about how 'macho dad' would take knowing his only son is gay, I didn't want to hurt mom, and I worry about Flower and Bird and how it might affect them."

"You're coming out now, and I'm proud of you. And, stuff your worrying right up your brown ass. Your girls will love you no matter what, Jimmy. You're a damn good father, and your mom and dad love you, too. They aren't going to judge, plus I'm here for you."

"I know. Thanks." And he smiled for the first time since arriving on her doorstep.

—

That night, Maggie slept twelve hours straight, and dreamt about Sally, the ravens, all sweet and pleasant, but the dream she had about her and Jake in a Dublin pub sharing a Guinness in a glass so big she could have fit Chester into it gave her the most joy and peace she'd experienced in months.

When Maggie finally woke, she discovered Jake had come home, gotten into bed next to her, slept all night, rose the next morning, showered, made coffee and toast, and went to work—all without disturbing her. But, on the counter next to the coffee pot, he left her a note.

"Sally says I could die and we may not have much time left. So, why don't you unplug your head from your ass, admit you love me, and let's get married?"

She smiled, folded the note, put it in her robe pocket, and sent him a text. "No." But she did include a gif of a dancing chimpanzee holding a bouquet of pink hearts.

CHAPTER 36

MAGGIE THOUGHT SHE'D fall over when she walked into O'Malley's to find Jake and Tom side-by-side at the bar swilling beer and yukking it up like old school chums who'd not seen each other in decades.

"Hello, guys," she said. "Good to see the two of you getting on so well, or rather I should say, good to see Jake not behaving like a chucklehead with you, Tom. Can I buy you both a beer? Stella for you?" She pointed to Tom.

He nodded and handed her his empty.

"Harp for you, Jake?"

"Lemme try one of those Stella's," he said.

———

The next day over coffee, Maggie sidled next to Jake on the sofa. "Looks like you and Tom are getting along. I suppose this means you've decided not to be jealous, and does this also mean he's cleared as a suspect?"

"You're right, Maggie, he's a good guy, and after he showed me photos of his long- legged, green-eyed, beautiful wife, Aimee, and told me Aimee is not only the love of his life but his best friend, I understand why he wouldn't be interested in..."

"Watch it, buddy." She glared at him in pretend offense.

"And, yeah. He's cleared. We've no evidence whatsoever he's connected to any of the murders, and I'm grateful he's good to you. I'd come to the pub, hoping he'd be around so I could thank him for what he's done for you, and then we got to talking. He's got some great stories." His face brightened. "Once this case is closed, we could get together with Tom and Aimee for dinner or have them over to the house. I know you aren't exactly a social butterfly, but would you be up for making friends with another couple? And, do you know the young deputy you call, Kiddo, is his nephew? Kiddo's wife is going to have a baby, and we're invited to a coed baby shower. We should go. It would be great to mix with other people."

The last time Jake and Maggie had socialized with another couple had been a few years back in her beloved Wicklow, and it was then she realized one reason she missed Wicklow so much was because of her personal connections there—Dawn who owned Mama's and now rented Maggie's A-Frame on the river, the late, great Sally, her best gal-pal ever, and even their young friends, Happy and Rosa, who she and Jake had been close to for a while. When things went south with the young couple in a way that Maggie couldn't allow herself to think about, she and Jake refrained from forming friendships at all. So, until she found Nola, Maggie keenly felt the absence of friends in her life, especially that of other women. She looked forward to also meeting Aimee, who she was sure she'd love as much or more than Nola.

"I don't know about getting together with Kiddo, though. I don't think it's a good idea to socialize with people we work with, Jake, not after our experiences in Wicklow."

"It'll be fine. He's young, but he's a good guy, and he told Tom you are a great mentor. He admires you, looks up to you. Besides, it can't hurt to have a few beers with everyone and celebrate his baby."

"Remember, I'm a crappy judge of character? Sure you want to hang out with people I like?"

"You get it right some time, like with Nola, Tom, Sally, Dawn, Diego, and maybe even me, you think?"

"Maybe."

"Tom is passionate about golf, too. He and Kiddo go to the links almost every week. They've invited me to tag along."

"You don't golf."

"I'll learn."

Maggie thought about it for a moment. "Sure. We'll do all that, and you can learn to golf, why not? But after you take me to Ireland. Deal?"

"Deal. If I don't die, that is." The look on his face turned cold, fearful, and sad.

"Forget about it, will you? Sally didn't say it was you, so quit it." Maggie worried, anyway.

—

The regular Sunday dinners at Danny and Cathy's would come to an end since Danny had taken care of the clean-up and rehab of the house in Wicklow. Maggie wondered if this venison stew Cathy had made especially for tonight might be the last she'd share with her family at the yellow table in Hemacinto.

"Cathy, I know you're busy with tribal business, and are getting ready to move back to Wicklow, but can I ask you for some help putting together a wake for Nola's husband?"

"I can cook somethin' like acorn muffins, or..."

"We're going with traditional Irish food, so Diego and León have that covered, but I want to decorate the place a little. Nola has photos and mementos we're putting up on A-Frame boards, and since we don't have a body, we are making an altar of sorts with his urn, some flowers, pictures, and candles, you know, a place where people can pay their respects. I'm not too good at that sort of stuff, and I can't ask Nola, so there's no one else."

"I will help if you want. Sure. Are you gonna want another bowl of stew? I made plenty and I ain't gonna be too happy if it goes to waste."

"Cathy and Danny, we will miss you so much," and Maggie meant it. "The people around this table are our only family, and I –both Jake and I will be sad when you move."

"You take care of Jimmy and the girls after we leave," Danny said. "We'll all see one another often. You visit us. We'll visit you, and I expect you all at the next Bear Dance." He gestured to Danny, the girls, Jake, and Maggie. "I not only want you there, you ought to take the girls for their first sweat in the women's lodge. They're old enough now to take the heat and they should be with Cathy and you.

Besides, I need Jimmy and Jake's help with building the sweat lodge, and Cathy will need your help with food prep in the Long House."

—

Déjà vu all over again, thought Maggie, as she sat at her desk perusing the files from the Wicklow investigation several years back in hopes for clues in the Hemacinto investigation. That Wicklow killer had been possessed by a manitou, a cannibal, and targeted twin children younger than eight. He killed Sally and would have killed her, too, had she not shot him so many times his torso resembled rotten Swiss cheese.

After a few hours of fruitless searching, Maggie, so frustrated she thought her head would crack open and her brains would spill out all over the keyboard, snapped shut her laptop and, although late, she decided to drive to O'Malley's to prepare for the wake.

She called Cathy. "I am taking a break from the investigation, and I'm going to the pub to get a head start on things for tomorrow since there's so much to do, and not much time to get all this done. I know it's late, but would you like to join me?"

"Can't. I'd help, but Flower and Bird are sleepin', Jimmy is out with that girlfriend of his, Danny's up north, and there ain't nobody to watch them little girls. I got everything already in the car, and I'll come early tomorrow."

Jake toiled at the sheriff's office, working late on the case with one of the other task force members who'd met him there, and when she called to tell him what she was up to, he said, "I'll see you home later. I assume you do have your cell with you, and is it actually turned on?"

"Just shut up, will ya?" She laughed. Maybe out of spite for Jake teasing her, or maybe from habit, she clicked off her cell, tucked it in her pocket, and headed for the pub.

Diego, León, and Salvador had already closed before Maggie arrived. She unlocked the door, poured herself a Jameson over the rocks, and set about the business of moving tables and chairs in preparation for the event. The pub would be closed tomorrow, and Cathy would meet Maggie in the morning with flowers, candles, and tablecloths to decorate before the musicians, the guests, and Nola made their appearance in the early afternoon.

Through a window, Maggie greeted the ravens who had gathered there. "Sorry, guys. No corn. But thanks for coming by to keep me company."

She'd moved the last bistro set and had begun to arrange chairs and set up a folding table for the altar, when the ravens began calling to one another. In her human form, Maggie didn't understand their language, so had no idea what the ravens were trying to tell her. She searched the kitchen for grain, nuts, bread or anything for them, at last scooping bar peanuts from a bucket and tossing them outside. "I know you're mad at me for not bringing your favorite corn, you spoiled brats. I got busy and forgot, okay? I'll make it up to you, you flying bastards, now leave me alone." But they didn't. Instead of flying away, more and more ravens amassed at the door, and in the few scrawny trees outside the windows where they could see her, and she could see them. "Suit yourself. I still don't have any corn."

Although the floor was spotless—"thank you, León, for always being so damned neat and thorough"—she grabbed a broom anyway and swept. She hadn't gotten too far with the cleaning when auto lights from the parking lot shown through the windows, and shortly after she heard someone at the door. Thinking it was Jake, she ran to open it, but when she did instead of Jake, there stood Jimmy with León.

CHAPTER 37

MAGGIE, WHO STILL held the broom in her hand, was so taken aback at seeing her nephew and León at the door, she dropped it, letting it clatter against the floor. She left it where it lay.

"What in God's name are you two doing here?"

The look on Jimmy's face told Maggie something terrible had happened. Her first thought is they were there to notify her Jake had been killed, and at that thought, her intestines turned to ice.

"No, no. It's not Jake, is it? Please don't tell me something has happened to Jake."

"What? No." Jimmy said. "Jake is fine, as far as I know. We've come for...another reason."

Maggie stepped aside to permit the two men passage. León picked up the broom. "I will return this to its proper place in the utility closet, Ms. Maggie, and I shall stay away for a few moments to allow you the time you require to converse with your nephew. Jimmy has something of grave importance to tell you."

León departed with the broom and headed in the general direction of the kitchen.

"What's up, Jimmy?"

His face blanched.

"Please, Jimmy. It's obvious something is wrong. Tell me what it is." She put her arms around him. When Jimmy left his arms hanging by his sides, and did not return her embrace, she released him and took a step back. "You have to talk to me."

"You know I love you, Aunt Maggie."

"And I love you, but don't bullshit me. Tell me what in the fuck is the matter, Jimmy."

He straightened and exhaled hard through his nose. "I'm here to turn myself in. I'm the Aunt Lorrie's Salt Killer."

Maggie was so stunned her knees weakened and she crumbled.

"Not you. No."

Jimmy extended a hand to steady her. She swayed, and the universe spun around her as though someone had knocked her on the head with a cudgel, then she caught her balance.

"León chose the victims and formulated the plans right down to the last detail, the kidnappings, the location for the kills, but I did the actual deed. It was his idea that we turn ourselves into you, personally." Jimmy choked up. "I had to do it, Aunt Maggie."

Maggie did her best to keep control, and to not sputter. She was nearly successful. "Why... why am I surprised to learn Le...León is behind this? Gimme a second to catch my breath, and let's take a seat in one of the booths. I've got a lot to ask you, all off the record for now, but we will be questioning you formally at the station."

The two sat in a dark corner away from the bar, and away from the kitchen where León puttered about.

"Before we get too far, I need you to tell me everything you remember, Jimmy."

"I kept something from you. I wasn't in trouble with the loan shark once, or twice, but León pulled me out of the fire at least a half dozen times. That loan shark would have killed me if he hadn't covered my debts."

"No bloody shit, you've kept something from me. But all this begs a question. You came to me once to ask for money...why didn't you come again?"

"I intended to keep you and all the family out of my gambling troubles. León held it over me—I mean the one time, he asked me to kill someone with him that I didn't want to, the butcher, because I'd finally had enough of murdering people. He refused to bail me out if I didn't help him with Bond, and I knew the loan shark would shoot me. I had nowhere else to turn for that sixty grand and I was desperate."

"And that's when you should have fessed up. Tell me again why you did it, Jimmy, because I'm struggling to understand, and I can't. The whole thing about you being a killer is incomprehensible to me."

'I am into him for a lot of cash, well over a hundred K, and I love him."

"Yes?"

"León had to help the family financially. I guess his mom and Graciela with the kids couldn't make ends meet. Diego helped, but León was the real money man. Look at it this way, what he has done is not as horrible as you think. He never hurts the innocent. He only takes out the worst criminals who have gotten away with the most heinous crimes. He's been ridding the world of bad guys for a long time, like you Aunt Maggie."

"No, not like me, not at all, goddammit! Don't even say that. And, what do you mean for a 'long time'?"

"He told me there were so many people throughout his life who'd gotten away with murder, or molesting children, and hurting animals that he felt it his duty to purge the world of these people, and so he did.

León began killing as a teenager, almost always with the help of a lover who did the actual slaughtering, so that way he could keep his hands clean. After trying it out of curiosity, and developing a taste for it, he discovered human meat is remarkably like tender pork, so along with odd jobs, he started a little business that made him some money over the years, enough to cover expenses at USC that fell outside his scholarship, enough for a small bachelor apartment, and enough to help his family."

"There is no organic pork farm in El Centro?"

"There is, but let's say he supplemented that meat with...the other."

"Why is he turning himself in? He's gotten away with this for so long."

"What made León want to be done with all this happened after we took out his aunt. He wasn't too crazy about her after her arrest as a gangbanger but finding out about her shooting that boy and getting away with it was the last straw for him. All those years León hadn't known about the shooting, not until he overheard Diego talking to his grandma when they both thought he was out of hearing range. But Graciela was his family, nonetheless, and her children were devastated. Killing her and leaving the kids grieving the loss of their mother did something to him. He hasn't been the same since."

"And then James Bond rejected him, and you wouldn't do León's dirty work for him any longer, so the little fucker had to do it himself." Although Maggie continued to speak, it was more to herself than to Jimmy. "This killing is different from the others, though, a crime of passion. He took the heart since Bond broke his, and although strong for his size, no way León could on his own follow his M.O. to kidnap a man as large as Bond, take him into a remote area, mount him on a spit, and roast him like the others. It all makes sense. Then, he couldn't take it that he had been the one to do his own dirty work this time, had murdered the man he loved, that's why you are both here." Maggie felt her world crashing in. "You've been killing for León because you're in love with him and would do anything for him, and you owe him for covering your debts. That establishes motive, all right. Why the liver?"

"León says his reason for taking their livers is to punish those who'd gotten off with heinous crimes, so deserved the pain, and as disgusting as it seems, he likes raw liver. He told me he blends it into his morning protein drinks because it gives him power. And he also says eating the raw liver of his victims has significance in some Native American lore that is important to him."

"One more question."

"Okay."

"Did Flower ever meet León?"

"Yes. I took the girls with me once to the pub to talk to León when you were off. Flower right away took to him. She said he was 'cute,' so she might even have a little crush on him."

Well, then Flower did know both of the killers. The raven is strong with this one. Maggie felt in her pocket for her cell., *I left it on the shelf on the bar, all the way the other end of the pub, and it's off. Fuck.*

"You know I have to get my phone and call this in, and I'll be arresting both you and León. What you have done is going to kill your mother, your father, and your girls, and after their loss, I cannot imagine the agony Diego and his family will go through. I don't even know what to say."

Jimmy didn't respond.

The weight of her heart as it broke, the heaviness of her grief, and the pieces of her sorrow growing hard in her chest almost took her to her knees, but she summoned all her strength to maintain her composure and keep herself in "cop mode."

"Wait here, while I call the sheriff's office. I mean it. Do. Not. Move."

She left Jimmy where they'd sat at the table in the back and went to the bar to fetch her phone. While her back was turned, it happened.

At first, she didn't feel the blade, only a shock of pain in her shoulder and upper back. When she realized she'd been stabbed, she spun to face her attacker, and there stood León with the biggest baddest German-made butcher knife from her kitchen, dripping with blood, hers.

She kicked at him. He twisted out of the way. He came at her again with the knife, and she ducked to one side to escape the blow, but the blade grazed her, making a sickening rasping sound as it sliced across her collar bone. Blood poured down her blouse. It took all her power to kick out again. This time she connected with León's gut. He doubled over, and made an "umph" sound, but kept his grip on the knife. He came up again, and faced her, his eyes on fire with rage and hate.

She screamed. "Jimmy! Help me! Jimmy!"

As she called out, she never took her eyes off León, who never spoke a word, entirely focused on his mission to kill her. She managed to duck most of his blows, but caught another wound to her upper arm where the blade grazed her as León attempted to plunge the butcher knife into her lung, and when she lifted her leg and crossed it over her torso to protect her stomach, the blade sunk into her thigh. She cried out more from surprise than pain.

Although wounded, her adrenalin ran on overdrive, and in shock, she didn't feel anything. She kept moving from side-to-side, twisting, turning, ducking down and coming back up, dancing from foot-to-foot like a skilled boxer in a champion match.

But, with her back against the corner between the bar and the stage, she had nowhere to run. She blindly kicked, and struck out, sometimes connecting with his shin or his ribs. He never let up, and he never allowed the butcher knife to drop, even when he skidded in her blood, and for a split second, lost his footing. He came at her, stabbing and slashing.

"Jimmy! He's going to kill me! Hurry!"

She thought she might lose consciousness, or maybe had already and only had not yet collapsed. She couldn't be certain. She didn't even know if she cared. Nothing felt real. The attack took place over maybe fifteen or twenty seconds, but it felt like hours had passed. *I can't hold on much longer.*

As she danced away from the knife blows, some slashing her skin, others barely missing her, she called out to Jimmy again, but she couldn't hear her own voice and thought he'd never come. *I can't die like this, please.*

She heard Jimmy. "Get away from her. Goddammit! Drop the knife!" She heard footsteps running from the back of the pub to the front where she leaned against the bar waiting to die, but still feebly kicking and missing, and punching the air. She heard her own breathing, her own desperate panting. She heard Sally whisper words of comfort. She heard her mother's voice, "It is all as it should be, my daughter."

As Maggie weakened from loss of blood and shock, and her kicks and punches slowed, León stood tall, his face bright with the sweetest and most beguiling of smiles. *He looks almost like he's in love with me rather than wanting to kill me. How odd.* That was her last thought before the room darkened, her eyes closed halfway, and she made her peace.

The triumphant León raised his arm to deliver what he must have intended to be a fatal cut through her heart, and although she continued to kick at him, Maggie knew it was over.

At the exact second the tip of the blade touched her chest, the blast of a gunshot echoed through the pub, followed by a spray of flesh and blood. She fell the same time León did, two bodies in perfect rhythm landed in synchronized thuds on the floor of O'Malley's, one person dead, the other almost dead, their blood co-mingling and spreading in an expanse wider than the River Liffy.

Through her half-conscious haze, Maggie heard them, the ravens. Hundreds. Thousands. Their kraas, grunks, and gronks deafened her; she heard nothing else, and was aware of nothing else, until the shadowy figure of a big man appeared above her. Her nephew. With the gun still in his hand, he knelt in the blood and cradled her head. "I've called emergency. An ambulance will be here any minute. Aunt Maggie. I didn't know he was going to try to hurt you. I know where you keep a sidearm at the bar so I grabbed it and killed him before he could kill you. Please forgive me for what I have done."

He'd leaned over to whisper something to her, and straightened just as someone crashed through the door, and once again, a gunshot blasted through the pub. More blood. So much blood. Jimmy Tall Bear Sloan fell over onto his Aunt, his eyes vacant, killed instantly when Jake's bullet found its target through Jimmy's brain. Maggie screamed and screamed.

The smell of Jasmine filled the room, mingling with the coppery smell of blood, and Sally covered Maggie's hand with her own. Although Maggie couldn't feel the hand, she was aware of her friend's attempts to comfort her, and she relaxed.

Sally smiled. "I am here, my friend, like I promised. I am here."

———

The ambulance driver rushed Maggie to the hospital with Jake and Sally following close behind. When the driver pulled to the entrance, the medical attendants rushed her into the operating theater, where the surgeon stood by.

Hours later, the doctor emerged.

"Is she going to be okay?" Jake asked.

"Hard to say. The knife missed her major organs, but she's lost a lot of blood, has sustained considerable muscle and tissue damage to her shoulders, arm, and neck, and the wound on her thigh barely missed a major artery. We've done all we can do but it's going to be touch and go for a time, I'm afraid."

—

Throughout Maggie's slow recovery and her lengthy hospital stay, Sally remained at her side as her constant companion, comforting her. "You know, my friend, it was I who told Jake to check on you. I sensed something awful."

Maggie wanted in the worst way to embrace Sally, but although in a world of pain and grief, she managed a grateful smile at least.

"I didn't know it would be Jimmy, but I knew you'd lose someone dear to you, and would need me, besides, your mother made me promise, and you two are so much alike, I knew she'd give me hell if I didn't keep my promise."

Maggie laughed. "Yeah, my mom is feisty and means business, even in death." She would have reached out to hold Sally's hand if she could have. "Thank you for being here, my dear friend. But, how ironic, don't you think?"

"What's ironic?"

"I'm supposed to be the cop, the protector, yet I am responsible for your death twice, and you are responsible for saving my life. If you'd not flown into Hank's eyes, he would have shot me through the face."

"Stop it. You aren't responsible for either of my deaths, so when are you going to quit blaming yourself, Maggie? Probably never, am I right? You're so damned stubborn."

—

Sheriff Mack called in now and again to check on her. She received a bouquet of flowers, balloons, and card signed by everyone at the sheriff's department. Cathy and Danny sent a note, but no visit, no flowers, no call. Maggie understood. One afternoon, Nola came by with fudge. "Thought you might need some chocolate, hon."

"I'd rather have a bottle of Jameson."

"Hahaha. When you're healed, and I've had a little more time to mourn James, we'll knock down a few together. I hope you know I don't blame you for his death, and I had no idea León could have done this on his own. You think someone helped him and no one knows who it is yet?"

"It's doubtful. Like you say, he's remarkably strong for a small guy, and it's possible he could have handled many of the killings himself but liked being in control, so enlisted help via manipulation and deceit so he could play the head honcho. Typical narcissistic psychopath, but we cannot find any evidence that anyone other than León murdered your husband."

"James' killer is dead, and that brings me peace, but I need more time to process my feelings about it all before you and I can get together socially. I know you understand."

Maggie patted Nola's arm. "It's okay, my friend."

———

Jake brought flowers and food and did his best to keep her spirits high, but Maggie could tell he concealed sorrow and bottomless guilt as he struggled to make sense of what had happened. "I did ring you after Sally came to me to tell me you were in trouble. It was so weird. I'd been working in the office, the other guy had left, so I was alone going over files and re-examining the evidence. I smelled the jasmine, and then she came out of nowhere and told me you needed me, and soon. I tried to call and left a message, but what a surprise: you'd left your damned cell phone off. Maybe if you'd gotten my call, I could have made it on time, and no one would have gotten hurt."

"This is my fault? Is that what you're saying? Jesus Christ, Jake. I can't believe you'd..."

"I don't think it's your fault, Maggie. Please. I just wish you'd keep your phone on because when I can't reach you, I panic out of fear something horrible happened to you. León was out to hurt you anyway. He probably figured out you weren't going to let go of the investigation until you found him, and maybe he thought you were getting a little too close. As for Jimmy, I don't know what to say, Maggie."

The look on Jake's face broke her heart. "Jimmy's death is not your fault, Jake."

"Yes. It is. I shot without thinking. I didn't even warn him. Had I known he was trying to help...God. I'm sorry, Maggie. I'm so sorry."

Despite injuries that hurt so badly she needed regular doses of Oxycodone and Percocet to get through a day, with some difficulty, Maggie managed to reach up with one hand to wipe the tears from his face.

———

The investigating team dropped by, crowding in, leaving standing room only.

"The nursing staff is only letting three at a time come in," Kiddo said to her. "The others have to wait their turn; they let the deputies closest to you in first." He laid a fistful of daisies on her bedside table and beamed at her.

After the last of the visitors finally left, Sheriff Mack stayed behind to talk. Maggie's slings and bandages had become a nuisance. "Crap. I can't even use my keyboard like this," she told him.

"You're going to be okay, that's what matters, Maggie, and you'll be back to work in no time."

"Thanks, but I am never coming back. I'm done."

The sheriff turned his attention to Jake. "The investigation into the shooting is underway. Despite your lack of warning before pulling the trigger, due to the circumstances, I wager the Shooting Review Board will rule this as a good kill, and you'll be cleared."

Maggie's heart lurched when she heard "good kill." *Jimmy, I'm so damned sorry you got caught up in this. I miss you so much.* As she thought about her only nephew and her grandnieces, she swallowed bitter tears.

"Thanks," Jake said to Mack.

"I thought you might be interested in knowing what we found in León's apartment when we searched it."

"Lay it on us," said Jake.

"His apartment walls were covered with drawings of a hideous demon that looked like a wild animal ripped half the flesh from its face. Upon questioning his grandmother, we discovered the demon is part of a Native American legend from the north, especially among the Micmac and Passamaquoddy tribes, a Chenoo it's called. It turns out Graciela's husband was full blooded Passamaquoddy. He told the story to his daughters and to León of the cannibalistic ice-demon who cuts the liver from his still living victims, eats it in front of them as they die, then severs their limbs and carries them in a sack as portable food. The grandmother says after hearing the story, León developed an unhealthy obsession with the Chenoo and spent hours online and at the library researching the legend."

"That makes sense as to why he chose that particular M.O." Maggie's wounds throbbed but she did not ring the nurse for more opiates. *I need to stay alert so I can catch all this.*

"We also found a list of his victims, and it's a long one, all printed nice and neat on a yellow pad in the top drawer of his bedroom side table, and as we expected each had priors as pretty nasty criminals, and each had been considerably overweight. For years, all were transients or derelicts with no family to miss them. León's biggest mistake was operating in his own community, especially in targeting the prominent community citizens, such as the dentist and his family. By the way, we found his 'souvenirs.'"

"The thumbs?" Maggie asked.

"Some raw, some cooked, all preserved nicely in formaldehyde-filled glass bottles of the exact same and size placed in neat rows on a shelf in his closet. The lab is processing the fingerprints now so we can notify the next of kin. And, in his pantry? Probably twenty or more containers of Aunt Lorrie's Seasoned Salt."

"He fell in love with the butcher, is that right?"

"We found in the bedroom dresser over a hundred hand-written love letters to the butcher returned unopened."

"Then Jimmy was right. León killed the butcher for rejecting him, but why did he target obese people?"

"The best pulled pork has a lot of fat, making the leg meat he blended with the organic pork from El Centro that he sold to butchers and restaurants worth quite a bit. Premium 'pork' for which León sold at a premium price. I know it will come out sooner or later that everyone who dined on pork at those restaurants, including your pub, ate their fill of human flesh."

CHAPTER 37

SALLY REMAINED EVER present, and Jake sat by Maggie's bedside day and night, too, but when it became clear to him she'd be fine and could go home soon, he kissed her, told her he loved her, then disappeared from her hospital room, and from her life.

Maggie grew alarmed when he didn't show up the next day, or the next, or the day of her release. She called him repeatedly, but no response.

Sally did her best to reassure her. "I could pop over to your house and check if he's there."

"No thanks. My guess is he is exhausted from all this and needs rest. I bet he'll be waiting for me when I walk in the door."

Nola drove her home. "Do you want me to come in, hon?"

"No. I'm okay. Besides, Jake is waiting for me, or will be home soon, I hope."

He wasn't there. She found his things gone, his clothes, his laptop, his manuscripts, every little precious part of him gone. He'd not even left a note.

She broke down, recovered, then started her search. She left him messages, texted him, called everyone she knew who might know where he'd gone, but no one had a clue.

———

Cathy, so devastated at the death of her only son, and so shocked at what he'd done, had to be hospitalized. Danny took the girls up north, and Maggie thought she might never see them again. She'd lost everything. She wanted to visit Cathy, but she felt as though Jimmy's death was still somehow her fault. She called Danny and the girls, but they were too broken to talk to her, not even Flower.

A few weeks later, she received a letter, an old-fashioned snail-mail, with no return address.

I'm so sorry, Maggie. I never would hurt Jimmy, but he had your Glock. I thought he'd kill you, and I had to save your life. I love you. I always have and always will, but I cannot face what I've done to you and your family, no, to our family, because you all are the only real kin I have ever known. I do hope you have the good life you deserve, and you make it to Ireland. I will see you in my dreams.

Love, Jake.

The mistake he made was in not mailing the letter from a town remote from his location. Maggie puzzled over it. "Wait. He's smarter than that, so no mistake. He wants me to find him and is testing to see if I care enough to do it, the rat bastard." Giddy with hope, she packed, loaded her car, and enlisted Nola to feed Samantha. "I'm sorry about the wake. When I find Jake, we'll do something about that. How are you holding up?"

"The question is how are *you* holding up? I'll take care of Samantha while you're gone, and when you get back with Jake, I'll drop by for a visit."

Maggie looked around the house to make sure she had everything. She opened the passenger door of her truck. "Come, boy." Chester jumped into the cab of her red 54' Chevy, and they headed to Wicklow.

—

After driving twelve hours non-stop, she pulled her truck into the driveway of the tiny cottage where Jake had lived while serving as sheriff. Although a dark night, no lights shown in the cabin. Her wounded thigh, arm, and shoulder ached. She popped a handful of Ibuprofen chasing the pills with bottled water she'd brought, let Chester out to pee, sat for a minute to compose herself, then exited the truck.

She pounded on the door. No answer. She beat against the door again until she heard someone moving inside. "Jake, open the goddamned door." No answer. "I will fucking bust this door down if you don't open it. Your choice."

At last, an inside lamp and a porch light came on, the door opened a crack, and a smell of sweat and urine assaulted Maggie's nose. "Open the goddamn door all the way, will you?"

When Jake admitted her, she found pizza boxes, burrito wrappers, and beer bottles strewn everywhere. Jake, though, shocked her the most. Although never a spiffy dresser, he'd always kept himself up. He hadn't bothered to shave in the weeks since he'd left. His eyes were so puffy and his face so drawn, he looked as though he'd aged ten years, and his clothes were filthy.

"Jesus, Jake. You stink. Get into the shower, now."

Up until that moment, Jake had not uttered a word. "You came."

"Of course, I did, you turd. Why did you leave?"

"You didn't get my letter?"

"The 'poor me, everyone hates me' letter? I got it, and you wanted me to find you, or you wouldn't have sent me a letter postmarked from Wicklow. What a bonehead move and don't dick around with me. I've driven straight through, and I'm sore and exhausted, and...."

He held her and kissed her in a way that opened her heart, and all the feelings she had for him billowed up like a cloud into her chest. "I worried you'd gone forever," she said. "I'm so glad to see you, oh God, so glad, but please take a shower."

He grinned and headed to the bathroom.

Once he left the room, she plopped down on the floor, put her head in her hands and sobbed, not with grief or sorrow, but with relief. The dog licked her face, and in return, she put her arm around him and patted his haunch. "We found him, Chester. And we aren't letting him run away from us again, are we, boy?" She knew what she had to do, then. She had to tell Jake the truth, the truth he already knew, the truth she never could say to him but should have years ago.

CHAPTER 38

EVERYBODY HAD BEGUN the arduous process of healing, and it took a long while for things to be okay, not normal because "normal" had become a dream left in the past for them all—so "okay" would have to do. Cathy, Danny, Flower, and Bird would never recover completely from Jimmy's death, but none blamed Jake or Maggie.

"We know it wasn't either of you who killed, Jimmy. My son brought it all on himself," Danny said, "And, Jake, I would have done exactly as you did if I ever thought for a second Cathy might be in danger. We will get through this as a family."

Jake went with Maggie to therapy sessions, and it seemed to help. One day while driving home after meeting with the psychologist, Jake turned to Maggie. "I have a question."

"Sure."

"You don't have to answer if you don't want to."

"What is it, Jake?"

"I'm not sure how to put this."

Maggie looked at the roof of her truck in exasperation, "Ask, and quit dicking around."

"What did Jimmy whisper to you?"

"He said he loved me, made me promise once again to take care of Bird and Flower, and said no matter what happened to him he would always watch out for us."

"Do you think he knew he would die?"

"He's smart enough to have understood the consequences of his actions, death being the end result, yes." She paused to take stock of her thoughts. "Jake, my heart is broken over Jimmy, and I know this is a weird thing to say, but one reason I don't want you to feel guilty is you may have done him a huge favor."

"I killed him, Maggie. I shot your only nephew through the

head. How can that be anything other than tragic?"

"For Jimmy, what you did was a far kinder way for him to go than to die slowly in prison where he would have spent the rest of his life. I know my nephew. He wouldn't have lasted in captivity for even a month, and he would have suffered every second."

Jake looked puzzled. "I understand, but something else is eating at me. If Jimmy knew he'd die, why did he say he'd always watch out for you?"

"Because he will."

—

Once things settled, and the doctors released Cathy from the hospital, Flower and Bird moved in with Jake and Maggie. They made plans to sell their house in Hemacinto and move back to Wicklow.

Maggie continued her raven lessons with Flower, although her own "hurt wing" made flight a little more difficult. "One day you'll have to do this raven thing completely on your own. I won't always be able to be with you."

Maggie Jake spent afternoons side-by-side in the Adirondack chairs on their back deck, taking in the balmy air, drinking tequila sunrises. With the case solved, they had more time to enjoy these slow, dreamy times.

The girls rode their bikes, swam in the local community pool, attended therapy, and cried for their father. Besides therapy with Jake, Maggie returned to one-one-one sessions with her psychiatrist, and for a while, she did not shift into a raven or see Sally.

Maggie waited for the right time to tell Jake her truth. It didn't take too long. One afternoon on the deck, the ravens settled into the Acacia tree and clucked and clicked among themselves, preening their feathers, swooping down periodically to nibble corn Maggie had spread on the lawn. Maggie spoke to them. "You know we are leaving. You are welcome to follow, but Jake and I, and the girls are going home."

Out of nowhere, Jake, staring at Maggie like a smitten teen, said, "Maggie Tall Bear Sloan, I love you."

Without changing her expression, or turning her attention away from the ravens, Maggie, at last, told him her truth. "And, Jake Lubbock, I love you."

———

Two years to the day Maggie rode in the ambulance to Hemacinto Hospital, she, Jake, and the girls boarded a flight on Air Lingus to Dublin. Cathy and Danny drove from Wicklow to Los Angeles Airport to see them off. "I made some acorn muffins for you to take in case you need a snack," Cathy said before kissing the girls goodbye. "You two be good in that Ireland place; we'll take care of your dog and cat, and we'll see you when you come home next month. This Autumn before the Bear Dance, even, you'll be startin' seventh grade in Wicklow with all your old friends."

Someone else came with Danny and Cathy to say goodbye. No one except Maggie and Jake could see her, of course. Sally. She smiled and waved at Maggie, blew kisses, and mouthed the words "Bye."

Maggie knew she'd never see Sally again and struggled to hold back tears. "See you in the afterworld," she mouthed back.

The four boarded the plane, the girls in seats in front of Jake and Maggie, and they flew like corvids through the skies over America, over the ocean, to Ireland.

It was early morning when they made the approach to Dublin Airport, and the sun shown on the Irish Sea, turning the surface a brilliant gold. Maggie had never seen anything like it, and she took it as a positive sign everything would be fine.

Before the "buckle your seatbelts, stash your belongings in the seat in front, and put your tray in the upright position," announcement, Flower turned, kneeling as to see over the tall seatback, and faced Maggie and Jake.

"Aunt Maggie, there's a magazine in this holder thing in front."

"I know. The airline puts those there in case you get bored playing video games or watching movies."

"But did you know there are a bunch of Irish stories in the magazine?"

"That makes perfect sense, don't you think?"

"But, do you also know about The Morrigan?"

"The what?"

"The Morrigan."

"New one on me, Skeeter. Tell me, who is The Morrigan?"

"Well, Auntie Maggie, I read she's a famous Irish goddess who changes into a raven, like you and me. When I took a nap earlier, she told me in a dream she's going to meet us in Wicklow, and not Wicklow, California where we're going to live again, but right here in Ireland. Isn't that cool?"

"Oh, shit."

www.ingramcontent.com/pod-product-compliance
Lightning Source LLC
Chambersburg PA
CBHW020618260626
47157CB00003B/1069